THE TEAROOM ON THE BAY

THE TEAROOM ON
THE BAY

Rachel Burton

An Aria Book

First published as an eBook in the UK in 2020 by Aria,
an imprint of Head of Zeus Ltd.
This edition first published in the UK in 2021 by Aria.

A CIP catalogue record for this book is available from the
British Library.

ISBN (PB): 9781800245945
ISBN (E): 9781800241138

Typeset by Siliconchips Services Ltd UK

Printed and bound in Great Britain by
CPI Group (UK) Ltd, Croydon CRO 4YY

Aria
c/o Head of Zeus
First Floor East
5–8 Hardwick Street
London EC1R 4RG

www.ariafiction.com

To Katey, with thanks

I

Isit down placing the teapot in front of me. The tea has brewed for exactly four minutes and I pour the reddish-brown liquid into my favourite blue and white striped china mug. No milk, no sugar. Just tea. I sit and watch the steam curling off the surface of the liquid as I allow it to cool and I wait for the subtle aroma of bergamot to hit me. I close my eyes and listen to the gentle click of knitting needles.

'Ellie used to be scared of Father Christmas you know,' my aunt Miranda says into the comfortable silence.

I smile to myself and hear a few chuckles interrupting the knitting. Most people here have heard this story before – it's one my aunt wheels out every year. It's the beginning of December and Christmas plans are in full swing – carol singing at the Model Village, a special New Year pub quiz and the inaugural tea and champagne celebration for New Year's Eve here at The Two Teas café.

I force my eyes open, knowing what's coming – Sascha won't have heard this story about my fear of Santa yet. I'm so tired I could just drift off to sleep in the warmth of the café. The last thing I want to do is knit or chat about my childhood fears.

As I suspected, Sascha is staring at me open-mouthed. 'Scared of Santa,' she says. 'But why?'

'I wasn't scared exactly,' I reply picking up my mug and taking a sip, but it's still too warm to drink. 'Just very wary.'

'She claimed that she didn't want some old man in her bedroom,' Miranda goes on.

'I think it showed common sense beyond my years,' I say.

I watch Sascha think about that for a moment, her eyes turning back to her knitting. 'It is a strange tradition when you think about it,' she says. 'Mostly children are told to have nothing to do with strange men.' She pauses and I think she's going to say something else but she doesn't. I think of the empty room in the flat at the hotel that she owns with her husband Geoff, the empty room that I know they both want to turn into a nursery one day.

It's no secret to the women sitting around this table that Sascha has struggled to get pregnant. It's one of the reasons she and Geoff moved to Sanderson Bay, thinking that the slower pace of life would help. They gave up their busy corporate lives in Leeds to move to this little town on the Yorkshire coast over a year ago. I'm not sure that turning a run-down seaside bed and breakfast into the luxurious boutique hotel it has become over the last twelve months has been particularly stress-free, but Sascha insists that despite the fact she still hasn't fallen pregnant, they are both happier here. Sanderson Bay has that effect on us all.

'Of course we always used to hang stockings by the fireplace,' Clara says. 'Santa Claus came in via the chimney, which is based on the Norse tradition of Odin who came into houses via fire holes on the solstice.'

We all groan at her because Clara knows everything

and she isn't afraid of sharing her vast wealth of useless information with us at any opportunity. As well as running the town's small supermarket, Clara Bellings is the trivia queen of The Black Horse and her pub quiz team haven't been beaten in over two months. Terry, the landlord, is thinking of having them banned.

The Knitting Club meet every Monday in my aunt and uncle's café. I suppose I should say that it's my café now but I still can't believe that I'm a business owner. I don't feel grown up enough to own my own café and, when I think about where I was just a year ago, I can hardly believe that it's my name on the deeds to this place, that it's my name on the brass plate above the door and that it's my name, Eloise Caron, on the Companies House website next to the words "The Two Teas Limited". It took five minutes to set up the limited company. I feel as though it should have taken much longer to do something that seems so grown up.

Miranda, my aunt, insists that nobody ever feels grown up enough to be doing whatever it is that they are doing – we're all winging it, or so she says. Even Bessie, who keeps her true age very close to her heart but must be seventy-five at least.

It was my idea to use the café in the evenings as a venue for groups to meet, just as it was my idea to sell our variety of loose-leaf teas along with cups, teapots and other tea drinking accessories. So far it's been a success. On Tuesdays the café plays host to the local book group and on Thursdays my uncle James helps me move all the furniture to one side for the Pilates class. But the Monday evening Knitting Club is the best night of the week in my opinion – nothing short of a biblical plague would stop the six of us turning up.

Miranda is Darjeeling, light and floral, which she drinks

like me with no milk or sugar. Clara is English breakfast with so much milk and sugar I wonder why she bothers with the tea at all. Lisa Martin is our newest recruit even though she has lived in Sanderson Bay longer than either me or Sascha – she is Assam with a splash of oat milk. Lisa works as a lawyer in Hull but bought a house here because she's loved it since she was a child and, despite her hellish commute, she always makes it in time for both the Knitting Club and the Pilates class. Bessie, the matriarch of our group who has lived in Sanderson Bay her whole life, even if nobody knows how long that life has been, is a hardened coffee drinker.

When I took over the café I didn't want a huge barista-style coffee machine because I wanted to concentrate on tea and I didn't want the place to smell of coffee all the time, but thanks to Bessie I always keep a pot of filter coffee on.

Sascha has given up caffeine in the pursuit of pregnancy and tonight she's drinking nettle tea, made from the dried nettles she helped me collect over the summer and which are supposedly good for fertility. It tastes disgusting and who knows if it even works, but Sascha is determined.

As for me, I'm Earl Grey – Chinese keemun tea and bergamot. I first discovered it at university and it soothes my soul, although I've had to cut down on the number of cups I drink these days, as I'm starting to notice I don't sleep as well as I used to. I probably shouldn't be drinking it this late in the evening.

Miranda taught me to knit when I used to stay with her and James on my holidays from boarding school. It's always been one of my favourite things to do, even though I was the brunt of a lot of jokes at university for my old-lady hobby. Knitting wasn't as fashionable then as it is now, but I've always found something meditative in watching a new project grow. It calms me down when I'm stressed or anxious. Not that I'm as stressed as I used to be, now I've moved to Sanderson Bay. I've started to feel different over the last few months, as though I have the space to breathe again, as though the walls have stopped closing in.

It breaks my heart that Miranda's arthritis is so bad that some days it is too painful for her to knit. But she never misses Knitting Club, sitting with us and joining in the gentle banter, her gnarled hands curled around her mug of Darjeeling.

'Nobody wants to hear any more about Saint Nicholas,' Bessie says now, clearly tired of Clara's stories.

'I'm just saying,' Clara replies. 'Traditionally we hung stockings by the chimney so children didn't have to be scared of somebody in their bedroom.'

'I wasn't scared,' I repeat. 'Just wary.'

Miranda catches my eye then and I know what she's thinking. If only I'd been a bit more wary about Marcus Dennison. I don't want to think about Marcus but sometimes, whenever I let my attention slip for a moment, there he is back inside my head. The fact that Christmas is nearly here doesn't help. I pick up my tea again, still too tired to think about knitting, and it's cool enough to drink. I take a sip, savouring the warm liquid for a moment and willing the ghost of Marcus Dennison to leave. It doesn't help though – nothing helps. Last week marked a year since he left, and I still don't feel as though I've put myself back together again.

The café door suddenly swings open bringing a blast of cold damp air with it, blowing all thoughts of Marcus away for the time being. At first I think that the wind has caught it but the cold air is followed by a man – a very tall, dark, handsome man. I put my mug down on the table in front of me and stand up.

The man frowns at me.

Out of the corner of my eye I see Bessie's eyebrows shoot up. 'Hello, young man,' she says. 'Would you like to join our Knitting Club?' Honestly if it was an old man saying that to a young woman, Bessie would be the first one shouting about sexism.

The man responds by frowning even harder, his eyebrows knotting together.

'I was just wondering if it would be possible to get a cup of coffee,' he says. His voice is deep and gruff and his manner overly formal. His accent sounds southern but there's a hint of something there, as though he came from Yorkshire once upon a time but doesn't want anybody to know that. He catches my eye then and it sends a brief wave of something almost unrecognisable through me. It's been so long since I felt anything. Over a year.

'But it looks like you're closed,' the man continues.

'We're always open to the passing traveller,' I say for some reason, sounding as though I'm narrating a nativity play. *Shut up, Ellie,* I think. He stares at me as though I'm mad and as I walk towards him grinning whilst he just keeps frowning. He's probably imagining scenes from *The Wicker Man*.

'We're all about tea here,' I babble on nervously. 'But I always have a pot of coffee on for Bessie.' The Knitting Club have fallen ominously silent behind me and I can feel their eyes boring into the back of me as the man stares at me from the front. The knitting ladies have been trying to fix me up with every passing man under fifty since I arrived with my

THE TEAROOM ON THE BAY

two meagre suitcases of belongings last year. This must be the best Monday night entertainment they've had in months.

I walk behind the counter and pick up the coffee pot, turning back towards the stranger.

'Drink in or to go?' I ask.

I watch his eyes dart over towards the Knitting Club again as he pulls a KeepCup out of his coat pocket.

'To go,' he replies.

Of course he wants it to go. He'd have to be mad to want to sit in here with all of us staring at him while he drinks his coffee.

I fill the cup noticing the picture of the whale on the side of it, the symbol of one of my least favourite coffee chains – not that I'm a fan of any of them really. I'm not a coffee person; I don't like the smell – but none of that is this man's fault so I swallow the small ball of rage that always springs up whenever I see that whale symbol.

'Are you in town for long?' I ask.

'Just a few days,' he says counting out his coins. 'On business.'

'Where are you staying?' I want to ask him what possible business could bring him to Sanderson Bay that none of the women sitting in this café wouldn't know about.

He looks at me then, his eyes meeting mine for the first time. They're pale grey and seem incongruous with his dark hair and eyebrows but it works. He really is very good-looking. 'I'm at the hotel up the road,' he says quietly.

'Oh Sascha and her husband own that,' I say.

'I've met Geoff,' he replies.

'Sascha's over there.' I point towards the knitting ladies again. 'Blonde wavy hair.'

Sascha waves and the stranger raises an eyebrow before turning back to me.

'I'm Ellie by the way,' I say, holding out my hand.

'Ben Lawson,' he replies taking my hand in his and squeezing it gently. I ignore the fizz that dances in my stomach when he does that. 'How long have you worked here?' he asks, the corners of his mouth turning up into what could almost be a smile.

'I've been here about a year,' I say. 'But I bought the café off the previous owners back in the spring.' I don't tell him that I bought it for a song from my own aunt and uncle; that's none of his business.

His face closes down again then, the almost-smile forgotten.

'You're Eloise Caron?' he asks.

'Yes, how did you—'

'I was expecting someone older,' he interrupts, his eyebrows knotting together again.

'I don't understand,' I begin but already he's turning towards the door. How did he know my name?

'Maybe I'll see you around,' he says as he leaves.

I shut the door behind him, putting the latch across so nobody else can blow in like Mary Poppins on this cold December evening.

When I turn back towards the table of knitters, I notice Bessie and Clara nudging each other.

'Stop it,' I say. 'No matchmaking. He'll only be here for a few days and he seemed quite rude anyway.' I don't tell them about the fizzing feeling in my belly, or about the fact that he knew who I was.

'He's a coffee drinker anyway,' Miranda says, smiling at me.

'I'm not sure he is,' I reply glancing back towards the door that he just disappeared out of as suddenly as he appeared. 'I think he might be Russian caravan.'

2

After everyone has left I load the dishwasher carefully with the mugs and plates and teapots that we've used tonight while Sascha, who always stays behind to help me clear up, sweeps the floor. I've only known Sascha a year but she's the closest thing I've ever had to a best friend and I don't know what I'd have done without her as I've turned my aunt and uncle's upmarket greasy spoon café into the tea shop of my dreams. Together we've both taken over rather run-down businesses and changed them into something special, something different.

Sanderson Bay has grown increasingly popular since the American singer Karol Bergenstein stayed here a few years ago. According to the news reports, her grandfather had visited Sanderson Bay when he was stationed in Yorkshire during the war and she wanted to get to see the places he'd been when she was in the UK on tour. As far as anyone knows she's never returned to Sanderson Bay but it's put us on the map and brought a lot of footfall and money to the town.

'So what did you say your handsome coffee drinker was called?' Sascha asks, leaning on the broom and looking at me.

'Ben,' I reply not quite meeting her eye. I'm still feeling a bit odd about him knowing my name.

'Well he'll be a nice distraction at least.'

'For you maybe. He's staying with you so you'll probably see him much more than I will. I doubt he'll be back here.'

'What makes you say that?'

'Like Miranda said, he's a coffee drinker. He even had a Moby's cup,' I reply referring to the coffee chain symbolised by the whale on Ben's KeepCup.

'But you think he's Russian caravan and I've never known you to be wrong.'

I can't remember when I first started to associate people with the tea I thought they should drink, but these days it's almost second nature to me. I can't meet anyone without wondering. Some people, like Ben, insist they're hardened coffee drinkers but there is always some sort of tea or infusion that they like, however hard they try to resist.

'Perhaps I am this time,' I say as I spray the counters down with disinfectant. 'I've always been wrong about Bessie.'

Sascha walks over to me then and sits on one of the stools on the other side of the counter.

'What's the matter?' she asks.

I hesitate, not sure if I want to tell her. The conversation I had with Ben had felt private somehow, hurried and whispered as though he was trying to keep it a secret from everyone else in the café at the time. I can't work out if the fizzing I'm still feeling in my stomach whenever I think of his grey eyes and that half-smile is attraction or unease.

'He knew who I was,' I say. 'He knew my name – he

called me Eloise Caron. Don't you think that's weird for someone who's just here for a few days on business?'

'Is that what he told you?' Sascha asks. 'That he was here on business.'

I nod.

'Who comes to Sanderson Bay on business?'

'Good point,' I reply and my stomach fizzes again, definitely unease this time.

'So why is he here?'

'And how does he know my name?'

'Well Geoff might have told him,' Sascha says. 'Or he might have seen it on the sign above the door.'

'Maybe,' I say as I put away the cleaning stuff and start to turn off the hot water and coffee pot for the night. 'We'll probably never speak to him again anyway – I doubt he'll stay for long no matter why he's here.'

I walk around the counter and take the broom off Sascha, putting it away in the cupboard. She follows me, sitting me down at the table by the window.

'Listen,' she says. 'I have some news that's much more important that Ben whoever-he-is.'

I look at her expectantly, hoping it's what I think it is but too scared to say the words myself.

'I'm pregnant,' she whispers quietly, as though she too doesn't want to say the words too loudly in case they turn out not to be true.

I grin at her, thoughts of Ben forgotten. 'Really?' I say.

'Definitely,' she replies. 'I did three tests this time and I've been patient.' Sascha has been disappointed by late periods before.

'How patient?' I ask.

'Ten weeks patient.'

I stare at her. 'You've known about this for ten weeks?' I say.

'I know,' she replies her face dropping slightly. 'Don't be cross with me for not telling you sooner. I had to be sure this time. Really sure. I didn't even tell Geoff for the first four weeks.'

I reach over and take her hands in mine. 'I'm not cross, Sash – how could I be? This is the best news I've heard in a long time. I'm so excited for you.'

'You have to keep it quiet though,' she says, whispering again. 'Other than Geoff and his mum nobody else knows.'

I mime zipping my lips together, but break into a grin again. 'I'm so happy,' I say.

'We have our twelve-week scan in two weeks' time.'

I stand up, feeling light-headed with excitement. 'I want to do something to celebrate,' I say. 'But I can't open champagne and it's too late to—'

'Just being able to tell you is celebration enough,' Sascha says. 'Plus I don't have to drink that vile nettle tea anymore!'

'I can't believe you've been drinking it for ten weeks when you didn't need to!'

'I couldn't stop drinking it or you'd have guessed.'

'I'll have to make up a nicer tea for you now,' I reply.

She stands up then and I notice, not for the first time, how pale and tired she looks. I can't believe I didn't guess she was pregnant. I suppose I didn't dare hope for her. I think we'd all given up hope.

'I should go,' she says. 'I'm exhausted.'

'Do you want me to walk back with you?'

'Don't be ridiculous.' She laughs. 'I'm pregnant not consumptive.'

I hold up my hands. 'Don't blame me if I want to wrap you in cotton wool. You've been waiting so long for this.'

She steps towards me and squeezes my arm. 'I know and I'm so grateful to you for just being there. But do me a favour and don't make it obvious until after the scan. We don't want to tell anyone else until then.'

I watch as she opens the door of the café and turns back towards me.

'I'll keep an eye on your Ben for you as well,' she says. 'I'll report back.'

'He's not my Ben,' I reply as she walks away.

But the first thing I think of when I wake up the next morning is Ben – his grey eyes and reluctant smile. I think of him before I think of the café, my usual waking thought. I think of him even before I think about Sascha and Geoff's baby.

My stomach fizzes. I must just be hungry.

I get out of bed and pad towards the kitchen to put the kettle on. My first drink of the day isn't tea – surprisingly. I start every day with hot water and lemon in an attempt to be healthy. I finish every day with leftover cake, so I suppose my life is all about balance.

The flat above the café feels quiet and cold this morning and I take my hot drink back to bed so I can check the café's social media accounts and reply to any comments or messages. I pull the duvet up over me and sink into the pillows.

This room used to be to my aunt and uncle's bedroom and I used to have the little room on the other side of the hallway when I came back for the school holidays. There are so many memories tied up in the walls of this flat – good ones and bad ones. Sometimes I'm almost overwhelmed by the nostalgia. And by the quiet.

Before I met Marcus I lived on my own in York, but York is never quiet. There is always the sound of people or traffic. Sanderson Bay is so still in comparison that some days it can unsettle me, especially when I've always been used to this flat being so full of Miranda's spirit and the smell of baking or cooking.

It isn't as though Miranda and James have died or anything. When my aunt's arthritis got too bad for her to manage the stairs, they bought a bungalow on the other side of Sanderson Bay with their savings and the money I gave them for the café. I see them nearly every day, but sometimes when I'm alone in the flat I miss them and I miss who they used to be before my aunt got ill and my uncle had that permanent groove of worry between his eyebrows.

Despite it being much quieter than it was when I lived in York, I don't feel that bone-aching loneliness I felt there before I met Marcus, and again after he announced he was leaving. I know I'm happier here; I know I made the right decision last year, but I still have this strange feeling of something missing as though I've gone out without my phone. I don't feel settled; I don't feel grounded. I want to finally be able to call Sanderson Bay home and to feel as though I have found my place in the world.

Because I haven't felt settled since I was thirteen years old.

I shake the thoughts away – Christmas always makes everything feel worse than it is. I probably just need to redecorate the flat and put my stamp on it to feel more at home, but I haven't really had time thanks to the success of the café. I turn back to the social media accounts. A few queries to answer, a booking for a Christmas party but not much else. Even the "no coffee lol" crowd are quieter than usual as everyone gets so busy with the festive season that they don't even have time to troll each other online.

The hardened Sanderson Bay coffee drinker can get their fix at The Black Horse. Terry and his wife Mo installed a barista machine a few years ago and now serve up every coffee imaginable, at least half of which I'm sure are made up. Terry and I aren't in competition; we complement each other.

During the week I always try and open the café by 7.30am. In December it's still dark at that time and I don't get many customers other than Lisa popping in for a take-away cup of Assam and oat milk. I've always been an early riser since I was a child – I used to use the time to read but these days I take up my Olympus Pen camera and, at this time of year, my brightest lamps, to update the café's Instagram account for the day.

Today I've known what I'm going to post about since the moment I woke up.

Ben. Or rather Russian caravan tea, the tea that Ben reminds me of, the tea that I'm sure I could get him to drink if he ever came back to the café.

Not that I want him to of course.

I set up the loose-leaf tea, teapot and cup for the photograph. I use the willow-patterned china to complement the Chinese tea, the silver tea strainer. Just as I'm about to take the photograph I hear somebody clearing their throat behind me. I jump, scattering tea leaves on to the floor.

When I turn around it's Ben, smiling that reluctant smile that is somewhere between embarrassed and smug. Scratch that, it's much closer to smug this morning than it was last night. Other than his grey eyes and his smile and his dark wool coat. I hadn't taken in many details about him the previous evening. His dark hair is neatly cut, and he has the beginnings of a five o'clock shadow on his chin.

'I was just thinking about you,' I say, regretting the words as soon as they come out of my mouth. I watch his smile change from smug to embarrassed. Embarrassed for me probably.

'I was wondering if I could get a coffee,' he says, taking off his coat. Underneath he's wearing jeans and a dark red V-neck jumper over a blue and white checked shirt. 'But I have a feeling you're not going to let me,' he goes on as he folds his coat neatly over the back of one of the chairs.

'No,' I reply. 'I'm not. At least not for the moment. There's a reason I was thinking about you and I want you to try something. If you don't like it, I'll make you a whole pot of coffee.'

'OK,' he says slowly, doubtfully. 'What is it?'

3

'It tastes like smoke,' Ben says as he puts the cup carefully back on the saucer. Everything he does is careful and meticulous.

'Is that good or bad?' I ask.

'Good, I think,' he replies. 'I've never tasted anything like it.'

'I bet you've never drunk tea that wasn't made with a bag, have you?'

He shakes his head and picks up his cup again. I smile to myself – I knew he was Russian caravan. But I'm not sure that the willow pattern china was the right cup to serve it in. It worked for the photograph but I think it would taste better out of something else.

I stand up and get one of the Hornsea mugs off the shelf. Miranda had picked these up at a car boot sale a few years ago and then never used them, so I purloined them as a perfect addition to the café.

I pour Ben a fresh tea into the mug.

'Try it in this one,' I say as I pass it to him.

'It tastes different in a mug?'

'Sometimes. The teacup was for aesthetics really – I was

setting up an Instagram photo. But if I was serving Russian caravan tea here in the café, I'd serve it in this.'

He takes a sip. 'Much better,' he says, but I can tell he's only humouring me. 'So only some teas work in mugs?'

'Well you wouldn't drink Earl Grey or an afternoon blend in a mug like that – they're too delicate and need to be drunk from china.'

He raises an eyebrow at me. 'So what else would you drink from a Hornsea pottery mug?'

He recognises the mug. Interesting.

'English or Irish breakfast,' I reply.

'So why Russian caravan?' he asks. 'When I told you I only drink coffee?' His words sound harsh but he smiles as he says them.

'I think there's a tea for everyone,' I say. 'Even people who say they don't like tea.'

'That doesn't really answer my question,' he says.

'It's a blend of oolong, keemun and lapsang souchong teas,' I begin. 'Which are all from the Chinese tea plant. Camel caravans used to transport the tea from the Mongolian Steppes all the way across into Russia.'

'Hence Russian caravan.'

I nod. 'It was a six-thousand-mile journey and took up to six months. Legend has it that the smoky flavour comes from all the campfires that the caravans stopped at along the way, but it's actually just the lapsang souchong, which is smoke-dried.' Clara isn't the only one full of useless information.

'And it's my tea because?'

'It's dark and brooding,' I say and I can immediately feel myself blushing.

'So that's why you were thinking of me?' His smug smile is back.

'Well I was thinking of the tea really,' I reply hurriedly. 'I was trying to take a photograph for Instagram when you arrived.'

'Sorry about that,' he says looking over at the spilt tea leaves on the floor.

'Don't worry, the light wasn't quite right anyway.' I stand up. 'I should probably clean that up.'

'And I should probably get going,' he replies, standing up and picking up his coat from the back of the chair. 'I had a look at your Instagram account last night actually.'

I prepare myself for a lecture about what I should be doing better to promote my business – I've never felt as though social media and marketing is my strong suit – so I'm surprised when he tells me it's good.

'You have a real eye for shape and light and colour,' he says, pushing his arms into the sleeves of his coat.

'I could do with some more followers.'

'Well I might be able to help you with that if you like,' he says. 'I work in marketing.' He shrugs as if to say it's no big deal, that it's easy to get new followers, even though I've been trying for a nearly a year.

'And what marketing business are you in Sanderson Bay on?' I ask. It's meant to sound light, amusing but I hear it more like an inquisition and I don't mean it to be like that at all.

'I'm sorry,' I mumble before he has a chance to answer. 'That's none of my business. I'm really grateful for your kind offer but I totally understand if you're too busy.'

He sinks his hands into his coat pockets and looks at his

feet. 'I may not have been entirely honest about my reasons for being here,' he says. It sounds as though he is going to make some great revelation. 'I'm just taking a bit of a break to be honest so I don't have much to do.'

'Any social media help you can give would be hugely appreciated,' I say. 'I don't think I'm very good at it.'

He smiles and it doesn't seem reluctant or embarrassed or smug this time, but it does make my stomach turn over.

After Ben has left I check my phone and see a text from Sascha: *Ben is up early and on his way to you! Tell me everything! He's even better-looking in the light of day!*

Sascha is a fan of the exclamation mark, but I can't deny the truth in her text. He is even better-looking in the light of day, but however good-looking he is and however that genuine smile made me feel, I know he's hiding something with his "here on business/taking a break" excuse. And later, when I see him deep in conversation with Eric Andrews, owner of the Sanderson Bay Model Village, I'm even more sure that he knows more about this town than he's letting on.

And it's only then that I remember I'd never asked him how he knew my name.

4

Thursday night is Pilates night in the café. This was the one night I wasn't sure would take off. When Seren, the Pilates teacher, first approached me about it I wasn't convinced, but over the last six months the class has grown from three of us – me, Sascha and Lisa – to at least ten every week. Bessie even came once, although we couldn't convert her, and Miranda comes every week and Seren gives her special modifications for her arthritis.

I only started going because I wanted the class to be a success but now I notice that if I don't go I really miss it. Joseph Pilates apparently said that "a man is as old as his spinal column" and although after a long day in the café my spinal column feels as though it belongs to an eighty-year-old, Joseph also said that "physical fitness is the prerequisite for happiness", so I continue to persist in my efforts, inelegant as they are.

It's a quick turnaround after Pilates to get to The Black Horse in time for the weekly pub quiz. Every week I try to persuade Lisa to join us but every week she refuses.

'I'm asleep on my feet, El,' she says. 'Maybe next week.' But every week she's too tired and sometimes I wonder what her life must be like, whether she's lonely, whether she ever gets sick of the long commute and the high-stress job. I tell myself that I need to get to know her better but somehow every week runs away with me and I forget and suddenly it will be Thursday again and she'll be telling me that she's too tired to come to the pub and it starts all over again.

Sascha, Geoff, Miranda and I, collectively known as The Teacups for pub quiz purposes, are determined to beat Clara's team before the end of the year so we can't afford to miss a week.

My aunt and uncle have lived in Sanderson Bay for fourteen years and in that time I've watched it change from a sleepy seaside town to the hip and trendy staycation location it's become today. I spent most of my school holidays here, unless my parents summoned me back to France, and it's always felt like a second home. The Black Horse is the pub in which James and Miranda bought me my first legal drink (there were several illegal ones before that at boarding school but we don't need to go into those now), and until a few years ago it was one of those very traditional, rather run-down British pubs with horse brasses on the wall, Anaglypta wallpaper stained yellow from years of cigarette smoke and a carpet that had seen much better days. The summer after Karol Bergenstein's much photographed visit, Terry decided to have the pub done out and it now boasts solid pine tables, perfectly white walls and every sort of coffee and cocktail under the sun.

As usual we're the last to arrive and Terry already has four ploughman's baguettes waiting for us. We settle down to eat and get ready for the quiz as Terry does his usual introductions.

'Welcome everyone to the Sanderson Bay pub quiz,' he

drawls as though there's anybody here who isn't aware that it's quiz night. 'Tonight I will be asking some of the toughest quiz questions on the planet and the winning team will get a bottle of champagne.' He announces it as though we're about to win a Rolls-Royce, but we all know it's just cheap prosecco and technically Terry could be done under the Trade Descriptions Act. The prize isn't the reason the pub is so full. The Teacups aren't the only team desperate to beat Clara's Brainboxes.

Just as we're about to begin the pub door swings open and Ben walks in. It's an unfortunate moment for him to arrive because we're all waiting with bated breath for the first quiz question and for once the pub is almost completely silent. Everyone turns to look at him and we're really not the sort of town that stares at strangers in the pub. We like to make them feel welcome – a lot of our livelihoods depend on holidaymakers and passing trade after all. We are not making the best impression on Ben Lawson.

Eric raises a hand in greeting and Ben goes over to talk to him as the pub falls back into gentle conversation.

'How does Ben know Eric?' I whisper to Sascha. 'I saw them talking the other day too.'

She shrugs. 'No idea.'

Terry starts his tedious introduction to the pub quiz again as though we're all goldfish and have forgotten in seconds why we're here.

'Get on with it,' someone shouts.

Ben goes to the bar to get a pint and as he's being served Terry asks him, over the microphone, what his name is and why he's here.

'Um, I'm Ben,' he says hesitantly very aware of all eyes on him. 'And I'm staying at Geoff and Sascha's hotel.'

'Are you joining a team?' Terry asks.

Ben looks around at us all and it seems to finally dawn on him that it's quiz night. He catches my eye and I beckon him over.

'Join us,' I say. 'We need all the help we can get. Are you any good at sport or politics?' The Teacups are excellent at music, TV, books and popular culture but ask us a question about cricket or who the foreign secretary was in 1987 and we fall apart.

Ben takes a long gulp of his pint and walks over to our table, sitting down next to Miranda.

'OK,' he says cracking his knuckles. 'Let's do this.'

The pub is suddenly in uproar, complaining about this sudden new arrival.

'How do we know he's not a plant?' someone shouts. 'Here to let Ellie's team win?'

'Oh don't be ridiculous,' Eric shouts back. 'It's just Ben Lawson, you know who he is.'

There's a sudden moment of quiet as everyone looks at Ben before Terry announces the start of the quiz for the third, and hopefully final time. All eyes turn down towards the answer papers, except mine as I look over at Ben and crinkle my brow in a question, trying to ask him how Eric knows him without the use of words. Ben shakes his head and looks away, taking another swig from his pint glass.

Once the quiz begins there is no time to talk or chat. Terry's questions are quickfire and relentless with barely time to write the answer down, let alone confer with team members. Whenever Terry comes into The Two Teas he always drinks English breakfast, but his rapid questioning style makes me wonder if he's actually gunpowder tea. I've never had the nerve to ask him though.

The Teacups have to trust each other as we write answers in the appropriate boxes on the answer sheet and try to keep up with Terry, hoping we've got at least a few right. Ben, it turns out, is good at both sport and politics as well as music and books. I look over at him as he writes his answers down and get that fizzing feeling in my stomach again. His writing is neat and meticulous, just like him, and I notice he's left-handed. He's wearing a dark green pullover over a red and white checked shirt and he hasn't shaved since the last time I saw him. When he looks over at me I let my eyes slide away. I don't want him to get the wrong idea.

'And the final question,' Terry announces dramatically. I hate Terry's final questions, they make no sense to me and they are not even questions. 'Damp fog solves nothing.'

I groan and Sascha rolls her eyes and throws down her pencil in disgust.

'I'll repeat that one,' Terry says. 'Damp fog solves nothing.'

'I have no idea what he's talking about,' I say.

But Ben grins and pulls the answer sheet towards him and writes "moist" carefully in the box. Sascha and I stare at him.

'Well done,' my uncle James says to Ben slapping him on the back. 'The Teacups never get those final questions.'

'Maybe we're in with a chance tonight, eh Ellie?' Miranda says winking at me.

'Let me get you another pint, Ben,' James says. 'What about you, Ellie, another glass of wine?'

I nod and everyone gives my uncle their drinks orders.

'So how do you know Eric?' Miranda asks the question that's been on my lips all evening.

Ben looks down into his empty pint glass and I see his cheekbones colour slightly before he looks up again.

'I know quite a few people in here tonight actually,' he says. 'Well I used to know them anyway. I used to live in Sanderson Bay when I was a kid, but I haven't been back for nearly fifteen years.'

He used to live here? Why hadn't he said that when he was drinking Russian caravan tea in my café two days ago? I catch his eye and raise my eyebrows at him, but he looks away again. He's definitely hiding something.

'Before our time,' Miranda says. 'We moved here fourteen years ago. We used to own the café before we sold it to Ellie.' She reaches over and takes my hand. 'She's made a much better job of it than we ever did.'

'That's not true,' I protest, glancing over at Ben who is blushing again. Is he embarrassed? Or just self-conscious at being the centre of attention? 'The café isn't better now, it's just different,' I go on.

'The whole town is completely different,' Ben says quietly.

'It must seem it if you haven't been back for fifteen years,' Miranda says.

'You know we were visited by a Broadway star and since then we've really had to up our game,' Sascha interrupts.

'Karol Bergenstein,' Ben says as my uncle comes back with the drinks. 'I saw it in the paper.'

'So where did you used to live, Ben?' my aunt asks as she picks up her glass of wine, and I see his face colour again.

'Um, just outside of town,' he says. 'Near the cliffs and the… um… lifeboat station.' He's staring into his pint again as though he doesn't want to talk about this.

Miranda nods. 'Oh yes,' she says. 'That little row of cottages. They're lovely.'

Ben doesn't say anything.

'Why did you leave?' my aunt ploughs on, clearly unable to sense his discomfort.

'I went to university,' he says. 'And Mum moved away around the same time.'

'And your father?'

I watch Ben go pale at the question. My aunt is wonderful and I owe her so much but she is so nosy. It's why she loves it here in Sanderson Bay – everyone here is fantastic but they do love to be part of each other's business. If you're shy or introverted or private or anxious it can be difficult sometimes. I know this because I'm all of those things – running a café has pushed me way out of my comfort zone – and I suspect that Ben is at least two of them. I can't let him suffer under Miranda's inquisition anymore.

'How the hell did you know that final quiz question?' I ask. 'Nobody ever gets those!'

He smiles at me and a flash of something that looks like gratitude crosses his face.

'Cryptic crosswords,' he says. 'It was a cryptic crossword clue.'

'Those things make no sense to me either.' I laugh. 'Explains why I've never been able to get what Terry is waffling on about though.'

'It's just patterns,' Ben goes on. 'Patterns in words and letters. They're easy to spot if you practise, if you know what to look for.'

Sascha and I exchange a doubtful glance. 'Easy for you maybe,' she says.

He holds his hands up. 'I've always just been able to see patterns in things,' he says.

'Do you do cryptic crosswords?' I ask. 'I've always been impressed by anyone who can make any sense of those!'

He smiles at me again now and it's not smug or reluctant. It's lazy and genuine and oh so sexy. I can feel the goose bumps springing up on my arms. 'I've done them for years,' he says.

'So how did you get the answer to this one?' I ask.

'Here look, I'll show you.' He gets up and walks over to my side of the table, squeezing on to the bench beside me, and pulls the pencil and paper towards him. His arm is pressing against mine and I'm very aware of the feel of him next to me. I take a shaky breath and hope he doesn't notice how his close proximity is making me feel.

'So first of all, what's another word for fog?' he asks.

'Um, mist?'

'Excellent,' he says and writes "mist" on the paper. 'And what's the symbol for nothing?'

'I don't know,' I say, feeling stupid.

'OK, another word for nothing then?'

'Nought,' I say. 'Or zero.'

He writes a "o" on the paper.

'And mist plus O is…'

'Moist!' Sascha and I shout out at the same time.

'That's a really simple one to be honest,' he says.

'If you say so,' I reply.

'I guess it's just practice. I've been doing them for years. I learned from my...' He pauses and his smile disappears. 'From my dad,' he finishes quietly.

Whatever it is that he is hiding, that he doesn't want to talk about, is to do with his father.

And it's nobody's business but his own.

Luckily, Terry chooses that moment to begin reading out the quiz answers. We all hurriedly swap answer sheets and listen as he goes through them. As Terry reads each answer out it starts to become clear that, thanks to Ben's help, The Teacups have done much better than usual. It could all rest on Terry's cryptic final question.

'And the answer to the final question,' Terry says dramatically. 'Is "moist".'

The various quiz teams begin their usual weekly moaning about Terry's final question. Ben and I exchange a look and I feel my stomach flip over again. It must just be the excitement of being in with a chance of winning the quiz for the first time ever.

All the answer sheets are passed up to Terry at the bar and he announces that he'll be back in a few minutes with the winner.

'I don't want to jinx it,' my uncle says. 'But I think we've done quite well this week thanks to you, Ben.'

'Don't tell anyone.' Ben smiles. 'They already think I'm a plant.'

'In third place...' Terry begins. He only ever announces the top three so as not to embarrass the teams, like The Teacups, who always do so badly. Although I am quietly optimistic tonight and find myself crossing my fingers in my lap. 'In third place is The Old-Timers.'

I uncross my fingers. There's no way we're going to get any higher than third place. I'm surprised by how disappointed I feel as I join in the applause and see Eric and Bessie high-five each other.

'In second place is The Brainboxes,' Terry says next. The pub erupts into cheers. It doesn't matter who has won now because for the first time in weeks it's not Clara's team. The Brainboxes are taking it well although Clara herself looks a bit put out.

'And in first place,' Terry says slowly and dramatically. 'The winners of a bottle of champagne are...' He pauses and everyone starts drumming on the tables with their hands. 'The Teacups!'

We all look at each other in shock.

'Oh my God we did it,' Sascha squeals.

'Fix,' someone else shouts.

'Well I think this calls for an actual bottle of champagne don't you?' James asks as he heads to the bar again. 'Lemonade for you, Sascha?'

'Push the boat out,' she replies. 'Lemonade and lime.' Sascha hasn't had an alcoholic drink in months in her pursuit of a baby so it doesn't look odd to anyone that she isn't having one now. Sascha looks at me under her eyelashes, her cheeks pink with happiness.

When James comes back with the drinks, we all pick up our glasses and clink them together.

'To The Teacups,' Sascha says. 'And to our plant who won the quiz for us,' she adds nudging Ben.

5

We're just finishing our champagne when Geoff arrives to walk Sascha home. I watch him help her with her coat and the gentle, protective way he treats her fills me with so much joy. I'm so happy for them and I find myself crossing my fingers again that they have a healthy, happy pregnancy.

Miranda and James leave not long after, James insisting Miranda needs to rest and Miranda insisting she's fine, although I can see the pain in her eyes.

Which leaves me and Ben.

'I should go,' I say standing up and reaching for my coat.

'Let me walk you back,' he replies.

'Don't be silly – I'm the opposite way to the hotel.'

'Let me see you safely home,' he insists. 'Where do you live?'

'Above the café,' I reply.

Eric raises a hand towards us as we leave the pub together and once we're outside Ben offers me his arm. I tuck my gloved hand into the seam of his elbow and, despite the layers of wool that sit between us, I feel a pulse of electricity, an unexpected spark. I look up at Ben but he's looking straight ahead.

'I'm sorry about my aunt,' I say as we walk down the main street towards the café. 'She's lovely, but like a lot of people in this town she can be quite nosy.'

'Small towns can be like that,' he replies.

'It took me a lot of getting used to. I'm not much of a sharer. I prefer my life to be private, not the property of Bessie Bower.'

He laughs and I remember that he must have known Bessie when he was a child as he grew up here. I want to know more about his time here and why he left. I want to know which house was his and who lives in it now. I want to know where he lives now but I also don't want to be nosy; his story is none of my business.

'Would you like to come in for a cup of tea?' I hear myself asking as we come to a halt in front of The Two Teas.

'Sure,' he replies and I'm suddenly glad nobody else is around as I let him into the café. I'd never hear the end of it. I wasn't expecting him to say yes. I was really just being polite, no ulterior motive intended. I hope he doesn't think there was one.

I cringe inside. Why am I so awkward with people? Running the café has helped and I'm much better at small talk than I used to be. But clearly I still need work.

I flick on the lights and realise that the tables are still pushed to the side of the room from the Pilates class earlier. My uncle usually comes early on Friday morning to help me put them back.

'Um, sorry,' I say. 'We came to the pub straight from the Pilates class. Let me sort out a table.'

I feel his hand brush my arm for a moment. 'Don't worry,' he says. 'I'll do it.'

I go behind the counter to put the hot water boiler on.

'Do you want me to make you some coffee?' I ask.

'No,' he says, surprising me. 'I'll have tea. I've not been sleeping very well recently so what do you recommend?'

'I recommend not drinking coffee,' I say.

I turn around to look at him, he's already put half the tables back in their place.

'I only expected you to put one table out,' I say.

'It's all right, I don't mind.'

I let him get on with it as I go back to preparing the tea. 'I've got just the thing for insomnia,' I say. 'You can try my night-time blend.'

'What's in that?' he asks.

'Lavender to calm your mind,' I say. 'Camomile to relax your muscles and valerian to soothe you to sleep.'

I hear him putting the chairs out behind me as I wait for the hot water to reach the right temperature. I don't want it to boil for herbal infusions. In fact there are only a few teas that you should use boiling water for and herbal tisanes are not one of them.

I put three spoons of the dried herbs into the teapot – a spoonful for each of us and one for the pot and when the water reaches ninety-five degrees, I pour it over the herbs. The steam smells of lavender and valerian and I take a few deep breaths of it before putting the lid onto the teapot. When I turn around Ben is standing on the other side of the counter waiting for me.

'It needs to brew for about five minutes,' I say. 'If you take it over I'll bring the cups.' I choose matching cups and saucers – dark blue with silver painted stars that I found in a shop in Hull that was closing down. I don't use them very often as not many people come in late enough for the soothing evening blends. Mostly I sell my night-time blends for people to drink at home.

'Do you make the teas yourself?' Ben asks, as I take the cups over and sit down.

'A lot of the herbal tisanes,' I reply. 'I have a herb garden in the back and then I dry them myself. I grew the lavender and valerian but I find camomile really hard to keep alive so I do order that in along with all the actual tea which obviously I can't grow here!'

'Obviously,' he says and smiles the smug version of his smile at me. 'What made you so interested in teas and herbs?'

'It started with the herb garden really,' I say as I pour the tea. 'I started growing herbs when I was about fourteen. We only have a small garden here but it's very sunny and I just wanted to do something nice with it as my aunt and uncle were so busy with the café. I wanted it to be something that didn't need much upkeep and that's the beauty of a herb garden. Once it's established it does its own thing.'

'You grew up here too?' he asks.

I shake my head. 'I grew up in France,' I say. 'But I came to England to go to boarding school when I was thirteen. My school was near Harrogate so I used to come back here for the Christmas and Easter holidays and I just went back to France in the summers.'

'So you didn't spend Christmas with your parents?' he asks, looking straight at me. I look away.

'No, but it was fine,' I lie. 'I loved Christmas at Sanderson Bay and things haven't changed that much despite appearances. We still have Christmas carols at the Model Village – you'll probably remember them from your childhood. They're tomorrow night actually, after the Christmas lights get switched on if you're still here and fancy coming along.'

'That would be nice,' he says. 'They used to mark the start of Christmas for me when I was a kid.'

'I was never back from school in time but my aunt always told me about them.'

When I look back at him, he's looking into his teacup as though he's about to see his future there. He has the same expression on his face that he had when Miranda questioned him about his father and I watched him stare into his pint glass.

'I'd already left when your aunt and uncle opened this café,' he says. 'Our paths never crossed.'

I don't know what to say to that and I wait for a moment to see if he's going to say anything further about when he lived here, but he doesn't.

'You were telling me about your herb garden,' he says instead.

'Well I wanted something to do with all the herbs I'd grown – lavender, lemon verbena, peppermint – and I discovered that if I dried them I could make teas out of them and it sort of grew from there. I wanted to sell the teas in the café, I even suggested to James and Miranda that I sell them to raise funds for the lifeboats but they were having none of it.'

I notice a look pass over his face when I mention the lifeboats, but I can't work out what it is. Most of the men who live in Sanderson Bay are either current lifeboat volunteers or, like Eric, they used to be when they were younger and I wonder about Ben's father and if he volunteered on the lifeboats too.

'Anyway,' I carry on. 'My aunt and uncle were adamant that the sort of customers they had in the café were not going to buy or drink herbal tea. This was before Sanderson Bay became a hip place to be of course.'

'And now look at you,' he says, looking around the café at the row upon row of different teas and tisanes – black, green, white, oolong and every herbal blend imaginable.

'It's a bit of a dream come true to be honest,' I say and I can feel my cheeks heat as he looks at me. I can't work out if it's the embarrassment of admitting that my dream was to sell herbal tea or if it's the intensity of his stare. I feel his hand covering mine gently on the table between us and that spark of electricity returns.

'I think it's fantastic,' he says. 'I think this and all the other changes are exactly what the Bay needed. Things can't stay the same forever.'

'Thank you,' I say. 'I had a bit of backlash about the changes at the beginning but most people seem to have come around to it now.'

'Did you stay in Sanderson Bay after you finished school?' he asks. 'Or did you go back to France?'

'Neither,' I say. 'I went to university in York.'

'Snap,' he replies. 'What did you study?'

'Art history, how about you?'

'Law,' he says.

'But I thought you worked in marketing?'

'Reading law made me not want to be a lawyer anymore,' he says and when he smiles it's that big genuine smile again that lights up his whole face and makes my stomach fizz and in that moment I suddenly realise how attracted I am to this stranger who blew into my café on Monday evening holding a whole host of secrets close to his chest.

And as clear as the attraction is, it's also clear that being attracted to him is a very bad idea.

'Did you stay in York after graduating?' he asks.

I pick up my blue and silver teacup and think for a moment about those long years I lived in York and how lonely I was. And then I think about Marcus and how I thought he was going to change my life.

'I stayed on at university for another year to do my masters,' I say. 'And then I got offered funding to do my PhD if I stayed on as an undergraduate lecturer.'

'That sounds amazing,' he says but he must see the look on my face and I watch his brows knit together. 'Wasn't it?' he asks.

'On paper it was an amazing opportunity, but in reality…' I pause. 'I'm quite shy and anxious and I felt sick every time I had to give a lecture. My professor told me it was just nerves and that I'd get used to it. But I never did.'

'You don't seem shy,' he says.

I laugh because I hear this all the time when I'm in Sanderson Bay.

'You're seeing me on my home turf,' I say. 'I know everyone in town and I've lived here on and off since I was a teenager. I'm comfortable here.'

'You don't know me though,' he says.

'Yes, but this is just a one-on-one situation. I'm fine talking to just one person, especially if it's about something I'm interested in.'

'Like tea?'

I smile. 'Yes, like tea,' I say. 'But also art. The problems came when I had to stand up in front of a lecture theatre of students who are only a few years younger than me.'

'How long did you do it for?'

'Nearly five years and then…' I stop and I look at him. I can't talk about what happened. Not tonight, not here with this beautiful dark-haired, grey-eyed man. I don't want to feel like this or think about Marcus or my unfinished PhD when I'm talking to him.

'I'm sorry,' he says. 'You don't have to tell me anything. Like I said you hardly know me.'

'How about you?' I ask. 'Did you stay in York after university? Have our paths crossed and we've never realised?'

'I went to work in London,' he says. 'But Mum had moved to York by then so I came back a lot at the weekends. I still do actually and I still have a lot of friends there. We've probably been sitting in the same pub on a Saturday night and never known!'

'Undoubtedly,' I reply. 'York is such a small place.'

Once again he's only mentioned his mother. I want to know about his father but I don't ask because I recognise something in him, something about that look that passes over his face and it's only now that I realise what it is.

Loss.

'Did you not want to go back to France?' he asks after we've talked about pubs in York for a few minutes. I lean back in my chair and sigh, because this is the question that everybody asks eventually, the question I never really want to answer.

'No,' I say. 'Not after Mum died.' I say the words quickly, like ripping off a Band-Aid. It's the easiest way to tell the story. I see that look, the one that I'm sure is connected to a similar loss, cross Ben's face again.

'I'm so sorry,' he says quietly.

'It was ten years ago now and I still miss her every day,' I say. 'It doesn't hurt as much as it used to but I feel as though when she died part of me died too, as though I'll never be the person I used to be when she was alive.' I stop. I have no idea why I'm unburdening myself to a virtual stranger at midnight in my café. 'I'm sorry,' I say. 'You don't want to hear all this.'

I feel his hand cover mine again, just for a moment. 'I do,' he says. 'If you want to tell me.'

'I was in my first year at university when she died. It was very sudden and unexpected. I went back to France for a few weeks and got special dispensation in my end-of-year exams. But after that I felt like I was just meant to go back to normal. Go back to York, get my degree and carry on with my life.'

He nods as though he understands and waits for me to carry on.

'So I did.' I shrug. 'What else could I do? I did what my mother wanted and stayed in academia.'

'Even though you didn't want to.'

'Even though I didn't want to,' I repeat.

'Did your dad move back to England?' he asks.

'No, Dad's French. They met when he was doing a year of his postgraduate degree at Oxford and Mum was an undergraduate there. They were both very academic so it was inevitable that I'd end up on that path.' I pause and look up at him and smile. 'Even though I didn't want to.'

'What about brothers and sisters?' he asks. 'Do you have any?'

Another question I hate answering.

'A half-sister,' I say. 'She's a lot younger than me. After Mum died, Dad moved from Paris back to the small town near Marseilles where he came from. A few years later he married again and they have a daughter, Marie. We don't see each other very often.'

He doesn't say anything, but being here with him feels comforting, as though I've known him for a lot longer than I have. He doesn't need to know that I haven't seen my father since Marie was born four years ago and that we only speak, awkwardly and briefly, on birthdays and at Christmas.

'I am sorry,' I say again. 'You don't need to hear all this.'

He looks at me for a moment as though he's about to

tell me something, but his eyes dart away and he seems to change his mind.

'You must have a lot of memories tied up here in Sanderson Bay,' he says.

I nod briefly, looking away from him again. There are so many memories and a lot of them are so complicated.

'Same here,' he says. 'I think that's why I've not been sleeping.'

'The tea should help,' I reply, and suddenly I need to stand up and put some distance between us. Everything feels too intimate, too close. I haven't spoken to anyone about my mum like this since Marcus and for some reason tonight, in the soft lights with the smell of lavender tea in the air, Ben doesn't feel like a stranger. He doesn't feel like somebody I set eyes on for the first time just three days ago. I push my chair away and stand up. I shouldn't have told him so much.

'I've got some night-time tea gift packs,' I say. 'A packet of the tea along with a special cup to brew it in. Let me get you one.' I go behind the counter again to get the gift pack and when I turn around he's walked up to me. I decide to stay behind the counter, to keep the solid wood between us as a barrier.

'How much do I owe you?' he asks.

'It doesn't matter.'

'No, let me pay,' he says. 'Please.'

'Pay me tomorrow,' I say, passing the tea to him. 'I'm all cashed up for today.'

He nods and looks down at the package in his hand.

'I should go,' he says. I watch him put on his coat and walk towards the door. Then he turns and looks at me.

'Thank you for telling me about your mum,' he says.

Before I get a chance to wonder why he thanked me, he's gone and I realise that I've shared so much with him but he hasn't said anything about himself and that I've been so caught up in talking to him and in trying not to notice the undeniable attraction there, that once again I've forgotten to ask him how he knew my name.

6

Friday morning is cold and wet with a biting east wind blowing in from the sea. The off-season in British seaside towns can be grim, but this morning Sanderson Bay is buzzing with life. Even when I open up the café at 7am the streets are full of people up ladders and shouting instructions at each other and a cherry picker travels backwards down the High Street, announcing that "this vehicle is reversing".

Tonight is the great Sanderson Bay Christmas lights switch-on followed by Christmas carols at the Model Village and everyone is up and about making sure all is in order for later on. I hope the weather clears up a bit and it stops raining.

Friday mornings are always busy at The Two Teas. A mum and baby group meet around nine o'clock and a lot of people who have second homes in the Bay start to arrive by mid-morning to get tea and snacks and catch up on any gossip. Most of the gossip this morning seems to revolve around Ben's arrival although it seems that not many people remember him from when he lived here. Fifteen years is a long time I guess.

'Tell me everything,' Sascha says in a stage whisper as she

leans across the counter. 'I want to know what happened with you and Ben last night.' Sascha might be closest person I've had to a best friend in my whole life, but sometimes she is beyond annoying.

'Nothing happened,' I reply. 'And until Abi gets here I'm way too busy to talk to you so go and find a seat if you want to wait.' Abi is my second-in-command at the café and I couldn't run the place without her.

'Sounds like somebody didn't get enough sleep last night,' she says, grinning at me.

I shake my head. Sometimes she's impossible but I can't imagine life without her anymore. Other people often make me feel small, as though I'm not enough. Funny people make me feel humourless, serious people make me feel like I'm trying too hard and even though I've a tendency towards being quiet myself, quiet people make me babble on unnecessarily – just as I've found myself doing with Ben. But when I'm with Sascha I feel calm and balanced. She's loud and over the top and enthusiastic about life to the point of being utterly irritating – even when life throws her nothing but rotten lemons – and the opposite of me in so many ways but she grounds me, settles me, stops me feeling like a strong wind could blow me away. I always feel like I'm enough when I'm with her.

'Do you want some tea?' I ask.

She screws up her face.

'I don't know what to have now I don't need to drink nettles anymore.'

'How about camomile?' I suggest. 'It might calm you down a bit.'

She sticks her tongue out at me.

'I'll bring it over,' I say.

Once Abi arrives I take a break and go and sit with Sascha who is clearly not going anywhere until she has all the non-existent gossip. The café is heaving and I love it when it's like this, on a cold, wet morning and everyone is inside enjoying tea and pastries and cake. It's cosy in here and the windows have steamed up.

'Before you ask,' I say holding up my hand. 'Nothing happened with Ben last night. He came in and put the tables out for me. Then we had a cup of tea and he went back to the hotel, as I'm sure you know.'

'Yes, I was quite disappointed when he turned up for breakfast this morning,' she replies and I roll my eyes. 'He's sitting in the lounge at the moment drinking coffee and doing the *Guardian* cryptic crossword.'

I raise my eyebrows. 'Hmmph, coffee,' I say.

'You can't force everyone to drink tea, Ellie,' she replies. 'But listen to me, he times himself!'

'What?'

'He times how long it takes for him to do the crossword. Like Inspector Morse.'

'What a dork.' I laugh but inside my stomach is fizzing again. I've always had a bit of a crush on John Thaw's Inspector Morse character and Sascha knows it.

'He's all dark and brooding and introverted, isn't he?' Sascha asks and I can feel myself blush as I remember the stupid thing I'd said to him on Tuesday morning. 'What is it?' she asks loudly.

'Shhh...'

'You're blushing!'

'I said something stupid to him on Tuesday,' I begin.

'Oooh do tell,' she says salaciously.

'I told him he was dark and brooding.'

'You told him?'

I nod. 'I didn't mean it,' I say. 'He wanted to know why I thought he was Russian caravan tea and now I suspect he thinks I'm completely mad especially as...' I trail off.

'Especially as what?'

'Well last night I ended up telling him about Mum and about Dad remarrying and about Marie.'

'But you never talk about those things.'

'I know and I definitely didn't mean to but I was tired and the tea was nice and...'

'And Ben is dark and brooding and the most handsome man who's passed through Sanderson Bay in a long time.'

'You're meant to be married,' I say with a smile.

'I still have eyes in my head,' she retorts. 'Anyway, while you were telling him your life story, did he get a chance to tell you anything about himself?'

'Not much,' I reply. 'He went to university in York five years before me, his mum still lives there and he works in London, maybe in marketing. That's it.'

'He didn't mention his dad?'

'No, and did you notice last night how he clammed up whenever his father came up in conversation.'

She nods.

'I didn't want to ask though,' I go on. 'I mean I know what it's like to have a bad relationship with your father so I'm not going to pry into his life.'

'I'm happy to...'

'No,' I interrupt. 'We barely know him – leave him alone.'

She looks at me over her teacup. 'You fancy him don't you?' she asks.

'We're not eleven years old,' I reply.

'But there's something there right?'

'Maybe,' I reluctantly admit. 'But I'm ignoring it. It's still too soon.'

'El, it's been a year,' Sascha replies quietly and gently. 'It's time to move on.'

'The café keeps me busy,' I say. 'And Ben will only be here for a few days.'

'I worry about you, El,' Sascha says. 'I worry about you here on your own. Don't you want to do something more with your life?'

I feel that stab then that I sometimes feel when I wake up, when I'm opening the café, when I'm uploading Instagram photographs. It's the memory of my mum and all the things she hoped for me and all the ways in which I feel as though I've failed. I wonder what she'd think about me running a café in a little seaside town. She always said that Miranda had "no ambition". Is that what she'd think of me too now?

Sascha must notice me hesitate because she apologises. 'I didn't mean it to sound like that,' she says.

'I know,' I reply. 'But this is what I want. It might not be what I want forever but I was so unhappy in York, even before Marcus left. I needed something new, something safe.'

I feel her hand on mine, but I know what my mother thought of people who took a safe option. I used to think the same, but now I think we have to put our own happiness first, our own stress levels. After years of worrying what people thought, after years of trying to live up to other people's expectations of me, I'm trying to do my own thing. I'm trying to make myself happy and healthy. Some days it even feels like it might be working.

What won't work is throwing a love interest into the mix, however much Sascha might disagree.

'Anyway how are you feeling?' I ask, changing the subject. 'We've barely had a chance to talk.'

'I'm OK,' she says. 'Excited, tired, terrified, nauseous—'

'Ginger!' I interrupt. 'That's what you need, ginger tea for nausea. I wonder if I can mix it with something else to help the terrors?'

She smiles. 'Do you ever stop thinking about tea?' she asks.

'Not really,' I reply. 'I'm sorry, tell me how you're feeling, tell me everything.'

She looks around the busy café. 'Not here,' she says. 'I know it's silly but I really don't want anyone else to know until I get this scan. Come over later on when you quieten down and we'll have a proper catch-up.'

The café door opens then, blowing in a waft of cold damp air.

And Ben.

Ben looking breathtakingly handsome in a dark blue roll-neck sweater and jeans with a newspaper tucked under his arm. His hair is damp and windswept and he runs a hand through it to push it out of his face.

And then he smiles at me.

'I'll leave you to it.' Sascha smirks as she picks up her coat and gets ready to leave.

★

He orders a pot of Russian caravan tea and a maple pecan Danish.

'Are you sure?' I ask. 'I can make a fresh pot of coffee?'

'I've had a coffee this morning,' he replies. 'I'm sure.' He looks around the busy café. 'I was hoping to talk to you,' he says. 'But you're busy. I'll have this and come back.'

'We're not that busy,' says a voice over my shoulder. 'I can cope for a bit,' Abi goes on.

I look at her and then back at Ben. 'Go find a table and I'll bring the tea over in a few minutes,' I say to him.

I take my time making his tea; a small red teapot, one scoop of tea for him and one for the pot, a red and white striped mug that reminds me of the red and white checked shirt he'd been wearing the night before. I need to stop thinking about him so much. He'll be gone as soon as he arrived and I'll probably never see him again. There's a reason he hasn't been back in fifteen years and I have a feeling that whatever has brought him back again is something that he's had to do reluctantly.

'He's gorgeous,' Abi whispers in my ear as she comes behind the counter to make tea for the other customers. 'I saw you together in the pub last night.'

'We weren't together,' I say.

She raises her eyebrows at me. 'Whatever you say.'

'You're as bad as Sascha,' I reply. 'Let me take this tea over to him and I'll give you a hand.'

'You will not,' Abi replies in her lilting Irish accent. She came to Sanderson Bay for a holiday eighteen months ago and never left. 'You'll sit with him and enjoy yourself.'

I sigh, but don't argue with her.

'Do you still want to take a look at your social media accounts?' Ben asks when I take the tea over.

'That would be great if you have time.'

'I do if you do.'

I sit down opposite him and take my phone and notepad out of my apron pocket. He launches straight into it without preamble or any acknowledgement of the previous evening, as though I imagined that moment we shared when his hand was on mine.

Perhaps that's for the best. It's not as though I want anything to happen.

'Everything looks so good,' he begins. 'Aesthetically your brand is fantastic, from the café logo, to the look you have in the café to your Instagram account. I can't fault any of it.'

I feel myself blush.

'And looking at the comments on your social media you've found a good balance of replying to followers and ignoring those who have nothing nice to say.'

'No point getting involved in a disagreement with a random stranger online,' I say.

He smiles. 'If only more people thought that,' he says. 'Do you do all of this yourself?'

I nod.

'In real time?' he asks.

'How do you mean?'

'Do you post the pictures as soon as you take them?'

'Yes, is that wrong?'

He tells me about apps for pre-scheduling social media so I can streamline my time more.

'You shouldn't be checking more than two or three times a day,' he says. 'Otherwise you're putting all of your energy into just one factor of the business, plus the less time you spend on the actual accounts, the less time you'll spend worrying about the stupid comments.'

Then he starts telling me about getting new follows; the sort of hashtags I need to use, the best way to use my captions and the link in my profile. I scribble notes madly in my notepad.

'You need to really get to that golden 10k on Instagram,' he says. 'Then you get the swipe-up feature and you can link to articles about tea and reviews of the café, that sort of thing.' He pauses and looks at me for a moment, his head tilted to one side. 'You could even open an online shop so people could order your teas.'

It's almost like he's reading my mind. Selling my teas a bit further afield than Sanderson Bay is a dream I keep in a little box at the back of my head because it feels too big, too ambitious. It feels like anxiety.

'I had a huge influx of followers last summer,' I say instead. 'When Sanderson Bay was heaving with holidaymakers and day trippers. Lots of them came here to take photos. The café is very Instagrammable apparently.'

He laughs. 'It is,' he replies. 'And the way you serve the teas and arrange your displays is as well.'

'Thank you so much for this – it's so helpful.'

'No worries,' he says. 'Really. It's my pleasure.' He catches my eye for a moment and looks away. My stomach fizzes.

'So where do you work in London?' I ask. I don't want the conversation to end – I want to find out how long he's staying and why he's here but I don't want to ask the questions directly.

'I started off as a junior in a big media marketing firm in Covent Garden,' he says. 'And then I got on to a graduate training scheme in the London office of a big corporate and I've worked my way up from there.'

'Which corporate?' I ask.

He doesn't reply straight away and I notice his cheeks colour and his eyes flick away again. I sit up a bit straighter because now I am interested. Why is he so reluctant to tell me?

'I already know what you're going to think,' he says. 'I saw the way you looked at my KeepCup on Monday night.'

I think about Monday night, the night he arrived. I don't remember his Keep...

Moby's.

'You work for Moby's,' I say quietly, trying not to say any more than that, trying not to say that I'm not interested in his marketing advice if it comes from Moby's.

'I work for Moby's,' he repeats and there's an expression on his face that looks like resignation or relief and I don't understand it.

I stand up, trying to keep the irrational anger at bay. He has a job, a good job, a well-paid job. He has a career he's probably been working hard at for years.

It's not his fault I feel like this.

'I have to get on,' I say. 'Maybe I'll see you later at the Christmas lights switch-on?'

'I have to pay you,' he says. 'For this and for the night-time tea set you gave me.'

'Abi's at the till – she'll see to it.'

He nods once but he doesn't say anything else and I walk back into the kitchen and take a few deep breaths.

'What the hell happened?' Abi says, popping her head around the door. 'He had a face like thunder as he paid.'

'Leave it, Abi,' I say, my voice sterner than I mean it to be. 'I'm sorry,' I say more softly. 'I don't want to talk about it.'

Abi looks at me for a moment, her head cocked on one side before going back into the café.

It's not Ben's fault, I tell myself. It's not his fault that I get so irrationally angry about Moby's. That same anger that I'd swallowed down when I saw his KeepCup on Monday. I try to pretend that I dislike all coffee chains equally but that isn't true. I may not be a big fan of coffee but nobody makes me want to scream the way Moby's does.

Two years ago when my aunt's arthritis had got so bad they were beginning to think about selling the café, and about a year and a half after Karol Bergenstein first put Sanderson Bay on the map, Moby's tried to buy the café.

I get it. From a business perspective Sanderson Bay suddenly looked like a winner, somewhere to put a franchise, somewhere people would want take-away coffees. But Sanderson Bay didn't want a Moby's and when my uncle first got the letter offering to buy the café he told them he wasn't interested, that he wanted a private sale.

But they didn't give up. They pestered and pestered, they upped their offer and, although we have no proof I'm sure they were doing something behind the scenes that meant the café wasn't selling because, although James and

Miranda had taken excellent advice from a business sales agent who knew the area, they didn't get any other offers. Just Moby's.

'Perhaps we should take the offer, love,' my uncle had said to me when this had been going on for over six months. 'We can't run this place forever and the twenty-first century has arrived in Sanderson Bay, maybe we should all embrace it.'

'And the money is not to be sneered at,' Miranda had added. I can remember looking at her hands then, hands that had been so good at knitting, sewing, baking; hands that were now riddled with pain and misshapen from inflammation. I'd almost given in.

'You can't,' I'd said. 'Just give it a bit longer – something is bound to turn up and we're coming into the quiet season. Let's see where we are in the spring.'

My aunt and uncle had agreed but before spring came, Marcus dropped his bombshell and everything I'd been clinging on to by my fingernails in York for so long finally fell away. And so I ran. I ran to the place I always ran to, the place I'd run to when I ran away from boarding school, the place I'd gone whenever York got too much, the place where I'd spent every Christmas and Easter since I was thirteen years old.

I had barely got through the door when I asked my aunt and uncle what their absolute minimum amount was to sell the café, the money they needed to buy the bungalow they dreamt of, the bungalow that would let them enjoy their retirement.

Then followed the most awkward telephone conversation

ever with my father, a conversation in which I told him my plan and asked him if it he would agree to allow me to sell the flat that he'd bought for me York. The flat he'd insisted on buying if I absolutely must stay in York and not set my sights and ambitions on somewhere further afield – New York, Paris, even London.

'You're a grown woman now, Eloise,' he'd said to me, his voice tight. We always speak in French and my father is the only person I speak French to these days. Sometimes I struggle to be fluent and when I'm anxious, as I had been that day, my French can be slow and he was already frustrated. 'Old enough to make your own decisions. The flat is yours to do with as you wish and if this is what you wish to do with your life, then that is your choice.'

My father, Michel Caron, used to be – until my mother's untimely death – professor of philosophy at the Sorbonne in Paris, while my mother sat in her tiny office and wrote ground-breaking biographies of feminist writers. I grew up in an apartment on the Left Bank that was lined with books – books that I was encouraged to read in both French and English – and, until I was sent away to boarding school, I spent my mealtimes listening to my parents talk about Socrates and Aristotle, Sartre and de Beauvoir. Later, after I'd finished my A levels – my father suffered the first of the many disappointments that I threw his way. I told him that I wanted to stay in Yorkshire, near James and Miranda, that I didn't want to go to Oxford and study English like my mother, that I didn't want to come back to Paris and go to the Sorbonne like him. I wanted to study art history and I wanted to do it in York.

He accepted it, in a fashion. But then my mother died

– the result of the aneurysm that had been quietly sitting in her magnificent brain bursting suddenly and my father left Paris too, returning to the south of France, taking up a position at the University of Aix-Marseille. But he never seemed to be able to accept how the academic life hadn't suited me and he certainly didn't accept it when I told him I couldn't take it anymore, that I was leaving and going back to Sanderson Bay with my PhD in pieces and nowhere close to being finished.

I swallowed down the guilt I'd felt at how obviously I'd disappointed him, at how disappointed the ghost of my mother would be, and tried only to think of my aunt and uncle, the two people who had been more like parents to me than my own parents.

I sold everything, not just the flat but all the furniture in it as well as half my wardrobe, my car – which I never used in York anyway but in hindsight would have been quite handy in Sanderson Bay – everything. It was just enough for the deposit, and my business plan was just enough for the bank to take me seriously.

Because I couldn't let Moby's buy it.

Of all the coffee shop chains in the world, the only man I'd found even remotely attractive since Marcus had to work for Moby's.

And there was more to it, I was sure of it. It seemed like more than coincidence that someone from Moby's was back sniffing around again. Everything about Ben's arrival since he asked me if I was Eloise Caron on Monday night – since he'd told me he expected someone older – felt like more than just a coincidence.

7

'Stop being so paranoid,' Sascha says later when I pop up to the hotel to give her the ginger and peppermint tea I've mixed for her morning sickness. 'Just because he works for Moby's doesn't mean he's up to something. Thousands of people work for Moby's and I expect some of them come here on holiday. Some of them probably even drink tea in your café, grateful to be away from the smell of coffee.'

We're sitting in her kitchen drinking tea – ginger and peppermint for her of course, Earl Grey for me – and eating the last two pieces of Bessie's walnut loaf that I brought from the café. We don't do lunches at The Two Teas, mostly because I don't want to be in direct competition with Terry and Mo at the pub but also because I don't want the café to smell strongly of soup and melted cheese. Tea has such delicate scents and flavours that I don't want them overpowered with anything stronger than a chocolate croissant or Bessie's amazing walnut loaf.

'Even I took the Moby's dollar for a while, you know that,' she goes on. Before Sascha had moved to Sanderson Bay she had been a corporate lawyer, although it's hard to believe when you see her now, and Moby's was a client of the firm she worked for. When I first took over the café she told me she was glad I'd stopped James and Miranda from selling to them. 'They have a habit of taking over,' she'd said.

'I'm sorry,' I say, realising that Sascha is probably right and that I am being paranoid. Or at the very least projecting my own hatred of Moby's onto Ben, an innocent employee. 'I'm not here to rant about Moby's all afternoon again.' Ranting about Moby's has started to turn into an obsession and I know I need to stop.

'Good,' Sascha says. 'Because I want to tell you about all the joys of being pregnant.'

For the next hour I listen to Sascha tell me about her nausea and her sore boobs and her constipation and her constant headaches that she can't take anything stronger than half a paracetamol for.

'Which is pointless,' she says. 'Paracetamol barely touches the sides. And then there's the mood swings.'

I raise my eyebrows. 'Sascha,' I say with a smile. 'I don't think the mood swings are anything new.'

'Don't you start – that's what Geoff said.' She laughs. 'But honestly I can go from being ecstatically happy to big snotty crying in minutes. It's exhausting.'

'Do you have any weird cravings?' I ask.

'Not yet, but give it time,' she replies. 'I'm only at the ten-week mark and baby is only the size of a strawberry.' She holds up her thumb and forefinger to indicate the size.

'That's a lot of symptoms,' I say, not really knowing what else to say or how I can be helpful in any way.

'It is a lot of symptoms.'

'But worth it of course.'

She puts her feet up on the chair next to her and drinks from her mug. 'Absolutely worth it,' she says. 'When I'm not too exhausted to remember my name.'

'Are you going to stay awake long enough to come to the lights switch-on this evening?' I ask.

'I wouldn't dare miss it,' she replies. 'What would people think?'

'They'd think you were pregnant,' I say.

'Exactly, and it's too early for anyone else to do any speculating.'

Before I leave she asks me if I'm all right and I shrug, still thinking about Ben and Moby's.

'It's just a job,' she says as if reading my mind. 'It doesn't mean anything.'

I know, as soon as she says the words, that she's right, but I can't let it go. Even when she'd been telling me about all the unglamorous symptoms of early pregnancy all I could think about was Ben and that Moby's coffee cup. I should have seen it as a sign as soon as he produced it.

Ben doesn't come to the great Christmas lights switch-on, but I barely notice because when my aunt and uncle arrive, I see Miranda is in her wheelchair.

'Before you say anything,' she says as I walk up to her. 'I'm fine so don't make a fuss.'

'You can't be fine, you hate being in your wheelchair,' I reply.

She takes my hand in her cold, gnarled one and gives it a squeeze.

'I'm not the chair's biggest fan,' she says, 'because of what it represents; but I'm also coming around to the idea that it helps me live the life I want to live. It's been a high-pain day – I don't know why, maybe because of the rain – but I knew that if I wanted to come to the lights switch-on and the carols then I had to use the chair.'

'So you're starting to get worse?' I ask.

'I have good days and bad days,' she says. 'The same as ever.'

'What can I do?' I ask. Sometimes I feel as though my aunt and uncle are keeping things from me, protecting me from the full extent of Miranda's illness.

'We're doing fine,' James says, touching my arm. 'The bungalow is perfect thanks to you.'

'But…'

'Honestly, Ellie, we'll tell you if we need anything. I promise.'

James wheels Miranda off to find a good place for her to see the lights and Sascha comes over, handing me a cup of tea in a polystyrene cup.

'It's just a teabag floating in an environmental disaster I'm afraid,' she says. 'But it'll keep your hands warm.'

'I'm worried about them,' I say, looking over at my aunt and uncle.

'I know you are, El, but you have to let them be as independent as possible for as long as possible. You know that.'

I nod, but before I can say anything else Dawn Hudson, the mayor of Sanderson Bay, takes to the stage wearing full ceremonial robes to begin the countdown.

'As always we have a whole host of volunteers to thank

for getting the town ready for tonight in some very wet weather,' she says. 'And a special thank you to Eric Andrews and the lifeboat crew for all their hard work. After this there will, as usual, be carol singing over at Eric's Model Village.'

We all cheer and applaud.

'Now let's get these lights switched on!' Dawn shouts and we begin to count in unison.

'Five... Four... Three... Two... One...!'

Ben finally turns up halfway through "Once in Royal David's City".

'Stop obsessing about Moby's,' Sascha whispers at me through gritted teeth when I nudge her. Geoff is singing the bit about the oxen very loudly and slightly out of tune on the other side of me. 'I've told you, where he works has nothing to do with why he's here, I'm sure of it.'

'Shhhh,' Bessie hisses from behind me, poking me in the back with a very sharp finger. Sascha looks at me as though it was me who was talking and we both start singing again.

Carols at the Model Village after the lights switch-on is a long-held tradition dating back to when Eric's father first built the model village in the 1950s. Everyone is welcome and there is a five-pound entrance fee and all the money goes to the RNLI to help the lifeboat volunteers across the country. After we've sung about a dozen carols – both traditional and more bizarre, a recent addition being a song called "I want a Hippopotamus for Christmas" – accompanied by Clara on the keyboard, there's mulled wine and mince pies for everyone. Carols at the Model Village definitely marks the start of the festive season in the Bay, although tonight I'm not feeling that festive if I'm honest.

I look over at Ben again who is deep in whispered conversation with Eric. I notice nobody is poking him and making him stop talking. Typical.

Then I notice Ben hand Eric a wad of cash in twenty-pound notes. I nudge Sascha again and she looks over, just in time to see Eric take the money from Ben.

'A bribe for something probably,' I whisper. But Sascha rolls her eyes and carries on singing. Bessie pokes me in the back again.

'Could it be,' Sascha says after the carols are over as she sips from her cup of hot orange squash – the non-alcoholic alternative to mulled wine, 'that you're obsessing about him not because he works at Moby's but because you have feelings for him.' She drags out the word *feelings* in a way that makes me feel uncomfortable.

'No,' I say abruptly, knowing that she might have hit the nail on the head.

'Moby's gave up on the café a year ago when you bought your aunt and uncle out,' she goes on. 'Why would they still be sniffing around now?'

I shrug. I know I'm being irrational, but all I can see is that desperate look on Miranda's face when she told me that the money Moby's was offering was not to be sneered at and all I can feel is the guilt that I've carried around all year because, although I've never known the price Moby's offered, I know it was a lot more than I bought the café off them for. Sometimes I wonder if I did the right thing after all, if I should have asked, no begged, them not to sell to Moby's and to let me run the tea shop I'd been daydreaming about as I sat in the university library in York not writing my PhD. Should I have let James and Miranda take the Moby's money while I actually gave that PhD a shot?

And I wonder if this guilt and indecision will always plague me. All my adult life I've wanted to live in Sanderson Bay, to find some way of making a living here and yet, now I'm here I wonder if I should be back there.

'I've never known,' I say quietly to Sascha, 'if I did the right thing by buying the café, by depriving James and Miranda of the money Moby's were going to give them just because I wanted to run away from York after Marcus left. Perhaps I should have given my PhD more of a chance.'

'The grass is always greener,' she replies. 'Do you think Geoff and I don't sometimes wonder if we did the right thing moving here?'

'I had no idea you thought like that too,' I say.

She laughs. 'We gave up huge corporate salaries and a gorgeous house to move here and do up a hotel with a leaking roof,' she says. 'Of course we feel like that too – everyone does sometimes, it's the human condition.'

'I don't know…' I begin.

'You did the right thing,' she says. 'You know you did. After all if you hadn't moved here when you did you'd never have met me and then where would you be?'

'Serendipity.' I smile.

'Exactly that.'

'Hello,' a low rumble of a voice says behind me and Geoff looks up from the phone he's been distracting himself with while Sascha and I have been talking.

'All right, mate,' he says shaking hands with Ben. 'Did you enjoy the carols?'

Ben nods. 'It feels like the start of Christmas now,' he says catching my eye. Sascha nudges me and I stumble a little, almost falling into Ben. Then she turns away with exaggeration as if to tell me I need to clear the air. She's right, I am being paranoid about Ben and I'm projecting my own issues, my own feelings of guilt and uncertainly, onto him when he's just here for a break.

'Um, I'm sorry,' I say.

'About what?' Ben asks.

'About being so rude to you this morning,' I say. 'You'd been so kind teaching me all those marketing tricks for social media and I was rude when you told me where you worked.'

'I'd already worked out that you don't think much of coffee chains,' he says with a smile I don't deserve. 'Or coffee for that matter.'

'I'm not a fan,' I reply. 'But especially not of Moby's. About a year ago they tried to buy the café off my aunt and uncle.'

He looks down into his cup of mulled wine but doesn't say anything. I wonder if he already knew.

'But none of that is your fault,' I go on hastily. 'It's your job, that you clearly love or you wouldn't have stayed there so long and we barely know each other so it's really none of my business.'

'I wouldn't say I love it,' he replies quietly.

'Well I'm sorry for taking my frustration out on you.'

'Apology accepted,' he says. 'Is that why you bought the café from your aunt and uncle?' he asks, still not looking up.

'It's one of the reasons,' I reply. 'Which reminds me, how

did you know my name on that first night when you arrived wanting coffee?'

He doesn't say anything at first, he just keeps looking down into his mulled wine. After a moment he looks up at me and smiles. 'There's a brass plate above the door with your name on,' he says. 'I'm guessing you have an alcohol licence for special events and you're the licensee.'

'Well guessed,' I said. 'We do champagne afternoon teas so I need the licence for that.'

Sascha was right, he did see my name above the door and formed a picture in his mind of what Eloise Caron looked like. He doesn't have a sinister agenda or hidden knowledge, he's just a guy back in his childhood home for personal reasons that are none of my business.

'So what did you imagine Eloise Caron looked like?' I asked.

'Nothing like you,' he says softly and, when his eyes meet mine my stomach flips over and I realise that Sascha is right. The reason this man can upset me so easily, the reason I'm so suspicious of him but can't keep away, is exactly because I have feelings for him.

I'm in so much trouble.

8

I wake up early on Saturday with a thumping headache right behind my eyes from the cheap red mulled wine the night before. I haven't slept well and what sleep I have had was disturbed by dreams of my aunt's wheelchair and a huge Moby's coffee franchise suddenly appearing where the Model Village used to be.

I get out of bed and pad over into the bathroom where I take two paracetamol and pour myself a large glass of water, which I take back to bed with me, drinking as much of it as I can before lying down and staring at the ceiling.

The celebrations last night mark the start of the festive season in Sanderson Bay but the start of Christmas doesn't fill me with a sense of joy and goodwill to all men like I want it to do. It fills me with a deep sense of indifference and something else, something that feels like loneliness.

Maybe it's just the aftereffects of the mulled wine.

My first Christmas in Sanderson Bay came after my first term at boarding school. I had only just begun to settle in when we broke for up for the holidays. I'd made a few friends and had started to get used to speaking English every day and sharing a dormitory with five other girls. I hadn't gotten used to how cold it was and the strange damp feeling of the sheets that never seemed to go away and I was looking forward to going back to France in the opposite direction to the way we'd come – driving south to Dover and crossing on the car ferry to Calais before driving again until we got to Paris. I was looking forward to being in our warm apartment, which my parents would have decorated for Christmas – my father dragging the six-foot fir tree up the narrow staircase that led to our fourth-floor home. But mostly I was looking forward to seeing *Maman* again, feeling her arms around me and inhaling the scent of her Chanel No. 5.

I'd been both surprised and disappointed when James and Miranda came to meet me on that first day of the Christmas holidays and I'd tried not to cry on the drive back to Sanderson Bay in my uncle's Volvo as he told me about the café they had opened and the plans they had for the Christmas holidays. I'd only met James and Miranda once before – the Christmas that I was eleven when they stayed with us in Paris and camped out on the living room floor in our tiny apartment. My mother got annoyed when the hot water ran out and my father spent more time at the university than usual and, by the end of that visit I had worked out that my mother and her sister didn't get on for some reason and that maybe having a sibling was more complicated than I imagined. From that summer onwards I stopped daydreaming about what it would be like to have a brother or sister of my own.

And suddenly I was in a car with my mother's sister who I barely knew, and nobody would explain to me why.

'You can call your mum as soon as we get back to the

Bay,' my uncle had said. But when I called her my mind hadn't been put at ease as I'd hoped it would. I wasn't just going to stay with my aunt and uncle for a few days until *Maman* came to pick me up, I was going to be staying with them for the whole Christmas holidays.

'I'm so sorry, Eloise,' my mother had crooned to me in French over the phone. 'But *Papa* is so busy and needs to spend some time outside of Paris this Christmas.'

'Why can't I come too?' I'd asked.

'I love you, *petite fille*,' she'd replied, not answering my question. But I hadn't thought she could love me very much if she didn't want to see me at Christmas.

I hadn't known it then, but I would spend the next fifteen Christmases in Sanderson Bay and I would never spend Christmas with my mother again.

Thinking about all of this now makes me feel even more lonely and despondent. Despite it coming up to my sixteenth Christmas in Sanderson Bay, sixteen Christmases without my mother. Despite it being ten years since she died and that sound of her voice getting more and more distant with each passing year, I always miss *Maman* the most at Christmas.

I rub my eyes and force myself out of bed.

Come on, Eloise, I say to myself. *You've got a café to run.*

I'm late opening up and Ben and Sascha are standing outside waiting for me. Ben smiles at me, that big genuine smile – a smile that has come on in leaps and bounds since the first night he arrived when it came across as part smug, part reluctant – and my stomach flips again.

'You're late opening,' Sascha says as she pushes past me into the café. Ben holds back, gesturing that I should go back inside first and holds the door open for me.

'And you're here very early,' I reply. 'Shouldn't you be serving breakfast to your guests?'

She waves dismissively at me. 'Geoff has it all under control,' she says.

'Isn't Saturday your busiest morning?' I ask.

'No Sunday, and not at this time of year.'

'So why are you here?' I ask, sensing Ben's presence behind me. I wonder what he's thinking, witnessing this back and forth between us. I know exactly why Sascha is here – she will want to know why I didn't invite everyone back to the café after the Christmas carols last night – but I want to see if she'll ask me outright in front of Ben.

'To have some tea of course,' she says. 'And one of those maple pecan Danishes.'

'What sort of tea?' I ask going behind the counter.

'That horrible ginger stuff you made me.'

'Right, glad you like it.' I turn to Ben. 'Can I get you something too?' I ask.

'Russian caravan,' he says. 'I'm growing quite fond of it.'

And I'm growing quite fond of you, I think to myself.

'Would you like a Danish as well?' I ask.

He nods and sits down at a table, opening the newspaper he's got tucked under his arm to the crossword page. I stop myself from staring and try to tell myself it's just the young Inspector Morse vibe he's giving off. That's all. It's got nothing to do with the way his smile makes me feel.

'So what happened last night?' Sascha asks quietly,

leaning over the counter as I make the teas – a grass green teapot for her, a pillar box red one for Ben. 'Why did you sneak off early?'

'I didn't sneak off,' I reply. 'I was just tired and I wanted to be on my own. You know how Christmas makes me feel.'

'Is this because your aunt was in her wheelchair last night?'

'Partly. It's hard watching her deteriorate and knowing there isn't anything I can do to make it better. It feels like a reminder that one day she'll be gone, just like Mum.'

Sascha reaches across the counter to squeeze my arm. 'Christmas can really make these things hard can't it?' I know that Sascha has a fractious relationship with her parents – they have never visited Sanderson Bay in the year I've known her and it's not something she talks about much. I also know that she and Geoff are staying in the Bay for Christmas on their own. 'Our last Christmas as a twosome,' Sascha had said with a smile. Whatever the story is with her family, I'm glad that she has finally got the chance to make a family of her own.

'It's impossible not to get nostalgic at Christmas,' I say, passing her the Danishes. 'Take these and I'll bring your tea over.' I don't want to talk about Christmas and the memories that always resurface.

The café begins to fill up quickly with both locals and weekenders, so I don't get much chance to talk to Sascha again, who is sitting with Ben as he patiently explains each cryptic crossword clue to her.

After the initial shock of realising that I wouldn't be spending Christmas in Paris with my parents wore off on

RACHEL BURTON

that first holiday at Sanderson Bay when I was thirteen, I tried to make the best of the situation. That seems to have been a personality trait of mine for most of my life – making the best of things. I learned to make the best of things at boarding school, at university, while I was doing my abandoned PhD – all the while knowing the disappointment my father was feeling. I hadn't really understood why my parents didn't want me to come home for Christmas but by Christmas Eve I'd realised I was, in fact, having fun.

I'd helped James decorate the flat above the café – the café itself had already been decorated when we arrived, much to my delight – and I'd helped Miranda make mince pies. We'd been to Hull to go Christmas shopping and to watch the Salvation Army band play Christmas carols and I'd spent my allowance on presents for my aunt and uncle, which I'd wrapped carefully in my bedroom and put under the big Christmas tree that took up most of the space in the tiny living room in the flat above the café.

The flat that was now mine, the flat that didn't have a single Christmas decoration in it. Neither did the café for that matter.

'Have you put Christmas decorations up all over the hotel?' I ask Sascha as I pass her table. I'd seen a tree in reception and the decorations in her and Geoff's flat the day before.

'We have,' she replies.

'The dining room looks like Santa's grotto on acid,' Ben grumbles quietly, not looking up from his crossword.

'Do I detect a Grinch?' I ask. He looks up and smiles at me.

'I'm not big on Christmas,' he admits.

'You're one to criticise anyway, Ellie,' Sascha interjects. 'I don't see a single bauble anywhere in the café.'

'No,' I say hesitantly. There's a reason I haven't put decorations up yet. 'When I was a kid, before I moved to England, we never decorated the apartment in Paris before Mum's birthday on the 14th of December.'

'New start, new traditions,' Sascha says, stopping me before I get too maudlin. I notice Ben is still looking at me. A little furrow has appeared between his eyebrows as though he wants to ask a question. 'All the businesses in Sanderson Bay decorate in time for the big Christmas lights switch-on. You've missed that now, so you need to get on it. You can get a Christmas tree this afternoon from the farm along the cliff road,' she goes on bossily.

'I was going to order one online,' I say.

'Get a real one,' Sascha says.

'But I don't have a car. Am I meant to drag it three miles home along a dual carriageway?' I remember the little blue Citroën that I sold to one of the undergraduates in my cubism class fondly. And I remember her telling me how much she'd miss me as she drove away. That had been a surprise.

'Good point,' Sascha concedes. 'Geoff's busy this afternoon or I'd get him to take you.'

'I can take you,' Ben interrupts. We both look at him. 'I mean, if you'd like me to.'

'You can leave as soon as Abi gets here to take over the café,' Sascha says before I have a chance to say anything.

And that's how I end up driving to the Christmas tree farm on the cliff road with Ben in his silver Audi.

*

'I sense a reluctance to decorate the café,' Ben says as we pull into the car park at the Christmas tree farm.

'The café has a certain look,' I begin.

'An Instagrammable look,' Ben says with a grin.

'Exactly, and Christmas decorations are just a bit messy. Plus I'll be sweeping up pine needles until the new year, which is why I wanted to order one online but I'm never going to be able to get away with that now!'

'Is Sascha always that bossy?' Ben asks.

'Always, but we love her for it. She gets things done in the Bay.'

'I can imagine.'

We get out of the car and start walking across the car park. It's a beautiful clear still day, sunny with big blue skies, but freezing and I wrap my coat more tightly around me.

'Is that the only reason you're reluctant?' Ben asks. 'Because it'll mess up the café aesthetic?'

'It's not the only reason,' I admit. 'What I said about Mum's birthday is true. It's ridiculous really – she's been dead for a decade and for five years before that I spent every Christmas in Sanderson Bay with my aunt and uncle who love Christmas and this year decorated their bungalow in mid-November but...' I trail off.

'But you always think of your mum at this time of year,' he says softly as though he understands and I nod, thinking again about how he always clams up when his father is mentioned. 'That's not ridiculous,' he says.

'When I lived in York I never decorated the flat until after her birthday. Not that I ever went all out like my aunt and

Sascha do because I'd always came to Sanderson Bay for Christmas even then.'

Ben stops walking and stands slightly in front of me.

'Can I ask you something?' he says. 'And please do tell me if this is none of my business.'

'OK,' I say slowly.

'Did you ever find out why your parents always sent you to Sanderson Bay at Christmas, why you never saw them?'

I think back again to that first Christmas with James and Miranda, remembering how scared I'd been, convinced I must have done something wrong. Convinced, as young teenagers often are, that everything was my fault.

'Not really,' I reply. 'Looking back at it now I think there might have been some problems in their marriage. Up to then everything had seemed fine and we had the most wonderful Christmases together in Paris – it would be so quiet because so many people left the city for the holidays and sometimes it felt like we had Paris all to ourselves.' I pause, looking away from Ben. 'But something definitely shifted,' I say. 'I'm not sure what it was though. I know they wanted another baby but the baby never came and I know sometimes in the summer when I went back to France and we all travelled down to Provence I'd sometimes find my mother crying when she didn't think anyone was looking and then my father married again. I don't really know though.'

A few weeks after that first Christmas in Sanderson Bay, once I was back at school, *Maman* had come to visit me. She flew in to Manchester airport and navigated her way across the Pennines in a rented car. She waltzed into my school, the first time I'd seen her since the previous September, looking like a film star and took me to a café in nearby Harrogate. Over tea and cream cakes she told me how much she loved me and how sorry she was that we hadn't spent Christmas together.

'*Papa* is unhappy,' she'd said. 'He wants to leave Paris and I don't know what to do.' I hadn't known what she'd meant at the time. I had seen the tears in her eyes but I hadn't really understood anything. I have no idea why I've never asked my father about any of this. Perhaps because I don't want to know the answer.

Ben squeezes my shoulder briefly. 'I'm sorry,' he says. 'I shouldn't have asked. It's just...' He stops and looks down at his feet.

'What?' I ask.

He looks as though he's about to tell me something but then he closes his eyes and shakes his head.

'Nothing really,' he says. 'I just wanted you to know that I get it, that Christmas isn't always joyful and fun. Sometimes it's...' He pauses.

'Complicated,' I say.

He doesn't reply but he does look up at me, meeting my eyes again and I know then that whatever happened to him to make him feel that way about Christmas, he genuinely does understand.

'Shall we get this Christmas tree?' he asks, changing the subject.

Conways Christmas Tree Farm has opened every November for as long as anyone can remember. My aunt and uncle always get their tree from here – I suspect, judging by how early their tree went up this year, that they were one of the Conways first customers this year. I wonder if Ben's family came here when he was a kid too, but I don't want to ask him, not after what he's just said. Perhaps that's why he's really come back here – to face his demons.

'We used to get our trees from here when we lived in Sanderson Bay,' Ben says, answering my unasked question. 'Another thing that hasn't changed a bit.'

'This is actually the first time I've been here,' I confess. 'I was always at school or in York when the Christmas tree was bought.'

'Well take your time to browse.' Ben laughs. 'Choose the tree that speaks to you!'

'Speaks to me?'

'Sorry, that's what my mum used to say – it just means you'll know which tree is yours as soon as you see it.'

'Aren't they all the same?' I ask.

'Philistine,' he replies. 'Of course not – every tree is an individual.' He strides ahead of me pointing out the different trees – the pyramid-shaped Douglas fir with its rich pine scent, the smaller, conical balsam fir, the magnificent Norway spruce.

'You might not want that one though,' Ben says. 'It sheds.'

We walk through the row upon row of Christmas trees and I inhale the pine scent, the definitive smell of the season. I've never seen Ben so animated or talkative and I'm glad that coming back here hasn't brought back whatever sad memories Christmas brings up for him. His mood bolsters me as well and I find myself excited to buy a tree for the café where before I had felt I was doing it under Sascha's duress.

'This might be your best bet,' Ben says stopping in front of some Scotch pines. 'Not too tall, not too wide—'

'The Goldilocks of Christmas trees,' I interrupt.

He ignores me. 'Sturdy branches for decorations and the *pièce de résistance…*' he pauses dramatically '… long-term needle retention.'

'So it won't make a mess all over my café floor?'

'Exactly.'

'How do you know all this?' I ask but before Ben can answer a woman comes out of the portacabin that we're standing near clutching a mug of tea.

'Ben Lawson?' she asks as she walks towards us. 'Is that you?'

The woman is about the same age as my aunt and wrapped up in a huge puffy coat, hat, scarf and mittens.

'Hi, Jennifer,' Ben replies.

'What are you doing here?' the woman asks.

'Just visiting,' he replies. His previous good mood seems to have disappeared and the reluctant smile is back, as though he wants to be anywhere but here.

'It's been a long time,' Jennifer says wistfully.

'This is Ellie,' Ben says, clearly not wanting to be drawn into nostalgia. 'She's buying her first Conways Christmas Tree.'

'Well in that case, we'll have to do you a special deal,' the woman says as I show her the tree I've chosen. I'm not sure it spoke to me exactly but it will look nice in the spot I've designated for it in the café. 'I'm Jennifer Conway,' she goes on. 'My husband and I own the farm.'

'I think you probably know my aunt and uncle,' I reply. 'James and Miranda Cunningham?'

She stops and turns around to look at me more

closely and I step back awkwardly wishing I hadn't said anything.

'Oh,' she says. 'You're James and Miranda's Ellie, so this Christmas tree must be for the old café.' I can't tell from her voice if she knows about the changes I've made or, if she does, whether she approves. 'In that case I'll definitely do you a deal. Is it just this one, my love?'

For a moment I wonder if I should have a tree in the flat too, like my aunt and uncle used to when they lived there. But what would be the point? It's only me and I won't be there for Christmas Day.

'Just that one,' I confirm. 'Although...'

Ben and Jennifer look at me expectantly.

'I don't have anything to decorate it with.'

'And you called me a Grinch,' Ben says, catching my eye and winking at me. My stomach goes wild and I look away quickly.

'Lucky for you we do a good line in Christmas decorations too,' Jennifer says as she hands Ben her mug and picks up the Christmas tree as though it were made of feathers.

'I used to work here when I was a teenager,' Ben says to me as we follow Jennifer back towards the portacabin. 'Christmas trees in winter, fruit picking in summer.'

'This really is a nostalgia trip for you, isn't it?' I say. 'I hope it's not... well...' I hesitate. I don't want to sound like I'm prying.

'What?'

'Oh just what you said earlier, that Christmas isn't your happiest time and I hope this isn't bringing back bad memories.'

'Far from it,' he says. 'And it's nice to spend some time with you.'

I feel his hand lightly brush the small of my back as he guides me up the steps into Jennifer's portacabin shop ahead of him and, for the first time, I don't think the fizzing in my stomach is a bad thing.

9

'Thank you for bringing me,' I say as we drive back to Sanderson Bay, the Christmas tree tied to the roof of Ben's car and a back seat full of other decorations, garlands and greenery. 'It's been fun.'

'I'm glad,' he replies. 'I thought maybe you were just humouring me and Sascha to be honest – that you didn't really want to decorate the café. I hope I haven't pushed you into buying something you don't really want.'

'Don't be silly,' I say turning to look at his profile, taking in the strong nose and brow, the dark stubble across his jaw, the way his hair curls at the back on his scarf. 'Seeing all the different Christmas trees helped put me in the Christmas spirit a bit. This time of year is tough but Sascha's right, I do have to make new traditions.'

'It helps,' he says, quietly. I wait a moment to see if he'll say anything else but he doesn't.

'I hope I haven't put you out by driving out here,' I say. 'You hardly know me.'

He turns to look at me, taking his eyes off the road for just a second. 'I think we're starting to know each other now though,' he says softly.

My heart is in my throat and I don't know how to reply

to that but luckily my phone rings before I say something stupid. It's Sascha.

'How's it going?' she says in a stage whisper. 'You've been gone a long time.'

'It's Sascha checking up on us,' I tell Ben and he grins. 'We're on our way back now,' I say into the phone. 'I'll close up for a couple of hours and get the place decorated and you can come and inspect it when it's done.'

'Is Ben going to help?' Sascha asks.

'I'll let you know when it's done,' I reply ending the call.

'I'm not going to ask why she's checking up on us,' Ben says as I put the phone back in my pocket.

'She thinks I've been single for too long,' I say, regretting the words immediately they tumble out of my mouth. I can feel myself blush.

'Well that answers one question I was going to ask,' Ben says as he indicates for the turn-off to Sanderson Bay. 'You're not seeing anyone.'

'Are you?' I ask.

'No and I'm free this afternoon if you want some help decorating the café.'

It's almost as though Sascha's stage whisper was so loud he heard what she was saying.

A year isn't too long to be single in my opinion, especially when you've had your heart broken. I loved Marcus so much, even though I know James and Miranda weren't too keen, and I'd allowed myself to picture a future with him – two academics researching art together. For the three years that we were together I'd convinced myself that I was cut

82

out for the academic life, that with him by my side I could get through my PhD and even a post-doctorate. Even my father, on our rare catch-up phone calls noticed a difference in me and my attitude to work.

But then a year ago Marcus left in the most unexpected way and everything I'd convinced myself was true unravelled and I came back to Sanderson Bay, to get away from the memories of Marcus and, it turned out, to buy a café. One of the reasons it felt like the right thing to do, aside from the café, was that Marcus never liked Sanderson Bay and it's the last place he'll come. If he ever sets foot in the UK again of course.

Spending time with Ben today has shifted something inside me. That closed-off part of me that has spent twelve months refusing to go on any of the dates Sascha and Miranda suggested, refusing to respond to flirtatious holidaymakers over the summer, refusing to even consider that there should be anything in my life other than the café and my friends, has opened up. Just a little, just enough to let the light in. Knowing that he finds Christmas difficult as well, even though he didn't tell me why, feels as though we have a connection. Coming back to the place you grew up when you've been away a long time takes guts. I know because I haven't been back to Paris since *Maman* died – and trust me being an art historian and avoiding Paris is quite an achievement; there's a reason I concentrated on Spanish painters. But recently I've begun to wonder if going back would help me get some closure or some sort of understanding.

That little connection has made me feel that being attracted to him might not be such a bad thing, even if he is only in the Bay for a short time. Especially as I'm fairly sure, from the way I saw him looking at me, that he feels the same way.

'Where are we putting it?' Ben asks as he drags the Christmas tree into the café.

'I thought in the back corner by the window,' I reply. There's a big plate glass window at the back of the café that overlooks my herb garden and I think it will look really good over there. 'Do you think it will fit?' I ask. 'I hope I haven't bought one that's too big.'

'Should be fine,' he says as he leans the tree against the wall and starts moving a table. 'We might need to squeeze some of the tables closer together.'

I go over to help him. 'That's OK – I'm sure people won't mind cosying up a little bit.'

In the end I decide to move one table out completely and put it in the storeroom until after Christmas.

'Do you have a stepladder?' Ben asks.

'What do we need a stepladder for?'

'To reach the top of the tree.'

'Can't you do that?' He's over six foot tall.

'I could but you have to put the star on the top of your own tree.'

'I'm not very good with heights,' I mumble. 'And yes, even a stepladder feels like a long drop to me.'

He looks over at the shelves of tea behind the counter. 'How do you stock your shelves?'

I feel myself blush at my own stupidity. 'My uncle comes over and helps me,' I say. 'But there is a stepladder in the back. Shall I go and get it?'

'I'll go,' Ben says. 'You start decorating the lower branches. I'll be back in a minute.'

I start to sort through the boxes of decorations I bought from Conways Farm, wondering if I've gone a bit over the top. At least I picked a colour scheme of red and gold and am not about to create a similar technicolour nightmare to the one that Ben says Sascha has put together at the hotel! I open the box of big red and gold baubles and start with them, putting them at intervals around the bottom of the tree and working up in size order – gold doves, red glittering stars – before I remember.

'Lights!' I say out loud as Ben comes back with the ladder.

He slaps himself in the forehead in the most comic way. 'I can't believe we forgot lights,' he says. 'Where can we get some?'

I pause for a moment. I can't think of anywhere in Sanderson Bay we can get Christmas tree lights – any that were being sold in the local shop will have sold out this week as everyone else had already decorated their shops, businesses and homes in time for the lights switch-on.

'How over-decorated is the hotel?' I ask.

'Very.'

'Lots of lights?'

'I like your thinking,' he says with a smile. I'm already dialling Sascha's number.

She arrives five minutes later with a box full of Christmas lights that she hasn't bothered to unravel.

'Here you go,' she says thrusting the box in my direction. 'And before you ask, they've all been PAT tested.'

'What tested?' Ben asks.

'Public appliance testing,' Sascha says. 'You have to have all your electrical equipment checked by an electrician every year if you use them in a business.'

Ben nods, probably wishing he'd never asked.

'And Ellie is a stickler for the rules,' Sascha continues.

'Is she now?' Ben says, raising an eyebrow at me.

'Are you going to stay and help?' I ask Sascha.

She looks between me and Ben and grins. 'Stay here and be a third wheel?' she says. 'Not likely.'

She leaves us to sort through the box of lights, which we slowly begin to unravel. I discard the multicoloured snowman-shaped lights in favour of the plain white ones, which Ben winds around the tree.

'Turn them on for me,' he says.

I plug them in. 'Perfect,' I say when I see them illuminated. 'You've got them completely even.'

'Well thank you.' He grins. 'And now we need some Christmas music,' Ben says.

I groan.

'You don't like Christmas music either?' he asks.

'A tastefully decorated tree is one thing, Christmas music is quite another – something I absolutely draw the line at. Sascha might think it's suitable to listen to "I Want a Hippopotamus for Christmas" while her guests are eating, but I do not.'

Ben gets his phone out of his pocket. 'Does that stereo connect by Bluetooth?' he asks.

I nod.

'Well you might like this.'

Gentle piano music ripples from the speakers, a piano version of "The Holly and The Ivy".

'This is actually quite nice,' I say. 'What is it?'

'It's just a playlist of Christmas music on Spotify – old-fashioned carols played on the piano. It's quite soothing and goes with your café aesthetic.'

I smile at him and we go back to decorating the tree.

'So why art history?' Ben asks after a while.

'I love art,' I reply. 'I grew up in Paris and spent wet Sunday afternoons wandering around the Louvre with my parents. I fell in love with the Venus de Milo when I was seven years old.'

'A lifelong love affair,' Ben says.

'Longer than any other relationship,' I reply. 'Anyway, I always loved art but I was never any good at drawing.' I change the subject quickly – I don't want to talk about ex-boyfriends thank you very much. 'No good at painting or pottery or any of the other classes my parents sent me to, so I started reading about art instead and it grew from there, especially once I discovered the surrealists – they were my big passion.' I pause realising that I've spoken in the past tense as though Ernst, Dalí, Magritte and their followers are no longer of any interest to me. 'They're still my big passion,' I say correcting myself. 'But just in a different way.'

'Your whole face lights up when you talk about it,' Ben says. 'And you can tell me to mind my own business again, but what made you give it all up?'

'Being passionate about something doesn't mean you have to make a living out of it,' I say. 'Especially when making that living means living by other people's standards.'

He nods at my cryptic answer as though he knows that's barely half the story, but he doesn't push it. 'What about tea?' he asks. 'That's obviously a big passion of yours too.'

'True,' I reply. 'But this time the only person setting the standards is me.'

He looks at me for a moment before going back to the tree and putting the last few decorations on the high branches. I want to ask him about his work, whether marketing fills him with passion and whether working for Moby's excites him or makes him feel as though he's jumping through other people's hoops but he doesn't give me a chance.

'Time to put the star on the top,' he says holding the big gold star out to me. I take it from him and he puts the stepladder in place. 'Face your fear, Ellie,' he says, smiling that devastating smile of his.

The fizzing in my belly propels me up the ladder and I place the star at the very top of the tree – it's almost brushing the café ceiling. Getting down again is another matter.

Ben can sense my hesitation and holds on to the ladder. 'I've got you,' he says as I make my slow descent, cringing with embarrassment. A grown woman should not be this scared of a stepladder.

I'm nearly at the bottom when my foot slips off the rung of the ladder and I fall backwards, straight into Ben's arms. Honestly, you couldn't make it up.

'I'm so sorry,' I say as he places me firmly back on the floor and I turn around. I notice he hasn't taken his hands off my waist.

'No harm done,' he says softly.

His eyes meet mine and electricity sparks through me. He ducks his head and he's so close I can feel his breath against my skin. He doesn't take his eyes off me as he takes his hand off my waist and brushes the hair out of my face, tucking it behind my ear. If I stood on tiptoe I could brush my lips against his.

'Ellie,' he says quietly and I don't know if it's a question or not as I begin to lift my heels off the floor. But before my lips meet his, there is a sudden banging on the café door and Ben whips his head away, the moment gone.

I move away from Ben towards the door.

'I'll start clearing up,' he says as I open up the café. A young couple are standing outside wearing those big waterproof jackets that people wear on yachts.

'Are you open?' the woman asks. I want to tell her that no, obviously not as the door is locked and the sign is flipped to closed. But I flip the sign over to "open" instead.

'We are now,' I say with a smile that I hope covers up my irritation. I don't know yet how I feel about the fact that Ben almost kissed me – it's something I'll have to unpack later when I'm alone. I would certainly have liked a chance to find out how I felt about him actually kissing me. But it's time I opened up. I've got some afternoon teas booked in for later that I need to get ready for.

The couple step inside and start looking around at all the different teas on the shelves, reading the handwritten cards I've made for each tea explaining what's in it and what it's for.

'We came here in the summer,' the woman says. 'We have a boat that we keep in the marina on other side of the Bay so we don't often come into the town itself, but we thought we'd come back this weekend to buy a few Christmas presents.'

'Well feel free to browse,' I say. 'Can I get you anything while you're here?'

'Can we get a pot of your Christmas tea?' the woman says, pointing at the chalkboard advertising it. 'And a couple of mince pies.'

'Coming right up,' I say.

I take one of the teapots I've bought especially for Christmas – dark red with sprigs of holly all over it and swill it out with hot water to warm the pot. Then three spoons of Christmas blend tea – black tea with small slices of dried apple and orange along with cinnamon, coriander and clove, it's the ultimate Christmas blend and just the smell of it will have you singing "Jingle Bells" no matter how much of a Grinch you are.

'I've put all the empty boxes and the ladder back in the storeroom,' Ben says as he comes back out into the café. 'If you tell me where the broom is I'll do a quick sweep-around.'

'Are you sure?' I ask. 'You only signed up to help me with the tree, not help out in the café.'

'Course I'm sure,' he says, and there's that smile again, the one that makes me feel weak at the knees.

'Thank you,' I reply with genuine gratitude. I love this café so much and I've never once regretted giving up my life in York to come here, but it is a full-on commitment with hardly a moment to myself to sit down with a book, or go to an art exhibition, or even to kiss a handsome man. I shake my head to make that thought go away. 'Can you just keep an eye on things here while I prep for this afternoon? We took longer with the tree than I thought we would.'

He nods and our eyes meet for a moment as unspoken words and that unfulfilled kiss float in the air between us.

I look away first, heading out into the kitchen to get the mince pies and the other cakes I'll be serving this afternoon – chocolate fudge, a brand-new walnut loaf from Bessie, Victoria sponge and thick slices of spiced Christmas cake.

When I come back the couple have chosen the gifts they want to buy – some packs of the Christmas tea, some china mugs and tea infusers and two of the night-time kits that I gave to Ben the other night. I cash it all up and take their payment.

'Go and take a seat,' I say. 'I'll bring your tea over.'

When I go over to their table they're talking about the Brass Monkeys Open, a sailing race that's held every Boxing Day on the other side of the Bay.

'Are you taking part?' I ask.

'Yes,' the man replies. 'We've got a Wayfarer dinghy so it's eligible. It'll be our first time doing the Brass Monkeys.'

'Have you been sailing long?' I ask.

'A couple of years,' he says. 'We're completely addicted!'

'We took the boat out this morning,' the woman says. 'We're trying to get as much practice as we can before the race.'

'Are you staying in the Bay over Christmas?'

She nods. 'Yes, but we're staying at the guest house over by the marina so we're closer to the boat.'

'You do know that the weather can turn on the flip of a coin at this time of year around here don't you?' Ben says from behind me. I turn around and he's standing nearby listening to our conversation, leaning on the broom.

'Well of course,' the man replies seeming a little flustered. 'And we're aware that the race could be cancelled if the organisers think that the weather will make it dangerous.'

'I don't think there should be a race,' Ben says quietly. His face is pale and his eyebrows are knotted together. He looks like the man who first walked into the café on Monday night, not the man who I've spent the afternoon decorating a Christmas tree with, the man who almost kissed me. 'There are too many risks,' he mutters as he turns away. 'December is not the time to be mucking about on boats.'

I turn back to the couple who both look a bit shocked.

'Can I get you anything else?' I ask, trying to draw the couple's attention away from Ben.

'No.' The woman smiles at me. 'This is great.'

'We're hardly mucking about on boats,' I hear the man whisper to his partner as I walk away.

I take the broom off Ben. 'What was that about?' I ask, trying to keep my voice soft. Ben shrugs, but his face is like thunder and I wonder where this anger has suddenly come from.

'I'm going to go,' he says.

'You don't have to,' I reply as he turns his back on me, picking up his coat from the back of the chair where he left it. 'I was just wondering...' I continue – but he's already gone, the café door closing behind him.

10

'He almost kissed you!' Sascha squeals clasping her hands together in front of her. 'I knew it, I knew the Christmas tree plan would work.'

'You didn't know any such thing,' I reply. 'And anyway, can we please concentrate on the more important issue. Have you seen Ben this evening?'

She shakes her head. 'He hasn't been back since the two of you went Christmas tree shopping. Until you arrived here, I assumed he was still with you.'

The afternoon had flown by in the café as we were completely full right up until closing with both bookings and walk-ins and the Christmas cake went down a treat. Being so busy meant that I hadn't had a chance to think about Ben's strange behaviour again until after closing. I'd seen Geoff head down towards The Black Horse so I wrapped up the last of the Christmas cake and took it to the hotel to share with Sascha and between us we had unpacked the afternoon from the almost kiss to Ben walking out of the café.

'So he helped you with the Christmas tree, you fell off a ladder into his arms, he almost kissed you, he helped tidy up the café and then he flipped out at a couple of customers and stormed off,' Sascha recaps, counting off the points on her fingers.

'He didn't flip out or storm off exactly,' I reply. 'It was quieter than that, but he was angry about something, the Brass Monkeys race I think.'

'What was the almost kiss like?' Sascha asks, completely ignoring me. 'Did he say anything beforehand?'

'Just my name in this really gentle voice,' I say, the memory bringing me out in goose bumps. 'But don't you think it's weird that his mood changed so suddenly?'

Sascha shrugs. 'Maybe he has a paranoid fear of the sea, or boats, or sailors?' she says.

'Nobody grows up in Sanderson Bay with a paranoid fear of the sea do they?'

'Who knows? I mean really, how much do we know about him?'

'Not much, although he did tell me that he finds Christmas hard too.'

'Why?'

'He didn't say and I didn't ask,' I reply. 'But it was nice to be with someone who understands that this time of year isn't all joy and goodwill you know?'

Sascha reaches over and squeezes my hand. 'I know you find this time of year hard, El,' she says. 'I'm just trying to get you to create your own traditions now that the café is yours. You shouldn't be hanging on to your mum's traditions after all these years, not if they make you sad.'

'It's not just that.'

'And you definitely shouldn't be thinking about Marcus,' she says firmly.

'You're right, I do need to start looking towards the future.'

'A future with a tall, handsome, grey-eyed stranger perhaps.'

'Not if he just keeps almost kissing me and leaving,' I say. 'Although…'

'Although what?' Sascha's eyes are like saucers, wide with curiosity.

'When I was with him today, when we were at the Christmas tree farm and afterwards…' I pause. 'Well I didn't feel as though I should be avoiding the way I feel. It's OK to be attracted to a good-looking stranger, even if he is only in town for a short while. It felt like a nudge from the universe to start living my life instead of hiding from it.'

'That's such a good thing, El,' Sascha says. 'Such a step in the right direction. Even if Ben turns out to be just a quick kiss before he disappears forever it will help you take that next step, I'm sure of it.'

'He seems to have disappeared forever anyway,' I say. 'And I haven't even had the quick kiss yet!'

My phone starts ringing and when I pick it up I see Geoff's name on the screen.

'That's weird,' I say showing it to Sascha.

She rolls her eyes. 'He'll be getting you to check up on me, to make sure I'm resting. He's been like a mother hen since I found out I was pregnant and it's doing my head in.'

'Hi, Geoff,' I say into the phone. 'I'm with Sascha now

and I promise you she's not doing anything more strenuous than eating cake.'

He chuckles. 'Glad to hear it,' he says. 'But it's not that I wanted to talk to you about.' I can hear the sounds of the pub in the background.

'What is it?' I ask.

'It's Ben,' he says. 'I think you'd better come down to The Black Horse, and do me a favour, El, make Sascha stay at home.'

Making Sascha do anything she doesn't want to do is easier said than done but I manage to persuade her that she didn't want to come out on such a cold night and that I would call her the minute I knew what was going on.

The pub is overcrowded and noisy when I arrive, the windows steamed up from the warmth of all the bodies inside. Christmas tunes are playing on the stereo and Terry seems to have gone completely overboard with the decorations since I was last in here.

I see Geoff standing by the bar and wave to him. He waves back and I walk towards him. It's not until I get closer that I see Ben, slumped on a bar stool next to Geoff, a half-drunk glass of whisky in his hand.

'Is he all right?' I ask Geoff quietly.

'Put it this way, that's not his first whisky,' Geoff replies. 'And he keeps saying he needs to apologise to you. I figured you might be able to help.'

'OK,' I say looking over at Ben again. He doesn't seem to have noticed me yet. He's just staring into his whisky glass in the same sad way he stared into his pint on the night of the pub quiz.

Geoff leans down towards me. 'Thing is,' he says into my ear, 'I'm not sure I want him to come back to the hotel in that state. It's not fair on Sascha.'

I want to disagree. I think Sascha is the best person to deal with this situation – she'd get Ben off that chair, back to the hotel and drinking coffee in no time and I wish Geoff would stop overprotecting her. I get it, of course I do, but I know it's driving Sascha mad. I don't say anything though – it's their marriage not mine.

'I'll see if he'll come back to the café with me,' I say. 'I can make him some coffee.'

'Thank you,' Geoff says squeezing my arm.

You owe me, I think as I walk over to Ben.

'Hey,' I say, nudging him gently.

'Ellie,' he replies. 'I was hoping you'd be here.' His eyes are glassy but his speech isn't slurred and I wonder if he's as drunk as Geoff thinks he is or if there's something else going on here. 'I wanted to tell you I'm sorry. I shouldn't have snapped at those customers and I shouldn't have walked out like that.'

'Why did you?' I ask. But before he can answer Terry comes over to ask if I want a drink or if Ben wants a top-up.

'I don't think so,' I say to Terry. Isn't there a law about not serving drunk people? 'Shall we get out of here?' I ask Ben. 'Go somewhere quieter?'

He nods and slides off his bar stool. Geoff slaps him on the shoulder.

'See you later, mate,' he says, but Ben doesn't reply. He just shrugs on his coat and walks out of the pub. He doesn't say anything as we walk down the High Street. He is a little ahead of me with his hands in his pockets and his head down. He looks like he knows where he's going so I catch him up and grab his arm. I don't want him going back to the hotel just yet – not because of what Geoff said but because I need to make sure he's all right. It was my café he was in when he got upset and it was my customers he snapped at. There has to be a reason.

'Shall we go to the café?' I ask. 'I'll even make you some coffee.'

'Tea,' he says, surprising me. 'That night-time tea. I like that.'

'Night-time tea it is,' I reply.

I unlock the café and reset the burglar alarm. Ben follows me in and sits at one of the tables at the back of the café near the Christmas tree.

I turn the hot water on and wait for it to heat up so I can warm the pot. Three spoons of night-time tea – lavender, camomile, valerian – and a scoop of dried rose petals for any anxiety Ben might be feeling. Well actually those rose petals might be for me. This whole situation is making me feel less than comfortable I'll admit, but I had one of the best afternoons I've had in ages when I was decorating the tree with Ben earlier and something is clearly bothering him. If he needs someone to talk to, I'll be that person even though my usual inclination is to run away.

When the water is warm enough I pour it over the herbs and rose petals and I put the pot and two cups – glass teacups bought on holiday in Morocco and carefully wrapped up in a sarong to transport home – on a tray and take it out to Ben but when I get there he's already fallen asleep, his chin on his chest.

I put the tray down and nudge him gently. 'Come on,' I say as he opens his eyes. 'I don't think you need night-time tea tonight. Let's get you upstairs – you can sleep on my sofa tonight.'

11

I check on Ben three times during the night, making sure he's hasn't rolled onto his back or choked on his own vomit or some other nightmare scenario that my overly anxious, and very awake, brain has conjured up. I wake up from a troubled sleep at 5am, which is early even for me.

When I come out of the shower, I can hear Ben moving about in the living room and I feel my shoulders drop away from my ears in relief that he has survived the night. Which is ridiculous because people get drunk all the time and survive the night and also I'm not sure he was that drunk at all – just completely exhausted. He had told me he hadn't been sleeping well.

'It's not that easy,' I hear him say and realise that he's on the phone to somebody. It seems very early on a Sunday morning to be on the phone to anybody. 'I'll be there this evening,' he goes on after a pause and I walk into my own bedroom. I don't want to be the person who eavesdrops on other people's conversations.

Once I'm dressed, I get some clean towels out of the airing cupboard and place them on the floor outside the living room before knocking on the door.

'I've left you a towel,' I say. 'Feel free to use the bathroom. I'll put some coffee on for you downstairs.'

The living room door swings open and Ben is standing in front of me wearing last night's clothes and generally looking dishevelled. Dishevelled but still very good-looking. My heart skips a beat.

'You don't have to do that,' he says. 'I'll get out of your hair.'

'No,' I say. 'Stay. If you want to anyway. I'm sorry it's so early but I have to open the café in an hour or so. At least have a shower – I've left a new toothbrush in the bathroom for you too.' I stop. I'm babbling again. 'Come downstairs when you're ready,' I say as I walk away.

There is a kitchen in the flat of course but I feel the need to put some distance between me and Ben, at least for a few minutes. Last night, before he fell asleep, he had been trying to tell me something and I'm hoping that if I give him some space this morning he'll be able to tell me whatever it was that upset him yesterday when the couple with the boat came into the café – other than them interrupting a moment that I wish hadn't been interrupted.

I put the café oven on to heat up some croissants and then put on a pot of coffee for Ben and heat up the water for my tea. I need something strong this morning and almost wish that I drank coffee. I make myself a strong black English breakfast tea in one of the Hornsea pottery mugs and wait for the croissants to heat through.

Ben comes down about fifteen minutes later, his hair still damp from the shower and his eyes slightly bloodshot.

'How are you feeling?' I ask as I pour him a coffee into a blue and white striped mug.

'I've felt better,' he says taking the coffee from me. 'Thank you for this, and for putting up with me last night. I owe you a massive apology.'

'Go and sit down,' I say, pointing him in the direction of the tables. 'I'll just go and get the croissants out of the oven.'

When I come back he's put the Christmas tree lights on and is leaning against a nearby table admiring the tree.

'It doesn't look too bad does it?' he says.

'Better than I expected,' I admit as I sit down.

He joins me and wolfs down his croissant in two bites.

'Hungry?' I smile.

'I skipped dinner last night,' he replies. 'Or rather I took my dinner in liquid form.'

I want to ask him why, I want to ask him what has brought him to the Bay and what unsettled him so much yesterday that he felt he had to turn to whisky. But I don't, because I know how much I hate it when people meddle in my life, however well intentioned that meddling is.

'Want another?' I ask instead, pointing at his empty plate.

'No,' he says. 'You've done more than enough for me. Thank you for looking after me last night. I'd got myself in a bit of a state. I'm so sorry – for that and for the way I treated those customers yesterday.' He blushes and looks away from me. 'My behaviour was—'

'You've apologised about fifteen times already,' I interrupt. 'It's fine, I promise. The customers were a bit shocked but I gave them some freebies and I think it placated them. I'm more concerned about you. Are you all right?'

He drinks his coffee and looks at me.

'It's just the time of year and being back here…' He pauses, shakes his head. 'It doesn't matter. I'm fine.

'I do have to get going,' he says before I can ask him anything else. 'I need to get back to the hotel and check out.' He picks his coat up from the back of the chair where he left it last night and steps towards me. 'Thank you again,' he says softly. 'You've no idea how sorry I am.'

'It doesn't matter,' I say as he takes another step towards me. My heart is beating so hard in my chest I'm surprised he can't hear it.

'It does matter,' he says. 'It matters to me. I've loved getting to know you over the last few days, Ellie.'

I don't know what to say to this man who appeared suddenly in my café just six days before and who now feels like part of the furniture, a very attractive part of the furniture, a part of the furniture I definitely want to get to know better.

'What are you thinking?' he asks gently and I realise that I haven't spoken for several moments.

'Nothing really,' I say. 'I have a feeling you're about to tell me you have to leave though.'

'I do. They want me back at work tomorrow and Mum called this morning so I should really go and see her on my way back.'

'Has coming back here done what you wanted it to do?' I ask, keeping my question vague. I don't want Ben to think I'm prying.

'Yes, it has actually. It's helped me make a few decisions,' he replies equally vaguely. He doesn't elaborate on what brought him back or what decisions he has had to make but I tell myself it's too soon for him to share that with me. I take a breath, still very aware of the sound of my heart beating. 'I'd really like to see you again, Ellie,' Ben says. He blushes and looks at me under his eyelashes as though he's embarrassed or apprehensive at what I might say.

'I'd like that too,' I reply, and I really mean it. These last few days with Ben have unravelled something inside me and finally allowed me to see that there is a life after Marcus, a life that could involve something other than work.

I step away from him a little as we swap phone numbers but when he's put my number into his phone he steps towards me again, closer this time, and reaches out to tuck my hair behind my ear, just as he had done yesterday afternoon when I almost fell off the stepladder. 'I'd like to come back if I can,' he says. 'Before Christmas.'

'If you've got time I'd love to see you,' I say, my mouth dry.

He leans towards me, drawing my lips gently towards his. My stomach is turning somersaults and I close my eyes in anticipation of the kiss… and I hear the café door open behind me.

'Morning,' says a gruff voice from behind us and we spring apart like kids who've been caught doing something they shouldn't. I curse myself for unlocking the door earlier.

'Morning, Eric,' I say plastering a smile on my face. 'The usual is it?'

'Aye,' Eric replies.

Eric is a very strong English breakfast with a splash of full cream milk and too much sugar. That's Eric all over – gruff on the outside and sweet in the centre.

'And a raspberry muffin?' I ask. Eric always has a raspberry muffin but he likes to pretend I force him into it.

'Ah go on then, if you insist,' he says.

'Morning, young Ben,' Eric says turning towards Ben as

I make his tea. The two men talk in slightly hushed voices and I find myself trying to make out what they are saying. I remember the money that Ben gave to Eric on the night of the carol singing and how I made a snide remark to Sascha about it probably being a bribe. How ridiculous that seems now. Sascha was right, although I'm never going to tell her that – Ben working at Moby's is just a coincidence. He's clearly in Sanderson Bay for very personal reasons.

'Have you told her?' I hear Eric ask as I turn towards him with his pot of tea and muffin. Ben shakes his head and Eric looks over to me.

'Where are you going to sit?' I ask, wishing I hadn't overheard any of that. Who is this "her"? Is it me?

'I'll be over in the corner,' Eric says, making his way over to a table and I follow with his tea. 'Do you want to join me, Ben?' he asks.

'No, I need to get going,' Ben replies.

I put Eric's tea down. 'Nice tree,' he says nodding towards the Christmas tree as he picks up his muffin.

'I'd better go,' Ben says.

I suddenly feel awkward again and don't know what to say but just as Ben reaches the door he turns towards me.

'I'll be back soon,' he says. 'I'll call you.'

'Nice lad that Ben Lawson,' Eric says as the door to the café closes and Ben walks away. When I look at him he winks at me over his muffin.

12

'Rumour has it that you went Christmas tree shopping with Ben Lawson on Saturday,' Bessie says.

Ben is, of course, the main subject of discussion when the Knitting Club meet the following evening.

'Apparently he nearly kissed her,' Sascha butts in. I feel my cheeks colouring and concentrate on the cardigan I'm knitting.

'Where?' Bessie asks.

'Here by the Christmas tree,' Sascha replies. 'While he was helping her decorate it, but they were interrupted.'

'Eric says he nearly kissed her yesterday too,' Bessie goes on.

'Is that so, Ellie?' Sascha asks. I look up and meet her indignant gaze. I hadn't told her about that yet.

'Why did he only nearly kiss you?' Clara asks.

'Because Eric disturbed them; the big lumbering idiot,' Bessie says.

They clearly don't need my input.

'It's a very nice tree, Ellie love,' my aunt says. She must be feeling better than she was on Friday as she walked over here tonight and is even managing to make some crocheted flowers. I feel a stab of guilt that I didn't go over to see her and James over the weekend because I was too wrapped up in other things. I smile my thanks at her for changing the subject. 'Did you get it from Conways?' she asks.

'That's where Ben took her,' Sascha says with a smug smile.

So much for changing the subject.

'Ben used to work at Conways when he was a boy,' Bessie says.

'Did Geoff get off all right?' I ask pointedly, hoping they get the hint that I do not want to discuss Ben right now.

Sascha's face falls. 'Yeah,' she says. 'Now I'm all alone at the hotel.'

'I thought Geoff's mum was staying to help out,' I reply knowing she'd rather be all alone forever than with Geoff's mum but she needs someone to help her run the hotel alongside the regular staff – even though it's quiet. Sascha sticks her tongue out at me and goes back to her knitting and I think that makes us even – for tonight at least!

'Where's Geoff gone?' Lisa asks. Lisa isn't here as much as the rest of us due to the demands of her job and the length of her commute, so she often catches up on the week's gossip at Knitting Club.

'He's on a mindful management course just outside Halifax,' Sascha says. The inevitable questions follow about what on earth mindful management is and I zone out because I was there a couple of weeks ago when Sascha encouraged Geoff to take the place on the course that had freed up at the last minute. It's a course about leading from the inside out instead of from the top down apparently, and about understanding the emotional intelligence of your team. Sascha suggested I should go on it too until I pointed out that one staff member does not make a team that needed to be managed – mindfully or otherwise. This led to another conversation (aka nagging session) about how I should be thinking of expanding, at which point I changed the subject.

'So,' my aunt says quietly to me. 'Do you like this Ben?'

I turn towards her but don't look up from my knitting. I can already feel my face colouring. 'He's…' I begin. 'He's nicer than I thought he was when he first arrived,' I say hoping to make it sound neutral, but when I do look up at Miranda I can see that the neutrality hasn't come across as I'd hoped.

'Well that's the first time I've seen you blush over a boy since you moved here,' she says with a grin. 'And Lord knows you had enough admirers over the summer.'

Both Miranda and Sascha keep insisting on this but all I could see was them pushing anything male towards me in some kind but ill-thought-out attempt to get me to get over Marcus.

'Perhaps that's true,' I admit. 'But don't get too excited. It's not like Ben's a local or anything. I probably won't see him very regularly – it might all just fizzle out into nothing. Besides, thanks to Eric he hasn't even kissed me yet.'

'He used to be a local,' Miranda says. 'So you never know.'

I can't help smiling. 'He did say he'd try to come back before Christmas.'

My aunt raises an eyebrow. 'Sascha tells me that he's booked a few nights at the hotel just before Christmas.'

That's news to me. I look over at Sascha who is still trying to explain mindful management to Clara and Bessie.

'Are you all just discussing my love life behind my back now?' I ask.

Miranda laughs and my heart melts, forgiving her gossiping about me immediately because it's so good to see her happy, to see her face more relaxed, less etched with pain – even if it is only temporary.

'We just want you to be happy,' she says.

'You seem much better than you did on Friday.'

'I told you it comes and goes and that's normal at this stage.' She reaches over and squeezes my arm. 'We are doing OK, you know,' she says. 'And I promise we'll ask for help when we need it.'

'I'm sorry I didn't come for lunch yesterday,' I reply. I often go to my aunt and uncle's bungalow for a late Sunday lunch while the café is quiet, but yesterday after Ben had left, I'd felt as though I needed to be alone for a bit while Abi looked after the café. Being alone had turned out to be a bad idea as I'd ended up thinking about what it was that Ben wasn't saying and why he didn't like Christmas much and that led me to think about *Maman* and all the Christmases she hadn't wanted me with her and how I'd never had a chance to find out why.

And then I'd started to think about Marcus and by the time I went downstairs to help Abi with the afternoon teas I'd been feeling very sorry for myself. It was a feeling I hadn't been able to shake even after Ben texted late last night to tell me he was back in London and was missing Sanderson Bay already, and even when he texted early this morning to tell me he was missing his Russian caravan tea and the person who made it for him.

I don't tell my aunt about Ben's texts. There is quite

enough gossip and conjecture around my love life as it is. I don't tell her that Ben works for Moby's either. There's no point upsetting her as it's still very early days and I'm not sure anything will come of whatever it is that's happening between Ben and me.

'It's fine, Ellie,' my aunt says. 'You don't have to come every Sunday.'

'I'll be there next week I promise.'

'So you're on your own at the hotel until Friday?' Lisa asks Sascha.

'Not on my own,' Sascha replies. 'As Ellie has so kindly pointed out Celia, my darling mother-in-law, arrived this morning.'

'Why didn't you just tell Geoff that you were fine on your own?' I ask, even though I know she needs the help.

She scowls at me. 'Because Geoff would insist I wasn't and his mother would insist I wasn't and I don't have the energy to argue with both of them.' She pauses. 'It's so annoying because she keeps criticising the way I'm doing things but every single thing she's criticised has been her beloved son's idea.'

'Why don't you correct her?' Lisa asks.

'Trust me, it's not worth it.'

Sascha glares across the café at nobody in particular and then pours herself another cup of ginger tea. When she gets haughty like this I can almost imagine what she was like as a corporate lawyer. Geoff, on the other hand, I struggle to imagine in his previous role in finance. Kind gentle Geoff with his too-long hair and his mindful management courses and his daily yoga practice (on the beach if the weather allows) could never have worked for one of those big multinational banks could he?

We all chat quietly about our Christmas preparations as we knit and I'm glad the focus has gone off me for now. Most of us will be staying in the Bay for Christmas – only Lisa will be going to her parents' house just outside Hull.

'I'll be back for your New Year party though, Ellie,' she says. 'I won't miss that!'

I grin at her. 'I'm so excited for the New Year do,' I say. 'Excited and nervous though. I hope people will come.'

'Of course people will come,' Miranda says.

'Won't they prefer to go to the pub, though, like they usually do?'

'I think a lot of people are planning to do both,' Sascha says. It's possible as I was planning the champagne tea to run earlier than Terry's New Year's Eve pub quiz. Perhaps I should talk to him about timings.

'How many tickets have you sold?' Lisa asks.

'About half of them but I'm hoping more will sell nearer the time, especially to the people who have holiday homes here who tend to arrive on Boxing Day.'

'Don't worry about it,' Sascha says. 'You'll sell all the tickets I'm sure of it.'

'Maybe Ben will be here for New Year,' Bessie says with a twinkle in her eye.

'Well you're the one who's known him since he was a baby apparently,' I reply. 'Why didn't you say you knew him when he first arrived?'

'Clara and I thought we recognised him that first night but we couldn't be sure,' Bessie says. I can remember them nudging each other while Ben and I had been chatting that night. I'd thought at the time that they were planning to set us up, but now I wonder if they know more about Ben than I do, especially about why he and his mother left in the first place. For two people that are constantly talking about everybody else's business, they can keep quiet when they want to.

We carry on chatting, without mentioning Ben too many times I'm glad to say, until my uncle arrives to pick up Miranda.

Around nine o'clock everyone starts to pack up their knitting and get ready to leave and I begin to clear away the tea things.

'Do you mind if I go straight back?' Sascha says as she comes up behind me. 'I'm exhausted today for some reason and I'd better get back and see what my darling mother-in-law is up to.'

'Of course I don't mind,' I reply. 'And you're exhausted because you're eleven weeks pregnant.'

'Shhh,' Sascha says with a smile, nudging me.

'Sorry,' I whisper. 'When's the scan?'

'Next Monday afternoon,' she whispers back. 'So if everything's OK I can tell everybody at next week's Knitting Club.'

When everyone has left, I lock the café door and pull the blinds across before putting the dishwasher on and making sure everything else is turned off. I'm just turning the Christmas tree lights off when there's a knock at the door.

'Just a minute,' I call, assuming that one of the Knitting

Club has left something behind, although I didn't see anything when I cleared up.

The knocking gets louder.

'OK, OK, I'm coming!'

I pull back the blinds and unlock the door.

'What did you forget?' I begin before I see who's standing there.

'Ellie,' he says. 'It's so good to see you.'

'Marcus?' I stare at him feeling as though all the breath has been knocked out of my body. 'What are you doing here?'

'Ellie, I think I made a terrible mistake.'

13

The first time I heard Marcus speak it reminded me of the old Simon & Garfunkel records my parents used to listen to, of the books I loved as a teenager – Hemingway, Fitzgerald, Wharton – of all the dreams I had but was too scared to follow. In five years of living away from New York, he hasn't lost any of that accent. He still speaks in exactly the same way that he did on his first day of post-doctoral research at York University.

He had asked me, later on that first day, why I'd stayed at York. He had asked me the same question that my PhD supervisor had asked, that my father had asked: "You could go anywhere, Ellie. You could do your PhD at the Sorbonne, at Columbia, anywhere in the world. Why do you want to stay here?"

I stayed because York was safe and it was the nearest thing I'd ever had to a home since I'd lived in Paris. After I met Marcus I lived vicariously through him. I didn't think I needed to be anywhere else. I thought I had everything I'd ever wanted.

On that first afternoon I fell in love with Marcus's accent and his smile and his sparkling blue eyes – in that order.

Later on I fell in love with him. Properly head-over-heels-this-will-last-forever love.

Until it didn't last forever after all.

That accent, that smile, those eyes are standing on the doorstep of my café now, the one place I thought Marcus would never come.

'What are you doing here?' I ask again.

'Can I come in, Ellie?' he says. 'It's freezing out here.'

It is freezing and there's snow on the air. Marcus pushes his blond hair, hair that has grown much longer in the twelve months he's been away, out of his eyes. 'Please, Ellie,' he says.

He's wearing a thin cotton jacket and a ridiculous pair of trousers that appear to be made of patchwork. I step aside to let him in and wonder why on earth he isn't wearing something warmer.

I shut the door behind me and lock it, pulling the blinds to again.

'Thanks, Ellie,' he says rubbing his hands together. 'Any chance of a cup of tea?' He smiles and his eyes glint and I can't help myself – I never could resist him.

I go behind the counter and switch everything back on again.

'Sit down,' I say. 'And tell me what tea you'd like.'

'Do you still have the tea you first made for me?'

He couldn't sleep when he first arrived in England. At first he thought it was just the jet lag but after a few weeks he confided in me that whenever he was at home on his own, particularly in bed at night, he couldn't switch his brain off. He said that thoughts and images just played over and over in his head – thoughts about not fitting in, about not being good enough. The next time I was in Sanderson Bay I made up a tea for him, one that I hoped would quieten his mind: rosehip, peppermint, chamomile, elderberry with dried apple pieces for flavour.

He came back to my flat after dinner to try it. He said he slept much better from then on but neither of us ever knew if it was the tea or the fact that after that night he didn't sleep alone again. At least, not until he decided to leave.

I spoon the herbs into a tea infuser to make him a cup of the tea he always swore by and pour over the hot water. I set a timer for six minutes and try not to think about Ben timing himself doing the crossword.

'Let it steep until the timer goes off,' I say putting the cup in front of Marcus.

'I know, El,' he replies. 'I haven't forgotten.'

'And while we wait perhaps you'll answer my question.'

'Why am I here?'

'Yes.'

'It's complicated,' he says. Everything is always complicated with Marcus. 'I've come straight from Manchester airport. I didn't know where else to go.'

'Marcus, you can't just walk back into my life like nothing has happened. You've been gone nearly a year. I've moved on.'

'So I see,' he says looking around the café. 'Did you just give up your PhD?'

'We both know that I was never going to finish it.'

'You could have done if you'd wanted to, El.'

'Maybe I didn't want to,' I admit. 'But we're not here

to talk about my lack of a doctorate. Why the hell have you turned up in Sanderson Bay, a place you've always claimed to hate, on a freezing cold Monday night in December when you're supposed to be in Thailand?'

He opens his mouth to speak but before he gets there someone starts banging on the door again.

'Hold that thought,' I say as I get up. 'And don't think you're getting out of giving me an explanation.'

I pull back the blinds for the second time that night and unlock the door. Sascha is standing on the doorstep shivering. She hasn't put her coat on.

'You have to help me, El,' she says. 'I'm bleeding.'

I usher Sascha into the café.

'We need to get you to a hospital,' I say.

'I know but how?' she replies. 'You don't have a car and Geoff has our car.'

'Have you told Geoff?' I ask.

She shakes her head.

'Have you told your mother-in-law?'

'No, Ellie, I can't bear to wake her up. Please help me, I don't want anyone else to know.'

'We'll have to call an ambulance,' I say taking my phone out of my pocket.

'I could drive you,' Marcus says.

Marcus. I'd almost forgotten about him.

'Who the hell are you?' Sascha asks.

'Sascha, this is Marcus,' I say and Marcus holds out his hand. Sascha doesn't take it, she just stares at me.

'Your Marcus?' she asks. 'The Marcus your aunt and uncle hate?'

'Charming,' Marcus mutters.

'Marcus who broke your heart?' Sascha goes on. She sounds almost hysterical. 'What about Ben?'

'Sascha,' I say quietly putting an arm around her waist. 'I'll explain everything later but right now we need to get you to a hospital.'

She squeezes her eyes shut as though she's trying not to cry and Marcus stands up taking a set of car keys out of his pocket.

'I got a hire car at the airport,' he says. 'It's right outside and if you give me directions, El, I'll drive.' I open my mouth to protest. 'I don't know what's going on but you know it's going to be quicker than waiting for an ambulance.'

I nod, knowing he's right. 'The nearest emergency department is about half an hour away,' I say.

'Let's get going then.'

I lead Sascha towards the door as Marcus follows. She has gone sort of limp in my arms now, as though she's given up. 'I knew it was too good to be true,' she whispers to me.

'Shhh,' I say. 'Everything's going to be fine.'

Marcus drives far too fast and gets us to the hospital in twenty minutes.

'It's not Monte Carlo,' I say.

'It's an emergency isn't it?' he replies.

Our eyes meet for a second and I remember everything that I used to feel for him, things that I know I'd feel for him all over again given half a chance. I tear my eyes away from him. Marcus can wait; Sascha has to be my focus tonight.

'It's good to see you, Ellie,' Marcus says quietly as we sit in the waiting area of the hospital together. 'Even if the circumstances are a bit…'

He trails off. Even Marcus has run out of words now – I ran out of them ages ago. I feel as though I'm on my last nerve and my head is pounding and I still have no idea why Marcus has turned up on my doorstep tonight or if Sascha is going to be all right.

'Can you get me something to drink?' I ask. 'A bottle of water or something? I should have brought something with me.'

'I'm on it,' he replies. 'No tea though right?'

Marcus knows me well enough to know that I would die of thirst rather than drink tea out of a machine. And I know him well enough to know that he's trying really hard to keep me happy. I just wish I knew why.

'Just water,' I reply. I watch him walk up the corridor away from me. Why is he wearing those ridiculous trousers? Why is he dressed for summer in the middle of a Yorkshire winter and why did he come to Sanderson Bay straight from the airport? How did he even know I was here?

I can't think about Marcus though, I need to know how Sascha is doing. It seems hours since the doctor took her away to examine her but it's probably only been a few minutes – my sense of timing is completely out. I start to look around for someone to ask but everyone seems too busy. I know they'll find me when there's news because Sascha wrote my name beside *"Next of Kin"* on the form she filled in when we arrived, but I'm still wound up with worry. I couldn't bear for anything to happen to this baby. Sascha and Geoff have been waiting for so long.

'Eloise Caron,' somebody says, mispronouncing my last name as though it's "Karen". I look up and see a doctor hovering near the seating area.

'That's me,' I say, standing up.

'Hi, I'm Dr Hargreaves,' the man says. He looks exhausted, as though he hasn't slept in a year. 'Mrs Jacobson is asking for you.'

I follow Dr Hargreaves down the corridor. 'Is she going to be OK?' I ask. 'Is the baby going to be OK?'

'We're just about to do an ultrasound,' Dr Hargreaves replies, not really answering either of my questions. 'We'll know more then.'

He pulls aside a curtain and ushers me inside the little cubicle. Sascha is lying on the bed looking pale and tired, but she's smiling.

'Ellie,' she says, holding out her hand to me. I take it and sit on the hard, plastic chair next to her. 'I've been asking for you for ages.'

'I'm here now,' I say. 'How are you feeling?'

'Nauseous and hungry at the same time but I'm not allowed anything to eat or drink until they're sure everything is OK.'

'They don't know yet?' I ask.

She shakes her head. 'There are lots of reasons it could

be happening.' Her voice sounds strained and slightly shaky. 'That's why they want to do the ultrasound – to see if everything is all right,' she goes on squeezing my hand. 'It will be all right won't it, Ellie?' she says, looking at me hopefully as though I have all the answers.

'I hope so,' I reply.

What else can I say? I look at her lying there. She seems so small and helpless in the hospital bed and I wonder where my larger-than-life, loudmouth friend has gone. She looks terrified and nobody apart from the two of us and Marcus know that we're here.

Marcus. Of all the people in the world.

'Do you want me to phone Geoff?' I ask, but she shakes her head again.

'Not until we know what's going on,' she replies. 'But while we're waiting for this ultrasound you can tell me why Marcus is here.'

I pull a face and she smiles. 'I have no idea why he's here,' I say. 'He just arrived on my doorstep about ten minutes before you did.'

'I thought you said he was in Thailand.'

'He was as far as I knew. I had no idea he was planning to come back – I haven't seen him since this time last year.' When Marcus left it had felt as though my life was unravelling but the threads of that unravelling had led me to Sanderson Bay, to the café, to Sascha, to a place where I could start again, a place where I could be myself again. A thread that brought Ben into The Two Teas just a week ago. How could that only be a week ago? It feels so much longer.

I'd almost got to the point of believing that what

happened with Marcus was for the best, because it allowed me to change my life for the better. But now he's back I no longer know what to think.

'Ellie,' Sascha says quietly. 'Be careful won't you? He broke your heart.'

'I know,' I say blinking back the tears I've been on the edge of crying all night. 'I don't really want him here. I don't know what to do with him or with the way I feel about him.'

'Have you heard from Ben?'

I feel myself smile a little at the mention of his name and a different sort of unravelling happens in the pit of my stomach. 'He's texted a few times,' I say.

'Good.' Sascha squeezes my hand again. 'Concentrate on that.'

The curtain opens again then and a nurse comes in wheeling what I presume is the ultrasound unit.

'Mrs Jacobson?' she asks.

'Sascha,' Sascha replies.

'Right, well let's see if we can get a look at baby shall we?'

Sascha sits up and pulls up her top as the nurse rubs gel all over her still-flat abdomen.

I can't look at the ultrasound screen and I can't look at Sascha, so I just concentrate on the gel on Sascha's stomach. Her grip on my hand gets tighter and tighter and for the longest minute nobody makes a sound.

'How many weeks did you say you were?' the nurse asks.

'About eleven,' Sascha replies in a small voice. I still don't look up. 'We have our twelve-week scan booked for next week.'

'That sounds about right,' the nurse replies and the reassurance in her voice makes me look up at Sascha who is, in turn staring at the monitor.

'There's your baby,' the nurse says pointing at the screen.

All I can see is a small white blotch.

'Oh my God,' Sascha whispers.

At that moment we start to hear the baby's heartbeat and it feels as though it's the only sound in the universe. Relief washes over me and when I look over at Sascha she's laughing and crying at the same time.

'That's a good strong heartbeat,' the nurse says.

She goes to get the doctor who tells Sascha that as far as they can tell everything is fine and lists a few reasons why she could have been bleeding.

'It was relatively light,' he says. 'You say there wasn't any pain and baby seems fine so don't worry, Mrs Jacobson. Is it possible you've been doing too much?'

Sascha shrugs and looks a bit guilty.

'Very possible,' I reply.

Dr Hargreaves checks his notes. 'You've an appointment for another scan next week,' he says. 'So I suggest that you go home and we'll reassess when we see you next week.'

Sascha starts to get up off the bed.

'And please, Mrs Jacobson,' he says, 'get as much rest as possible.'

'Who has time to rest?' Sascha asks when he's gone. 'I bet he doesn't rest.'

'He's not eleven weeks pregnant with a much-longed-for baby,' I reply. 'You'll be resting from now on if I have to tie you to the bed.'

'Oooh kinky,' she replies, picking up her bag. Sascha is very clearly back to her old self. 'Right let's go and see what Marcus is up to,' she says walking down the corridor ahead of me.

I groan inwardly. The last thing I need is Sascha asking Marcus a bunch of nosy questions. All I can hope is that Marcus will get us home as quickly as he got us here.

14

I wake up early again the next morning to the sound of rain battering the windows. I don't seem to be able to sleep past 5.30am at all at the moment so I get up and I make myself a cup of hot lemon, listening out for sounds of life from the living room where Marcus is sleeping. I'm dreading him waking up and having to have the inevitable conversation with him, the conversation I put off last night because I was too tired and too wound up. All I'd wanted to do when we got back to the Bay was to make sure Sascha was OK, work out what to do about Marcus and go to bed. My desire to sleep overtook my desire to speak to Marcus so I gave him some blankets and directed him to the sofa. This flat has become a refuge for waifs and strays – it's hard to believe that only a week ago I was feeling lonely.

But in an hour or two Marcus will wake up and I'll have to face the conversation I hoped I'd never have to have.

When Marcus left I didn't understand what had happened and I wanted him to explain it to me properly. But now I realise that perhaps he couldn't explain it to me, that perhaps he just knew in his heart or in his gut that he had to take a break from his life and go to Thailand, just as I'd known – after he left and after Moby's started pressuring

James and Miranda – that I had to find a way to buy the café myself.

In the four years that Marcus and I were together I was able to pretend, by living vicariously through him, that my life was exactly as it should be. I was able to pretend that I was happy, that I was in the right career, that my PhD was going well. Marcus was so focused, his PhD from Columbia a huge success, his post-doctorate research going well – but I knew that at home he could be anxious about his work, worried that it wouldn't be well received and constantly concerned that he didn't fit into the department at York. He made me feel that my own anxieties were normal, that my own career must be going well because, after all, nobody had said it wasn't.

I had thought, on the night that he told me he was leaving, that he was going to propose. All the signs were there, or so I believed – he had talked about our future a lot, where I saw myself in five years' time, did I want children – and he'd become more affectionate; not that he wasn't affectionate anyway but it was as though he wanted to spend every free moment with me. I had thought it was nerves, that when he did ask the question and I accepted (which I knew I would), everything would go back to normal.

But he didn't ask. Instead, when he took me out to dinner on that cold November night and told me that he wasn't happy, that his life wasn't going in the direction he wanted it to go in and he needed to do something else, something that would help him work out his next steps. That night didn't end with a diamond ring and falling into bed together wrapped up in our own happiness as I'd dreamed it would, it ended with a one-way ticket to Bangkok and Marcus moving into his friend's flat until it was time for him to leave. He told me he was going ten days before his flight left for Thailand. He claimed he'd been too scared of hurting me to tell me before.

'It sounds like a cliché I know,' he said. 'But honestly it isn't you, it's all me.'

I left the restaurant then and wandered through the cold, damp streets of York passing drunk students and early Christmas revellers and knowing, even then in my confused heartbroken state, that without Marcus there, I couldn't pretend that I would finish my PhD anymore and that it wasn't just him who needed to work out their next steps.

I'd run away from boarding school once, in the second year that I was there, just after the second Christmas spent at Sanderson Bay and not in Paris with my mother. I'd thought that nobody loved me, that nobody cared about what happened to me. When I'd run from the school while everyone else was eating dinner I'd realised, suddenly, that although my plans to escape were carefully hatched, I hadn't actually planned anywhere to escape to. It was then that it had hit me, that Sanderson Bay was that place and that, actually, somebody – two people in fact – did care about me very much.

Which was why when I finally went back to my flat on the night Marcus told me about Thailand, the first people I phoned were James and Miranda and it was during that phone call, when they mentioned Moby's had upped their offer again, that I knew what I had to do.

The last year in Sanderson Bay has changed me more than I ever thought possible and, although when I let my mind drift back to Marcus I still miss him and my heart still hurts, I know I can never go back to the life or the person I used to be.

I wonder if he found what he was looking for in Thailand.

I wonder why he's back.

And I wonder what this terrible mistake he's made is.

After an hour of scrolling through social media and replying to comments (and maybe a little bit of time rereading the texts that Ben has sent to me), there are still no signs of life from Marcus so I get up and bang on the living room door.

'I have to open the café in an hour,' I call. 'I'm just having a quick shower and then I need you to get up.'

He grunts something at me. He never was a morning person.

The café is already open when he finally appears wearing a less colourful outfit than the night before. He leans against the doorframe and watches me as I make Lisa's tea and I can tell by the look on Lisa's face that she's seen him.

'Long story,' I say. 'I'll tell you later.'

She raises an eyebrow and tells me to have fun and I'm thankful that she always running late for her long commute into Hull. God knows what she's thinking when only last night I was singing the virtues of Ben.

I turn around and look at Marcus. He's exactly how I remember him, tall and laconic with that slow easy smile that belies his more anxious interior. His hair is longer, and his skin is more tanned but he's still the same person I lived with for nearly four years, the same person who I thought I knew almost as well as I knew myself.

The same person who broke my heart.

But he's not exactly the same. There's something else there now, as though he either found what he was looking for and didn't like it or realised that what he wanted couldn't be found.

'Tea or coffee?' I ask him.

'Tea of course,' he says.

Marcus is a Yunnan tea, a smoky (but not as smoky as Russian caravan), caramelly black tea from China. Until he met me, the only tea he'd ever drunk was the iced variety, so my tea obsession confused him. He soon discovered his own tea and, although I knew he drank the cheap machine coffee at work, Yunnan became the tea he started every morning with. It's Yunnan I brew for him now as I send him to sit down.

I have a slow trickle of customers first thing that dies off quite quickly and I know I'll have an hour or two before things pick up again. It's time to ask the question.

I sit down opposite him.

'I'm going to ask the question for the third time,' I say.

'What am I doing here?' he replies.

'What are you doing here?'

'Honestly?' He sighs and pinches the bridge of his nose with his thumb and forefinger. 'I don't know. I didn't know where else to go. I've been thinking about you a lot recently, Ellie, thinking about us.'

I feel a sense of panic rising up from my stomach. I know that if I sit here and listen to that accent, lose myself in those blue eyes, I could fall for him all over again.

'There is no us,' I say as convincingly as I can. 'There can't be any us.'

He looks at me with a strange expression on his face

as though I'd thrown him, as though I'd said something he didn't think I'd say. Was he just expecting me to fall back into his arms as though the last twelve months hadn't happened?

'You've met someone else,' he says. 'I'm guessing that's who Ben is.'

'Sort of, not really. But that's irrelevant. It's not about whether or not I've met anyone.'

He reaches over the table and takes my hand. 'We were so good together,' he says quietly.

He's as hard to resist as he ever was but I pull my hand away. 'Until you broke my heart,' I reply remembering Sascha's warning from the night before. When I first turned up in Sanderson Bay I was such a mess, thanks to Marcus, that Sascha was able to remember it on one of the most frightening nights of her life. She told me to be careful – I can't let his soft accent or his lazy smile or his blue eyes suck me back in.

Sascha.

'I have to call Sascha,' I say pushing my chair away from the table.

'I'm not going anywhere, El,' he says. I can't work out if it's a threat or a promise.

I take my phone out of my pocket. I've got two messages. The one from Sascha simply says: *I'm fine, don't worry. I'll see you later.* She knows me too well.

The one from Ben makes me smile: *I found somewhere that sold Russian caravan tea, it says. But it's not as good as yours. I'll have to come back just to buy some tea if nothing else xx.*

I stare at those two kisses for longer than I should, trying to analyse what they mean and thinking about the two kisses we almost had. I must have a dopey smile on my face as I look at it because Marcus interrupts my thoughts.

'What's so funny?' he says. 'I take it Sascha is better?'

I look up at him. 'Nothing, Sascha's fine,' I snap.

'So,' he goes on. 'You and me—'

The café door opens interrupting him and we both turn to see Eric come in. Today I am grateful for Eric's interruption.

'Morning,' he says looking first at me and then at Marcus.

'How are you, Eric?' I say as I stand up. Marcus says nothing.

'Middling,' Eric replies. 'Usual please.' He takes a five-pound note out of his pocket and gives it to me, along with a sidelong look at Marcus.

'Himself is back then is he?' Eric says in what I presume he thinks is a whisper but I can tell Marcus has heard.

'He just turned up on my doorstep last night,' I whisper back. 'I've no idea what he's doing here.'

'Be careful there, love,' Eric says as he takes his change. Marcus used to come to Sanderson Bay with me sometimes when we were together. He didn't like it much; he always claimed it was parochial and small-minded and he could never understand why I loved it so much. Most of the locals knew who he was and I'm pretty sure they had the same rather low opinion of him as my aunt and uncle, who are bound to find out he's here now Eric knows. I sigh inwardly – it is typical of Marcus to show up just when I'm feeling as though I'm moving on.

'Have you heard from young Ben Lawson?' Eric asks in a louder voice, intending Marcus to hear this time. I see Marcus look towards us.

I can feel myself smile. I can't seem to think about Ben without breaking into a stupid grin like an idiot. 'He's texted a few times,' I say.

'He'll be back next week,' Eric replies authoritatively, as he takes the tea tray I've made up for him over to a table on the opposite side of the café from Marcus.

Eric is the first of a sudden rush of customers, both local and visitors, and I leave Marcus almost forgotten with his Yunnan tea and his insistence on talking about "us". A few of my regulars who recognise Marcus raise their eyebrows at me, but I repeat what I told Lisa, that it's a "long story", which I know will only whet their appetites and they'll all be wanting more as soon as they see I'm not busy.

'Wow it's busy for a Tuesday morning in the middle of winter,' Abi says when she arrives, unwinding her scarf from around her neck.

'Sheltering from the rain,' I say, looking at the water running down the outsides of the windows. 'They'll decamp to the pub as soon as it's lunchtime.'

'It's sleet actually,' she says taking off her coat and putting on her apron. 'Maybe it'll snow and we'll get a white Christmas.' Her eyes light up with excitement but Marcus getting snowed into Sanderson Bay for the duration is the last thing I need.

Abi spots Marcus then and I see her eyes light up even more.

'Who's that?' she whispers, her voice much quieter than Eric's had been.

'That's Marcus,' I reply.

'*The* Marcus?' Abi has never met Marcus as she didn't live in the Bay when we were together, but over the last year

THE TEAROOM ON THE BAY

she has heard all about him and his sudden calling to South East Asia. 'What's he doing back?'

'He seems to think he's made some sort of mistake. I've a horrible feeling he wants to get back together with me.'

'What about Ben?'

'Does everyone in this damn town know my business?'

Abi looks at me for a moment and then turns her attention back towards Marcus.

'He's very handsome,' she says. Marcus is staring at his phone. He hasn't changed so much on his travels if he still stares at his phone all the time.

'You can have him,' I reply. 'But first can you look after things for me for half an hour?'

'Sure,' she says and I signal Marcus to follow me back up to the flat. Disappearing upstairs with him will no doubt give everyone even more to speculate on but right now I don't care. I need to know why he's here.

'Look, Marcus,' I say as we sit down in the living room. It's surprisingly tidy in here considering Marcus usually manages to spread his belongings far and wide. 'You left last year without talking to me about it first, telling me you needed to "find yourself",' I make air quotes with my fingers. 'You can't just walk back in and tell me how good we were together and expect me to just drop everything to be with you again.'

'That's not what I expect,' he says. 'It might have been what I hoped when I was driving here last night but now I've seen you here, seen the café, seen the community you've created around yourself I don't necessarily expect you to leave it.' He takes my hand and I don't pull away this time. 'I can see that you're happy here in a way you never were in York.'

'I wasn't unhappy because of you,' I say, remembering the days when Marcus was the only reason I got up in the mornings. 'You were—'

'You were unhappy because of me in a way,' he interrupts. 'Without me you'd have realised much sooner that academia wasn't where your heart lay; you'd have realised you were just doing it for other people and not yourself. Trying to keep your dad happy wasn't a reason to make yourself miserable.'

'I wasn't miserable exactly…' I begin.

'But you wouldn't go back to it now would you?' he asks.

I shake my head. 'But that's why I was so surprised when you were the one who left first. You loved your job so much and it was your love for the work and for the department in general that kept me going for so long. What happened?' I ask. 'Why did you leave so suddenly?'

'It wasn't really so sudden,' he says. 'I'd been thinking about it for a while, months really – maybe even longer. I'd been looking to change something for years. That's the reason I came to England in the first place. I only meant to stay for an academic year; I didn't expect to fall in love.'

I don't say anything at first, instead looking down at where our hands are entwined. There are too many questions I want to ask all at once – like why did he leave if he was in love with me and why did he never tell me that he wanted a change, that he only meant to come to England for a year?

'Why did we never talk to me about all this before?' I

ask. 'Why didn't you try to work through this with me? Why did you just announce you were leaving that night? I thought—'

'I know,' he interrupts again softly. 'You thought I was going to propose that night didn't you?'

I look away from him and I can feel the heat rising in my cheeks and my heart breaking all over again. What an idiot I was.

'Believe me I thought about it,' Marcus goes on. 'I thought about asking you to marry me. I even thought about asking you to come to Thailand with me but I knew it wouldn't be the right thing to do. I knew I was holding you back, stopping you from working out what you really wanted to do.'

'None of that explains why you didn't talk to me about this.' My voice sounds sharp now and I can't work out if I'm angry or upset or both. 'Why did you just leave, making me feel as though it was my fault?'

'None of it was your fault,' he says stroking the knuckles of my hand. I look down to where our hands are joined again. It feels so familiar, as though our hands are meant to fit together.

'I handled the whole situation badly,' Marcus goes on. 'I never meant to hurt you. We were so good together.'

'We were good together for a while,' I say.

'And that's why I'm here,' he says quietly. 'To show you that we could still be good together.'

I pull my hand away. 'No, Marcus,' I say. 'That's not how things work.'

'What do you mean?'

I lean back on the sofa and rake my fingers through

my hair. I don't know what I mean. Even a month ago I'd been dreaming of this moment – of Marcus coming back to England and telling me that he'd made a mistake, that he missed me and wanted to try again. But today all I can think of is Ben and the way he tucked my hair behind my ear just before he almost kissed me. As I think of that, I realise that at some point I've moved on and I've stopped being the person who was waiting for Marcus to come back. It crept up on me so quietly that I didn't even realise it had happened.

'I'm guessing you didn't find what you were looking for in Thailand?' I say, not answering his question.

'It's hard to find what you're looking for when you don't know what it is,' he replies cryptically. 'The first six months were fantastic – I travelled all over Thailand and across south east Asia – Cambodia, Vietnam, Malaysia, Indonesia. It was so eye-opening, El, there was so much I didn't know.' His eyes light up as he speaks. 'But then afterwards I went to live with this community of travellers in Koh Samui and… I don't know… everything just seemed wrong and all I could think of was you and everything I'd left behind.'

'And that's why you came back?' I ask.

'I wanted to retrace my steps to find out where I'd gone wrong – not just with my career but with you. I might not have found the answers I was looking for but I have changed and I want to prove that to you, Ellie.'

I stand up and walk to the other side of the room to put some distance between us.

'What's the point, Marcus?' I say. 'It doesn't matter anymore.'

'I wondered if it was my job I missed at first,' he goes on, ignoring me. 'So I spoke to Professor Doyle to see if there were any positions.' Doyle had been our supervisor at York. 'That's how I found out you'd left, that you'd come back here.'

'Were there any positions?' I asked.

'Why? Do you want one?'

'God no!' The words are out of my mouth before I even know what I'm saying and Marcus smiles.

'You really don't want to go back do you?' he says.

'I guess not.'

'No there's nothing suitable,' he goes on. 'But like you, once I knew there were no vacancies I realised that wasn't what I wanted anyway. What I wanted was you.'

I turn to look at him then, my heart in my throat. I'd been waiting so long to hear those words and yet now they have been spoken they are the last thing I need.

'Marcus, it's taken me a long time to realise this but breaking up with you was the right thing to do. It was the only way I was going to do something for me for once.'

'And now you have,' he says and I have a feeling from the look on his face he isn't listening to me trying to explain that me and him are history. 'The café looks amazing, everything you ever dreamed of eh?'

Marcus was one of the few people I ever spoke to about my dream for the café and even then I only spoke tentatively as though it was all imaginary. I didn't think he'd ever taken it seriously.

'I can see this is where you're meant to be, Ellie,' he says. 'I knew that as soon as I walked into the café yesterday. It's beautiful, totally unrecognisable from when your aunt and uncle owned it and it's so you. This is where you are meant to be.'

I wish I could be as sure about that as he seems to be. I want this to be the right thing so badly but there's still that voice in the back of my head, my father's voice, telling me that maybe I was the one who made a mistake, not Marcus.

'I think so,' I say, hoping that by realising Sanderson Bay is my home now he will give up on this ridiculous plan to prove to me he has changed.

'And it works out even better this way.'

'In what way?'

'Well it's as clean slate for both of us this way isn't it?' Marcus says, standing up and walking over to me. 'If you were still in York we'd have all that baggage from the past with us but this way we can start again in a new place together.'

'You want to stay in Sanderson Bay?' I'm astonished. He always hated it here and was very vocal about that.

'I want to be wherever you are, Ellie. Haven't I made that clear?'

I turn away from him then, walking towards the door.

'I don't know how many times I have to say this, Marcus,' I say turning back towards him, one hand on the doorknob. 'I don't want us to try again. I don't need you to prove to me you've changed. If you want to stay in the Bay you can, but don't do it in some ill-thought-out attempt to get back together with me because it isn't going to happen. Like I said, I've moved on.'

Marcus's face drains of colour, pale beneath his tan, and I feel a surge of guilt. I don't want to hurt him, but equally

I don't want him to think there is even a tiny chance of us becoming a couple again.

'Is this about Ben?' Marcus asks quietly.

'Of course it's not about Ben,' I snap, 'I hardly know Ben. This is about me and the life I've made for myself since you left. I haven't been sitting around pining for you, Marcus.' That last statement might be a bit of a lie, but he doesn't need to know that and I want him to understand that coming back to Sanderson Bay and opening the café is the first thing I've done entirely for myself in my whole life.

'I've seen your face light up whenever anyone mentions his name,' Marcus says with a hint of petulance.

'This isn't about Ben,' I repeat. 'Or any other guy. This is about me.'

Marcus turns away from me and walks towards the window looking out on to the High Street below. I'm about to leave him to it when he speaks again.

'What am I going to do, El?' he asks quietly.

I sigh, hoping this means he's listened to what I've said and is changing the subject permanently.

'I take it you've got nowhere else to go,' I say, leaning against the door.

'How did you guess?' he asks.

'Because I know you, Marcus. You're impulsive and you won't have sorted anything out before you left Thailand.'

He turns towards me smiling sheepishly.

'Have you got any idea what you're going to do?' I ask.

'Honestly? No. Not a clue.'

'Do you think you'll go back to New York?' Marcus is

the only child of two very wealthy Manhattanites. He has a trust fund and has spent his entire life, apart from the last year, in academia. I was always surprised he ever left America, but he pulls a face at me.

'I don't know, El,' he says.

'Perhaps whatever it is you're looking for is back to New York,' I suggest. 'Perhaps you need to keep retracing your steps.'

'Perhaps,' he says.

I pause, knowing I'll probably regret what I'm about to say.

'Look, if you help me sort out the second bedroom you can stay while you think about it, if you like.'

I can't believe I'm doing this – giving the man who broke my heart a place to stay. But I know now that without that heartbreak, without that moment that brought me to my lowest since my mother died, I wouldn't be where I am now – running my own business, being a part of community, surrounded by friends and family.

Without that heartbreak I wouldn't be happy and it's taken seeing Marcus again to make me realise that I am happy.

Besides, I can hardly kick him out on to the street when he doesn't even seem to have a winter coat can I?

'Your old bedroom,' Marcus says.

'It's that or nothing,' I reply, trying not to remember the handful of times Marcus stayed here when the flat belonged to Miranda and James – who made him sleep on the sofa as I had done last night. I try not to remember the times Marcus would sneak into my bed after everyone else was asleep, the two of us crushed together in the single bed that

I'd slept in as a teenager. 'But I'm warning you that the folk of Sanderson Bay have very long memories and it will take them a long time to forgive you for your outburst in the pub last time you were here.'

He cringes at the memory of the evening, after too many glasses of wine, when he announced to the whole of The Black Horse that he thought Sanderson Bay was a 'hateful, gossipy sort of place' and he couldn't understand why I loved it so much.

'So it's up to you,' I go on.

'You're an absolute doll, Ellie,' he says hamming up the New York accent in that way that always used to make me smile.

'And you can help me out in the café,' I go on. 'Abi will show you the ropes.'

Because I'm going to need some time to explain to my aunt and uncle why the hell Marcus is sleeping in my spare bedroom.

15

'But what's he doing here?' Miranda asks as I clear the dirty dishes into the kitchen for her.

In hindsight it may have been a mistake to bring Marcus to Sunday lunch at my aunt and uncle's. I'd thought that, as we're no longer together, they would tolerate him more but it seems not. Like I told Marcus, the residents of Sanderson Bay have long memories.

'He had nowhere else to go and he's trying to work out what he wants to do next,' I reply. I haven't told my aunt that Marcus came here initially to try to win me back. He hasn't mentioned that again since our conversation earlier this week and I'm hoping he has given up on it, despite me having caught him looking at me in strangely once or twice over the last few days.

'And he's going to be doing this soul-searching here in the Bay is he?'

'It's as good a place as any,' I reply. 'After all it's where I worked out what to do with my life.'

Miranda raises an eyebrow. 'After Marcus broke your heart.'

'I do wish people would stop reminding me of that.

Marcus and I could have gone on pretending forever but that's not much of a life is it?'

'You really believe that? You really believe that he did you a favour?'

'I didn't at the time but I do now,' I reply. 'He could have gone about it in a different way I'll admit, but I wasn't happy in York – I know that now.'

'And you're happy now?'

I hesitate. 'Yes,' I say. 'Yes I am.' But Miranda has noticed that hesitation.

'Do you want to get back together with Marcus?' she asks. 'It's understandable if you do, especially now he seems to have come all this way to find you again.' Not much escapes my aunt. 'I just think you need to be very careful—'

'No,' I interrupt. 'I don't want to get back together with him.' I pause. 'And he doesn't want to get back together with me.' That last part might be a little fib, but it doesn't matter what Marcus wants. I know now that I have moved on, moved past the heartbreak that he caused.

'And you're sure you're happy with how things have worked out?' Miranda asks.

'Definitely!'

'Then I'll try to be nice to him,' she says with a smile. 'How long is he here?'

'I'm not sure but he's been quite a help in the café so he's pulling his weight while he's here.'

Marcus and Abi have been getting on like a house on fire and she's taught him everything she knows about the café. With that and what he already knows about tea from four years of living with me, I've been able to leave him and Abi to it most afternoons so that I can spend some time helping Sascha while Geoff is on his course. Helping her mostly seems to involve keeping her away from her mother-in-law who has been ruling the hotel with an iron fist in Geoff's absence, but it's felt like a relief to spend just a little time away from the café and the exhausting relentlessness of it. I love what I've achieved but perhaps it's time I admitted that I needed more than one staff member to help me out.

'It's quite romantic really,' Sascha had said one afternoon.

'What is?'

'Marcus flying halfway across the world to see you,' she'd replied.

'Foolish more like. I mean really what was he thinking? He doesn't even have a winter coat.'

'I don't suppose he was thinking much about the weather.'

'No, perhaps not,' I'd said.

'I can't believe he thought he could just waltz back into your life though.' I'd told Sascha the real reason for Marcus's return.

'But it's helped me realise that I don't want to get back together with him,' I'd replied. 'Plus if it hadn't been for what he did I wouldn't be here.'

Sascha had grinned. 'And you'd never have met me,' she'd said. 'Imagine how awful that would have been.'

Somehow Sascha also managed to persuade me that I should be the one to tell Geoff about our impromptu trip to the hospital on Monday night when he got back from his course. I could see, as I'd explained, that there was nothing to worry about, that he was angry we hadn't told him but I could also see that concern and love overtook that anger.

'It's all going to be fine,' I'd said to him. Because for the first time in a very long time it felt as though it just might be.

'Have you heard from Ben?' Miranda asks me now as I start to stack the dishes in the dishwasher.

'We text every day,' I reply. 'He's promised to come back to the Bay before Christmas.'

'Well he'd better hurry up; that only gives him a week.'

'He'll be here,' I reply and my stomach does backflips at the thought of him walking back through the café door. I hope it's me there when he does and not Marcus.

As Miranda and I walk back into the living room to join Marcus and my uncle, she asks me if Sascha is pregnant. I look at her for a moment, taking her in. She looks well today, better than she has in a while, and I hope that this good patch will last over Christmas so she can enjoy it.

'What makes you ask?'

'I just noticed she's not drinking that nettle tea anymore.' Like I say, not much gets past my aunt.

'I'm not at liberty to divulge any information,' I reply.

Geoff and Sascha's baby is the main subject of conversation at Monday night's Knitting Club meeting. The twelve-week scan has taken place and all is well, so Sascha can share her happy news. I'm glad of it because it stops everybody questioning me about Ben and Marcus, the latter of whom nobody is exactly over the moon to see again.

'Why is he here if he hates us so much?' Bessie had said the other day in a loud enough voice for him to hear.

So I'm very happy for Sascha's baby to be the number-one subject of discussion.

'You're the first people I'm telling,' Sascha says. 'Apart from Ellie of course.'

Miranda catches my eye and winks, but I know I've kept my promise to Sascha. I didn't tell anyone. My aunt worked it out for herself.

'Oh look at the little nose,' Bessie says as she takes her turn looking at Sascha's sonogram picture. 'Isn't modern technology wonderful!'

I still can't see anything except a white blob, but at their appointment today Geoff and Sascha were told that everything was absolutely fine and, as there had been no more bleeding, there was nothing to worry about. Sascha had been given a lecture about taking it easy which she was trying to ignore to no avail.

'Geoff has me resting in bed like a consumptive woman in a Victorian novel,' she says. 'Every afternoon I have to go and nap like a naughty toddler. It's infuriating.'

'He loves you,' I say. 'You've both waited so long for this. Just do as you're told for once.'

'I was on full bed rest for the whole of the last three months of one of my pregnancies,' Clara tells us. Clara's three children, who are all in their late twenties and early thirties now, no longer live in the Bay but are all coming back for Christmas together for the first time in years.

'My great-niece had that hyperemesis whatsit,' Bessie replies. 'Where you're throwing up all the time. She had to go into the hospital and be put on a drip.'

I hold up my hands. 'OK, everyone, enough with the pregnancy horror stories. Sascha doesn't want to hear them.'

'I do not,' she says. 'This is the happiest moment of my life. I don't want to know about bedrest or throwing up and I definitely do not want to hear any stories about labour. Ignorance is bliss.'

'I'm so happy for you,' Lisa says.

'Thanks, Lisa,' Sascha replies.

'Shall we have some champagne?' I ask. 'I know you can't have any, Sash, but we should celebrate.'

'Have you got some of that elderflower fizz that you serve with the afternoon teas?' she asks.

'Coming right up!' I say, getting up to go to the fridge to collect the drinks.

I pour the champagne and hand Sascha her elderflower drink.

'To Sascha, Geoff and baby,' Bessie says holding up her glass.

'Sascha, Geoff and the baby,' we all repeat as we clink glasses.

'Hello, ladies, what are we celebrating?' asks a voice from the doorway. We all turn around as one unit.

'Ben,' I say. I feel my face heat up and break into a grin so wide I might split in two. He's even more handsome than I remember, his dark hair falling into his eyes, and I want to run up to him and wrap my arms around him but I'm not doing that in front of Sanderson Bay's foremost gossips, so I stay where I am. He stands with his hands in his coat pockets and smiles back at me. 'I didn't hear you come in.'

'You really need to start locking this door,' he replies. 'You never know who might walk in.'

'We're celebrating Sascha's news,' Bessie says. 'She's having a baby!'

Ben walks over to us. 'That's wonderful, Sascha,' he says. 'Congratulations to you and Geoff.'

'Are you staying at the hotel?' Sascha asks. 'You're not booked in until later this week.'

'No this is just a flying visit today,' he replies and I feel my stomach drop.

'Well come and have some champagne at least,' Bessie says.

'I'd better not as I'm driving. I was just wondering if I could borrow Ellie for a few minutes.'

'Sure,' I say. 'What do you need?'

He steps a little closer to me. 'Can we go for a walk?' he asks quietly. All eyes are on us, burning holes in our backs.

'Just let me get my coat.' I run upstairs as quickly as I can so as not to leave Ben alone with the knitting ladies for too long. As I leave I stick my head around the living room door where Marcus is watching TV.

'Hey,' I say. 'I've got to go out for a while. If the ladies need to leave can you lock up after them? I've got my key.'

'Where are you going?' he asks.

'Just out,' I reply, not wanting to tell him that Ben is here. It's not really any of his business anyway.

He looks at me for a moment knowing I haven't told him the whole story.

'OK,' he says turning back to the TV screen.

Once I'm back downstairs I tell Miranda to call Marcus down if they all want to go.

'He'll lock up after you,' I say, unsure of how long I'll be.

'Have fun,' Bessie calls after us.

16

'Who's Marcus?' Ben asks as we step outside. He offers me his arm and I slip my hand into the crook of his elbow just as I had done after the pub quiz.

'My ex,' I reply.

He doesn't say anything but I can feel his body tense.

'He turned up out of nowhere last Monday night,' I continue. 'People seem to be making a habit of appearing in the café on Monday nights.'

He lets out a breath of air, somewhere between a laugh and a sigh.

'I'm sorry,' he says. 'It's none of my business – you don't have to tell me.'

'We used to work together at York University,' I begin. 'We broke up just over a year ago. It was really sudden and came out of nowhere.' I miss out the part where I thought Marcus was going to propose. 'He took me out for dinner one night and told me that he had quit his job and was leaving to go to Thailand in two weeks. It was...' I pause.

'A shock?' Ben asks.

'Amongst other things yes.'

'Were you living together?'

'Yes, it kind of threw my whole life into disarray to be honest. But it worked out for the best in the end.'

'Because it brought you here,' Ben says quietly. We're walking down the High Street towards the beach. It's a freezing cold night and the sky is very clear so that you can see the stars and the fingernail whiteness of a crescent moon. I stop and look out over the sea.

'It brought me here at exactly the right time,' I say. 'Moby's were really pressuring my aunt and uncle to sell the café. It was a really stressful time for them.' I pause and turn to him. 'My aunt has an arthritic condition that is just getting worse – you might have noticed she was in a wheelchair on the night of the carol singing?'

He nods and looks at me so intently I can barely hold his gaze.

'By leaving my job, selling my flat, moving away and persuading the bank to lend me a large amount of money, I was able to raise enough to buy the café off them, which shut Moby's up once and for all.'

My hand is still on his arm and I feel him tense up again.

'It's OK,' I say. 'I don't blame you personally for what Moby's does. I know it's just a job.'

I watch as he swallows. 'I'm sorry you had to go through that,' he says solemnly and I'm not sure if he means splitting up with Marcus or dealing with Moby's.

'Like I said, it all worked out.'

We start to walk towards the sea again.

'I missed this place,' Ben says. 'I'm surprised by how quickly I came to love it again after avoiding it for so long.'

I want to ask him why he's been avoiding coming back but I don't. He will tell me when he's ready.

'It has a habit of getting under your skin really quickly,' I say instead.

He stops by the railings of the promenade and turns me towards him, his hands on my forearms.

'It's not just the town that's got under my skin,' he says quietly and I feel my stomach somersault, my mouth go dry.

'I really like you, Ellie,' he says his eyes flicking away from me for a moment. 'I might have totally misread this but I think you maybe feel the same?'

'You haven't misread it,' I reply. My voice is barely more than a whisper.

'I'm sorry to just appear suddenly without telling you like this and I'm sorry if I was quiet and standoffish when I was here before.'

'That's OK,' I say.

'On Sunday morning when Eric interrupted us…' he begins.

I don't say anything, I just hold my breath and wait.

'What about Marcus?' he asks eventually.

I let go of the breath I'm holding. 'What about Marcus? He isn't… We're not…'

Before I've managed to finish the sentence, Ben ducks his head and I feel his lips brush against mine gently, tentatively. I put my hands on his waist and draw him closer as he deepens the kiss and I respond, my tongue finding his as my hands slip inside his coat, exploring the muscles of his back through his jumper. I feel his hands in my hair, his thumbs massaging the nape of my neck as he pulls me against him and I can hardly breathe for the intensity of it. Kissing Marcus had never felt like this.

After a few moments I pull away just to catch my breath. Ben rests his forehead against mine.

'I've been thinking about that for days,' he says.

I reach up gently, running my gloved fingers over his cheekbone. 'Me too,' I say. He smiles and wraps his arms around me, kissing the top of my head.

'I was hoping to take most of this week off work but...' He pauses and shifts uncomfortably as he always does when he talks about work. 'Something's come up and I have to go back to London tomorrow. I was working at Mum's and I came here as soon as I found out. Perhaps I should have phoned first.'

'No, this was a nice surprise,' I say, standing on tiptoe so I can kiss him again. 'A lovely surprise.'

'I didn't want to just keep texting and not knowing how you felt about...' He breaks off and shrugs. 'You know.'

'I've been thinking about you too, about those almost kisses all week,' I reply. 'Does that put your mind at ease?'

As confirmation he kisses me again and there's nothing tentative about it this time. Kissing Ben feels glorious, like the kisses you read about in books but that never seem to materialise in real life. I hear him growl softly at the back of his throat and pull away.

'I should... um,' he mutters. 'I should... Will you... Sorry, I'm not very good at this.'

I laugh. 'I don't know, you seem pretty good from where I'm standing.'

'Will you have dinner with me on Friday night?' he asks. 'Somewhere other than Sanderson Bay perhaps.'

'Somewhere where we're not being watched you mean?'

'Exactly.'

'I'd love to,' I say. 'Would you like me to book somewhere?'

'Please,' he says. He's so close I can feel the warmth of his breath against my skin. I feel as though I could kiss him all night.

'Leave it with me,' I reply, my mouth dry again.

'I'm sorry that I have to leave so quickly. There's just something I have to do before Christmas.'

'It's OK, I'm happy you're here at all even if it is for literally just a few moments.'

'A few very nice moments,' he whispers kissing the side of my neck.

I feel my breath catch in my throat. If we stay here much longer I'm going to start undressing him regardless of the probable hypothermia risk.

'You must be freezing,' he says. 'Let me walk you back to the café.'

He kisses me again before we start walking back towards the High Street, our arms wrapped around each other, as though we don't want to let go.

'I really am sorry,' he says again as we approach the café. 'I wish I could stay longer.' For a moment I get a feeling that he's apologising for something other than his fleeting visit but I shake the thought away before I have time to analyse it unnecessarily.

'I wish you could too,' I say. 'But I'll see you on Friday.'

'I'm looking forward to it,' he murmurs as he turns towards me again, dropping his lips to mine. I reach up, sliding my hands across the back of his neck and into the hair on his nape as his hands drop onto my waist and suddenly I'm desperate to feel those hands on my bare skin.

'Too many clothes,' I whisper and he laughs against my lips. Something must catch his eye then because he looks up, over the top of my head, and I turn to follow his gaze.

'We have an audience,' he says.

Standing in the window of the café, their noses pressed against the glass, are all the members of the Knitting Club, including Miranda who really should know better. They all wave when they realise we've spotted them and that's when I notice that Marcus is there looking out of the window too.

'God I'm so sorry,' I say feeling completely mortified. 'They are all so nosy.'

When I look up at him he's laughing, his grey eyes sparkling in the streetlights.

'Don't worry about it,' he says. 'It could be so much worse. If they didn't approve of me I think they'd probably have let me know by now so it feels like I've passed some sort of test.'

'I think you probably have,' I reply thinking of the rather low opinion they all still have about Marcus – even though he seems to be in with them right now, staring out of the window unnecessarily.

'Which is why I need to get back,' Ben says, suddenly serious, his eyebrows knotting together in that way they had on the very first night I met him. 'I need to sort this work problem out so I can give you my full attention on Friday.'

'Go before they come out here and start asking questions.' I want him to smile again, I want him to stop looking so serious every time he thinks about work. About Moby's.

He takes both my hands in his. 'Until Friday,' he says. He drops my hands and kisses my forehead before he turns and walks away. I watch him get into his car, I watch him drive away and I stand watching the road where he was long after he's gone, not wanting to go inside and hear what Marcus has to say about everything.

17

'Oh my God it's so romantic!' Sascha squeals, throwing herself dramatically against the back of the couch we're sitting on. The two old ladies drinking tea in the opposite corner of the lounge of the hotel give us a hard stare.

'Shhh,' I say. 'For goodness' sake, not in public.'

'Is there a problem, Sascha?' says a voice from behind me. I turn around to see Celia who has glided into the lounge unnoticed.

'Why would there be a problem?' Sascha replies impatiently.

'You seem…' Celia pauses. 'Agitated.'

'I'm fine,' Sascha says, giving her mother-in-law a hard stare to rival the old ladies in the corner.

Celia doesn't say anything, she just glides away again.

'This is what I'm talking about,' Sascha begins. 'Every day…'

I hold up a hand. 'OK, I get it.'

'Anyway where was I?' Sascha ponders. 'Oh yes, how romantic it is to drive all the way from York – which takes over an hour by the way—'

'I know where York is,' I interrupt.

'Driving all that way just so he can kiss you!' She puts her hand to her chest. 'Your life is like a romance novel at the moment what with this and Marcus flying in from Thailand to try to win you back. Nobody has ever done anything like that for me.'

'Geoff adores you,' I reply. 'Stop being so ridiculous and remind me why we're sitting in the public lounge instead of upstairs in your apartment.'

'Because I'm watching,' she says, her eyes narrowing. 'Every time I go upstairs for a rest she changes something, so now I rest down here.' She pauses. 'Watching,' she repeats, pointing to her eyes.

'Right,' I say. 'Perfectly rational behaviour.'

Celia did not go home when Geoff got back from his course. After I'd told him about the hospital trip, Celia insisted on staying to help so Sascha could rest more. Now Sascha is convinced that Celia and Geoff are changing everything behind her back.

'What are you going to do when you've had the baby?' I ask. 'You can't be watching all the time then – you need to be watching the baby so it doesn't roll off something.'

'Roll off something?' she asks.

'I don't know what babies do.'

'They shouldn't be on something to roll off it in the first place,' she says. 'But I swear if Celia is still here when this baby comes I'll—'

'OK, OK,' I interrupt. 'I get it.'

'So just leave me alone to quietly watch and you tell me more about Ben.'

'There's not much else to tell,' I say. 'He arrived, he kissed me, he told me he'd been thinking about me, he asked me to dinner on Friday night and then he left again.'

'Have you heard from him since?'

'He texts every day.'

Sascha raises an eyebrow. 'What sort of texts?' she asks. 'Flirty, saucy, downright filth?'

'Sascha for God's sake,' I say but I'm laughing, and I can feel myself blushing.

'I'm assuming by your red face that it's filth,' she replies.

'Not quite filth but...' I trail off, looking away.

'Let me see!' she says, reaching for my phone, which is sitting on the table beside me. I make a grab for it but she gets to it first, punching in my security code and scrolling through my messages.

'Is nothing private?' I ask.

'Nope.'

'How do you even know how to get into my phone?'

She looks up at me. 'Because all your security codes are your birthday. I could steal your whole identity if I wanted to.'

'Why would you want to?' I ask.

'I'd happily steal your identity for messages like this,' she replies, her eyes wide. '*All I can think of is that kiss. I can't wait to see you again,*' she reads out.

'Give the phone back Sascha,' I say but I know this is a fight I won't win. I should have just told her what the messages said in the first place.

'*Sweet dreams,*' she goes on reading out another message before pausing. 'Oh maybe I won't read that one out loud after all,' she says, glancing over at the old ladies. 'Don't want to give anyone a heart attack.'

I can feel myself blushing as she hands the phone back to me.

'Filth,' she teases. 'Just as I thought.'

'It's just flirting,' I reply and she laughs, nudging me playfully.

'I know, El, and I think it's brilliant. He's clearly really into you.'

'Do you think?' I ask, my stomach churning with excitement at the thought.

'I know,' she says. 'So are you excited about Friday?'

'I am...' I begin.

'What's the matter? You sound like you're having second thoughts. Are you? You shouldn't be, those messages are pretty clear.'

'No, not at all. It just all seems to be moving so fast – three weeks ago I didn't even know Ben existed and now he's driving here from York just to kiss me and ask me to dinner. Don't you think it's weird?'

'Life is weird,' she replies. 'We bump into people seemingly randomly and they turn out to be the loves of our lives and you wonder what would have happened if you hadn't been in that place at that time, like me and Geoff.'

'I don't think we're quite at you and Geoff levels just yet.' Geoff and Sascha had met in a Moby's of all places. She bumped into him because she was checking her email instead of looking where she was going, and he spilt an iced coffee all over her.

'Well what about you and me?' she asks. 'We both arrived in Sanderson Bay at the same time, more or less, completely by coincidence and ended up being best friends. You never know what life might throw at you and, in my experience, it throws a lot of bad stuff – so when the good stuff comes along you have to grab it with both hands.' She speaks a lot of sense sometimes. 'And stop worrying about Moby's,' she goes on.

'I'm not worrying about Moby's.'

'It's just his job; it doesn't really mean anything. It's just another weird coincidence.'

'Why does he get so uncomfortable whenever he mentions his job then?'

'Ha!' she laughs. 'I knew you were worried. Maybe it's because you've made it very clear how much you hate Moby's.'

I shrug. 'Maybe.'

'Or maybe he just doesn't like his job that much. Lots of people don't. I hated mine for years. So did you.'

'Fair point,' I reply.

'You have to talk about all this stuff with him – not me, El,' she says, sensible for once. 'But—'

'But what?' I interrupt. I'm not in the mood for "buts", I'm nervous enough about Friday as it is.

'What about Marcus?'

'Urghhh,' I groan.

'Did he say anything after he saw you and Ben together?'

'It's not what he's said,' I reply. 'He was really standoffish with me at first, asking me how much I knew about Ben and where had he come from all of a sudden, but now he seems to have changed tack.'

'In what way?'

'He's trying to be super helpful in the café, constantly telling me to take some time off and to trust him and Abi with everything – as if I can ever stop thinking about the café. I've told him clearly that there isn't any chance of us getting back together and I'm only letting him stay until he works out what he's going to do next but I'm not sure he's got the message.'

'Even after he saw you kissing someone else?'

'I know. I don't know what to do. Miranda thinks I should ask him to leave but that seems cruel.'

'Oh forget about Marcus for now,' Sascha says with a wave of her hand. 'Concentrate on Friday. What are you going to wear?'

As Friday approaches I find myself getting more and more nervous and with less and less idea what to wear. I haven't been on a date since I first met Marcus and I haven't got dressed up for a night out since he left. I've been too focused on the café, on our evening events and on trying to make my life in Sanderson Bay where the most glamorous thing anyone wears is a raincoat.

I haven't been anywhere that I need to dress up for since the night I thought Marcus was going to propose. That night I wore my green vintage dress, but after he left I sold it, knowing that I'd never be able to wear it again. For the first time I regret that decision – the green dress would have been perfect for my dinner with Ben.

Marcus meanwhile is settling into Sanderson Bay life surprisingly well for somebody who always claimed to hate "parochial small towns". He continues to help out in the café and valiantly ignore all the snide remarks that the locals make about him.

'I have to get them to trust me again,' he says mysteriously. 'Just like I need to get you to trust me.'

'How much longer are you staying?' I ask, but he just shrugs and avoids the question. I wonder if I should spell it out to him that I have a date with somebody on Friday but he must already know – nearly everyone has asked about it every time they come into The Two Teas.

I try to take my mind off my date with Ben – and take advantage of Marcus working for free in the café – by going to Hull for the day to finish my Christmas shopping. I meet up with Lisa for a quick lunch.

'So Friday's the big night,' she says.

I smile. I always smile when I think of Ben. 'Why do I get the feeling that everyone is living vicariously through me at the moment?'

'We're just excited for you,' she says. 'It's good to see you moving on. Although isn't it weird that your ex is living with you?'

'Yes, but I'm trying not to think about that,' I reply. 'And I'm hoping Ben won't get the wrong end of the stick.' It is a weird situation, even though I've told Ben there is nothing left between Marcus and me.

'Maybe you should just introduce them to each other,' Lisa suggests. 'It might make things clear to Marcus that you are definitely moving on while showing Ben that he has nothing to worry about.'

'Maybe,' I reply although the thought of it practically brings me out in hives. I'm anxious enough.

In the end I decide to wear my grey wrap dress with my black stiletto boots.

'How do I look?' I ask Abi who is staying late at the café to give it a deep clean.

'Perfect.' She smiles at me. 'It's nice to see you dressed up to go out.' I don't think Abi has ever seen me in anything but the black trousers and T-shirt I wear in the café, my Pilates clothes or my uniform of jeans and a shirt that I wear off duty. It wasn't much more than a year ago that I was dressing up several nights a week – be it departmental dinners in college, nights out with friends or meals with Marcus. My life has changed beyond recognition in the last year and if Marcus coming back has taught me anything, it's that I have no regrets about that at all. But Abi's right, it is nice to get dressed up to go out again.

'You're sure you don't mind staying to do this?' I ask, gesturing towards all the cleaning materials.

'Absolutely not,' she says. 'I could do with the overtime.'

'Well if you get bored or need a hand, Marcus is just upstairs.'

'No I'm not,' Marcus says from behind me. 'I'm here to help.'

Abi doesn't look up but I notice her cheeks colour. I have a feeling she might have a bit of a crush on Marcus.

'Don't rush back tonight,' she says. 'I can open the café in the morning.'

'Don't be ridiculous – I'll be back by midnight.'

'Why? Will you turn into a pumpkin if you aren't?'

I laugh nervously. I don't want to have this conversation in front of Marcus. 'It's just dinner,' I say.

'Are you sure you know what you're doing, Ellie?' Marcus asks.

'I'm perfectly sure, thank you,' I begin, but before I can say anything else the café door opens and Ben walks in.

'Oh sorry,' he says. 'The door was open... and...'

'I'm ready,' I say putting on my coat. I don't owe Marcus any sort of explanation and I turn to give Ben my full attention. He smiles at me and my heart is suddenly in my throat again and it's not from the weird nerves and concern that I've had all week. It's because he has the most beautiful smile I've ever seen and I can't believe I ever thought it was smug. He holds out his arm for me and I tuck my hand into his elbow.

'Look after her,' Marcus says from behind us as we leave.

Ben stops and turns around. 'I intend to,' he replies.

18

'Is everything all right?' Ben asks as he parks the car outside the restaurant I've chosen – an upmarket gastropub about five miles out of Sanderson Bay. I'm fairly sure we won't see anyone we know here.

I undo my seatbelt. 'Yes of course,' I say. 'Why wouldn't it be?'

'I don't know, I felt as though I was walking in on something there. I'm assuming that was Marcus?' I'd told him during the week that Marcus was still staying with me and showing no signs of moving out.

'That was Marcus,' I reply. 'And also Abi who works with me at the café. I'm sorry I didn't introduce you; it just felt a bit weird. But you didn't walk in on anything.'

'OK,' he says.

'Abi was just telling me that she'd open the café for me in the morning.'

Ben reaches over and takes my hand. 'Is she not expecting you to be back in time?' he asks quietly. I look up at him and he catches my eye.

'Clearly not,' I say as I desperately try to look calm while my stomach turns cartwheels.

'So you're sure everything is OK?'

'I think I'm just a bit nervous. It's a long time since I went out on a date and it feels as though there's a lot of pressure.'

I watch his eyebrows draw together. 'I'm so sorry,' he says. 'If you've changed your mind about tonight—'

'No!' I interrupt a little too eagerly. 'No, I haven't changed my mind and I didn't mean that I felt pressure from you. Just...'

'Ah,' he says, realisation dawning. 'The knitting ladies.'

'They seem so invested in this and I feel if I don't get it right I'm letting them down. I know that sounds ridiculous.'

He squeezes my hand gently. 'Relax,' he says. 'I just want us to get to know each other better. Forget about everyone else. Tonight is about you and me and if at any point you feel uncomfortable or want to go home, just tell me.' He tucks my hair behind my ear with his free hand, his fingers lingering in my hair. 'Your wish is my command.'

'Thank you,' I say quietly and he moves away to get out of the car. I reach for the door handle.

'Wait,' he says. He gets out and walks around to my side of the car. He opens the door and holds out his hand to me. I don't say anything. I just let the warm fuzzy feeling wash over me and try to do what everyone keeps telling me and relax into the moment.

He wraps his fingers around mine and draws me into his side as we walk to the restaurant. It's freezing again and I snuggle into the warmth of his body.

'So how's work?' I ask. 'Did you get everything sorted out?'

I feel him tense against me again. 'Um... yeah, yeah,' he says. 'Everything's fine.' It doesn't sound fine. He stops and turns towards me.

'I don't want to talk about work,' he whispers. 'And I don't think I can wait until after dinner to kiss you again.'

'Nor do I,' I reply.

Our fingers still entwined he lowers his lips to mine and kisses me so gently, so teasingly as though it's a taste of what's to come, an appetiser for the evening ahead. It knocks the breath out of me.

'Let's eat,' he says as he pulls away. But I can see the longing in his eyes and I'm suddenly glad that Abi offered to open up tomorrow.

'As you know all about Marcus,' I say as our starters arrive. 'I'd say it's your turn to tell all about your exes.'

'There's not much to tell really.' He's wearing a charcoal suit that's immaculately cut, and a white shirt that's open at his throat and I can barely take my eyes off him for long enough to look at the food on my plate. I need to pull myself together.

'Rubbish,' I tease. 'There must be something.'

He blushes. 'I mean, obviously I date but I'm never in one place for very long. My job's in London but I have to be in York for Mum as much as possible. The relationships I've had haven't really worked out long term.'

I feel my heart drop and he must notice the expression on my face.

'God, Ellie, I'm sorry,' he says, and I feel his leg press against mine. 'That came out all wrong. It sounds like I've brought you out for dinner and told you I'm not interested in relationships, which isn't the case at all. I just need to be honest about my life.'

I take a breath and allow myself to soften.

'Tell me about your mum,' I say. 'Do you go back to York every weekend?'

'Most weekends.' He pauses and looks at me. 'Mum hasn't been very well.'

'Oh I'm so sorry. Is she OK now?'

'She has anxiety,' he goes on. 'And she's not very good at managing things. I make sure her bills are paid, that she has the right money in the right accounts, that all her appointments are made. She phones a lot when I'm in London to check things so I need to have everything straight in my head.'

I notice once again that he doesn't mention his father.

'It's hard to maintain other relationships when my mum needs me so much,' he says.

'Only if the other person in the relationship isn't very understanding, I would have thought,' I say quietly.

He holds my gaze for a moment, not speaking, and a shiver runs down my spine. He looks away first.

'Does she know that you've come back to Sanderson Bay?' I ask. 'What does she think? Do you think she'll join you here one day?'

He does that thing again where he looks tense and uncomfortable, the same thing he does whenever he talks about his work, and then he smiles.

'I don't think she's very interested in coming back to the Bay,' he says. 'Although she might be if I tell her I've met you.'

I have a feeling he's trying to change the subject, that whatever has happened in the past is off limits and he's not going to talk about it. But I see that expression pass over his face again, the one that reminds me of loss, and I know we have so much more in common than either of us are really talking about. I know there is a connection here and Ben will tell me the real reason he is back in Sanderson Bay in his own time. It doesn't matter right now and I'm not going to push him, curious as I am.

As the waiter clears away our plates and brings our main courses, Ben asks me about boarding school.

'When I was a kid I always thought it would be fun to go away to school,' he says. 'Like *Harry Potter*.'

I laugh. 'Trust me, it's absolutely nothing like *Harry Potter*. It's always cold, mostly boring and the food is rubbish – there isn't even any pumpkin juice can you believe!'

He tells me about growing up in Sanderson Bay.

'It was mostly boring too,' he says. 'And the only place to go then was the greasy spoon café on the clifftop.'

'All the schoolkids still hang out there,' I say. 'They don't come into town that much. I guess with the school being that side of the Bay it makes sense.'

'They don't come to your café?'

'Come on,' I reply. 'Would you have gone to an artisan tea shop when you were fourteen?'

He smiles and my heart turns over. 'No,' he says. 'Probably not.'

When Ben isn't talking about work or his mother, he's quick and funny and I laugh more over dessert and coffee than I can remember laughing in a long, long time. At some point between the dessert menu and our friendly argument over who is paying the bill (he wins that one in the end), I suddenly feel as though a part of me has become uncaged. After buying the café and moving to Sanderson Bay, I've spent the last year of my life playing everything as safely as I can – not thinking about the future, about my dreams, or even about having fun and it has taken a stranger walking into town one December night to make me realise that life after Marcus doesn't have to be like that.

Whatever happens between us, wherever this goes, I will always be grateful for that.

It's snowing heavily as we come out of the restaurant and Ben takes my hand as we walk back to the car.

'We should probably get back as soon as we can,' he says. 'Before we get snowed in.' He stops walking then and turns towards me. He has snowflakes in his eyelashes and melting into that lock of hair that falls into his face. 'Not that getting snowed in with you would be a bad thing,' he whispers and even as the snow settles into the collar of my coat, making me shiver, I can't resist lifting my heels (because even in three-inch stilettos I still have to stand on tiptoe) and kissing that beautiful mouth.

Ben reacts instantly, pulling me into him, his tongue tracing the seam of my lips. I tilt my head back as he deepens the kiss and I draw his hips towards me, feeling the press of him against me.

'I'm so glad I came back,' he whispers against my mouth.

'Do you remember when we were at the Christmas tree farm and I told you that I found Christmas difficult too?' Ben asks as he drives slowly and carefully through the snow.

'Yes of course,' I reply.

'There's something I need to tell you.'

'You don't have to tell me anything you don't want to.'

'You've shared so much with me,' he says his eyes not leaving the road ahead.

'That doesn't mean that you have to—'

'My father died at Christmas,' he interrupts.

'Oh, Ben, I'm so sorry,' I say, turning towards him in the car seat even though I know he can't look at me.

He shrugs. 'It was a long time ago, nearly eighteen years, and it's why Mum moved away when I went to university, why she's so anxious now. I just wanted you to know that I understand that weird awkwardness Christmas can bring.'

'Thank you for telling me,' I say.

I wait to see if he's going to say anything else, but he doesn't. Instead, without taking his eyes off the road, he reaches over and gently strokes his finger down my arm. 'I came back to the Bay to lay some ghosts to rest,' he says. 'And after tonight I'm very glad I did.'

'I guess that's why your mum isn't interested in coming back,' I say quietly, but he doesn't answer.

We arrive back in Sanderson Bay and he pulls into the small carpark behind Sascha and Geoff's hotel, turning off the engine. He undoes his seatbelt and twists towards me, taking my hand.

'Ellie, I've really enjoyed tonight,' he says.

'I'm not sure I want it to end just yet,' I reply, surprising myself.

'Me neither,' he says before I get a chance to be embarrassed about being so forward. Things between us seem to be moving much faster than I'm used to, but then I know I can't hide away from my life anymore, pretending the café is all I need.

'I'd invite you back to mine,' I say quietly, trying not to blush. 'But Marcus is there and that will be weird.'

'I can sneak you into the hotel,' he says.

'Why do you need to sneak me in? My best friend owns it!'

'These signs have appeared in the rooms about not having overnight guests,' he replies, his eyes twinkling, the corners of his mouth turning up into a smile. 'And I don't want to be seen breaking the rules.'

'That doesn't sound like the sort of thing Sascha would…' I stop, realising who is responsible for the signs. 'Celia.' I say.

'Who's Celia?'

'Sascha's mother-in-law,' I reply. 'She's staying at the moment and Sascha is convinced she's changing things. I thought she was being paranoid but apparently not.'

He still looks confused.

'Basically you can ignore the signs,' I say. 'Leave Celia and Sascha to me.'

He gets out of the car and walks around to the passenger side to open the door for me.

'Are you OK in those heels?' he asks as I swing my legs out. The snow is quite deep now and still coming down at a fast pace.

'I'm fine,' I reply. 'Good traction.'

He shuts the car door and presses the button on the key to lock it. 'Because I can carry you if you like.' He smiles.

'That's not—' I begin, but before I can finish he's picked me up as though I weigh nothing and slung me over his shoulder. I squeal with laughter.

'Shhh...' he says, barely containing laughter himself and walking towards the front of the hotel. 'Guests who return after 11pm must use their keys and make as little noise as possible.'

'Is that from the notice in the rooms too?' I ask as he places me down on the front step of the hotel and unlocks the front door.

'Yes,' he says. 'So please don't make any noise – I don't want to get thrown out.'

The hotel is in darkness and nobody else seems to be about, for which I'm grateful. An interrogation by Sascha or her mother-in-law is not what I need right now.

We walk along the first-floor corridor and he unlocks the door of his room, holding it open for me to walk inside. I take my coat off and drape it over one of the chairs as I look about the room.

Each room of the hotel is decorated differently and Ben has been given one of my favourites – it has a nautical theme with blue and white striped wallpaper and chambray-style bedding.

'Can I make you a cup of tea?' he says as he takes his coat and suit jacket off. 'Sorry stupid question, you're not going to want tea from a teabag are you?' He smiles at me and something inside me that I've been holding on to for far too long melts away. 'I've brought some of that night-time tea you made for me if you—'

'No, no tea,' I interrupt. My mouth feels dry again.

'Come here,' he says gently and I step towards him. He ducks his head, kissing the side of my neck, my throat, his hands caressing my lower back. I trail my fingers down the front of his body until I find his belt buckle and as I do so he unties the bow of my wrap dress and lets it slide off my shoulders on to the floor.'

'God you're so beautiful, Ellie,' he says.

I close my eyes, breathing in the scent of him, forgetting about all the things I know he hasn't told me yet. The time will come for us to share more about ourselves with each other. Right now I know I'm exactly where I want to be.

19

'I should go,' I say very early the next morning as I snuggle into Ben's embrace, showing no eagerness to leave whatsoever.

He groans softly. 'Do you have to?' he asks kissing the top of my head. 'Can't you just stay a little bit longer?'

'I can't risk Marcus on his own at the café for too long,' I reply. 'Plus I need to sneak out before anyone else is up or you'll be in trouble for having overnight guests.'

'I don't care,' he says. 'Let them throw me out. I have no regrets.'

I prop myself up on one elbow and look down at him. 'No, me neither,' I say and he draws me towards him, kissing me softly.

'But I really do have to go,' I say, pulling away from the warm temptation of him and getting out of bed. The nearest item of clothing I can find is Ben's shirt so I wrap that around me and go to the window to see how deep the snow is. 'How long are you staying?' I ask.

'Until tomorrow,' he says, sitting up in bed and stretching. 'Then I'm going to see Mum for Christmas.'

I peek out of the curtains. It's still dark outside but I can see the snow lying like a thick white blanket on the ground and the roofs of the cars in the car park.

'Well I hope you'll be able to get back to York,' I say. 'The roads are going to be blocked for a while – come and see.'

He gets out of bed, wrapping the sheet around his waist, and stands behind me snaking his arms around my waist and kissing my neck. 'Like I said, getting snowed in with you won't be so bad.'

'I still have to go,' I say dragging myself reluctantly away from him and towards the bathroom.

'You look good in my clothes,' he says.

I end up leaving later than I intended after Ben decided to join me in the shower and my hopes of getting out of the hotel without the Spanish Inquisition are dashed when I see Sascha standing by the front door as I come down the stairs.

'Well, well, well,' she says, her arms folded across her chest and a huge grin on her face. 'I can see that somebody didn't go home last night.'

I can feel myself blushing. 'Shh,' I say as I walk up to her. 'Keep your voice down. I don't want your mother-in-law to hear.'

'What's it got to do with her?'

I smile innocently. 'Haven't you seen the notices she's put up in the rooms? I thought you were watching,' I say pointing to my eyes.

'What the hell?' She turns away looking for Celia and I take my opportunity to leave as quickly as possible.

'Bye, Sascha,' I call. 'I'll talk to you later.'

I walk along the High Street towards the café. I must be one of the first people out this morning as there are hardly any footprints in the snow. I'm not wearing the most suitable footwear and I'm definitely not wearing enough clothes but I can't stop smiling to myself. Spending the night with Ben might have been wildly out of character, and I'm fairly sure the gossip will be all over town by lunchtime, but I can't remember the last time I felt so content. Last night felt right, as though it was meant to be and all my doubts about Ben and the fact that he works for Moby's have disappeared. There is so much more to him than his job and it feels good to spend time with someone who understands why Christmas can be so hard, someone who seems to just get me as I am without wanting me to be something different.

Despite the fact that Ben doesn't live here, that his life is in York and London, for the first time since I was a teenager I feel as though I'm home.

Marcus is already up and about when I get to the café, setting out the tables and chairs.

'I thought Abi was going to open up,' I say. I feel awkward and uncomfortable that it's Marcus here to witness me coming home in last night's clothes.

'I told her I'd do it,' Marcus says. He sounds pissed off. 'I wanted to make sure you're OK.'

'I don't need you checking up on me. I just need to pop upstairs and get changed and I can take it from here.'

'Ellie,' he calls after me.

I turn around. 'Yes.'

'This Ben,' he says. 'How well do you know him?'

'Marcus…' I warn.

'Do you know he works for Moby's?'

'Of course I know.'

'Well don't you think it's a bit of a coincidence that he just turns up here out of the blue? It was Moby's who were trying to pressure your aunt and uncle into selling this place to them wasn't it?'

'Look, Marcus, I was suspicious at first too but that's not why he's here.'

'Are you sure?'

'I'm sure,' I reply. 'He grew up here and...' I pause. None of this is Marcus's business.

'And what?' Marcus asks. 'Admit it, he hasn't told you why he's here, has he?'

I have no intention of admitting any such thing. 'How do you know he works at Moby's anyway,' I ask.

'I googled him.'

'You what?'

'Don't you google new people you meet?'

'No,' I reply. 'Not unless I'm about to employ them.'

'So you googled Abi?'

'Yes, did you?'

He has the decency to look abashed. 'Yeah.'

'Marcus, don't you have any faith in human beings at all?'

'Not really,' he says. 'Abi's OK though.'

'Well I won't tell her you've been stalking her online. Now let me go and get changed and please stop checking up on me.'

'I'm not checking up on you. I'm just—'

'Whatever it is you're doing stop. You don't need to prove that you've changed – it doesn't matter anymore, Marcus—'

'There's a pile of post from yesterday on the counter,' he interrupts as though he knows I'm about to tell him for the umpteenth time that there is no chance of us getting back together and he just doesn't want to hear it. I don't know what I'm going to do to make him understand or to make him try to move on with his own life. He can't stay in my spare room forever.

I pick the post up and put it on the shelf at the back of the café. It can wait until Monday.

It's a busy day at The Two Teas with Christmas afternoon tea bookings taking up most of the afternoon, so by the time I finish up I've got seven text messages from Sascha demanding to know all the gory details from last night. Before I call her back I reply to the message from Ben.

Are you doing anything tonight? he asks. *Can I see you?*

'What are you doing tonight?' I ask Marcus as he stands at the counter nearby.

'Nothing,' he says, his face lighting up. 'Would you like to do something?'

'No, Marcus, I wouldn't,' I reply more harshly than I mean to.

'We could do something, Marcus,' Abi says as she comes towards us with a tray of empty cups. 'There's a film on in Hull I was thinking of going to. Do you fancy coming with me?'

I could kiss her and I can't work out if she's trying to get Marcus to go out with her because she likes him or because she's worked out I would quite like the flat to myself tonight.

Marcus sighs. 'I suppose so.'

'There's no need to sound so eager,' I say. 'It'll be good for you. A change of scene might help you work out what you're going to do next.'

'Ellie,' Marcus says as Abi goes to serve some new customers. 'About Ben…'

'Don't start again, Marcus,' I say holding up my hand. 'I don't know how many times I have to tell you that. I've moved on and I thought you had too.'

'He works for Moby's,' Marcus presses on regardless. 'Doesn't that ring any alarm bells for you?'

'I thought we'd talked about this.'

'Are you seeing him tonight?'

'Yes and I'd like to invite him over if you're going out.'

Marcus looks at me for a moment and then walks away to talk to Abi. I make an assumption that he's going to go into Hull tonight.

Would you like to come here? I reply to Ben. *I'll cook.*

And then I go into the storeroom to phone Sascha. She answers on the first ring.

'Tell me everything,' she says.

'Stop being so nosy,' I reply.

'I'm so bored here, always resting. Let me live vicariously through you.'

'Did you find out about the new notices in the rooms?' I ask. 'The ones about no overnight guests and not making noise?'

'Yes I did and I've been into every room and taken them down,' Sascha grumbles. 'That woman has no right to make rules in my hotel. I apologised to Ben about it too.'

'You didn't!' I'm slightly embarrassed at the thought of her talking to Ben about it.

'I did of course. I told him he could have overnight guests whenever he liked.'

'Oh my God, Sascha! What did he say?'

'He blushed bright red and mumbled something before walking away.' She laughs. 'You two are made for each other.'

'Sascha, for heaven's sake—' I begin.

'So come on, tell me,' she interrupts. 'What was it like?'

'We had a lovely evening, we got along really well and the food was fantastic.'

'And the sex?'

'Sascha, I'm not telling you about the sex.'

'Good?'

'Yes,' I mutter in reply.

'How good?'

'Very – now shut up.'

She's cackling in my ear.

'I'll be glad when this baby is born and you have something to occupy your time,' I say.

'They say it's going to snow more tonight you know,' Sascha says seemingly changing the subject. 'And they won't get the snowploughs out until Monday from what I've heard, so lover boy is snowed in until after the weekend at least.'

'How did he seem when you saw him?' I can't help myself from asking.

'Fine,' she says. 'Certainly about you. He did say he was looking forward to seeing you again. But he's been shut in his room working all day.'

'Yeah, there's something going on at his work he's reluctant to talk about but he seems quite stressed.'

'Typical Moby's,' Sascha says.

'Hmmm…' I reply, thinking about what Marcus said again. Should the fact he works for Moby's still be ringing alarm bells?

'They just work their staff really hard,' Sascha says, as if reading my mind. 'Or at least they did when I was their legal consultant. That's all it is so stop worrying.'

'I'm not worrying.'

'Yes you are,' she replies. 'You are OK aren't you?'

'Of course I am – why would I not be?'

'Joking aside I wasn't expecting you to stay last night. You seemed so reluctant to move on a week or so ago.'

'I know it's a bit out of character but much as I hate to admit it you were right.'

'Can I get that in writing!'

'Marcus coming back has made me realise that I'm not the same person I was a year ago and I do need to have a life of my own again. I do need to do something other than work. I know there probably isn't much future in this, but it's a chance to have some fun.'

'Good for you,' she says. 'And good for me, always being right.'

20

Ben arrives bearing a bottle of wine and a huge bunch of flowers. He knocks the snow off his boots and kisses me chastely on the cheek. For a moment I wonder if he regrets last night, if we moved too quickly.

But then I remember his words – *I have no regrets.*

And neither do I, for perhaps the first time in my life, even though I know this isn't going to be easy, that Ben and I have different lives in different parts of the country. It might not be anything at all.

'Whatever you're cooking smells fantastic,' he says.

'It's just lasagne,' I reply.

'Can I help at all?'

'No, it's nearly ready,' I say taking the flowers and wine from him. 'Thanks so much for these. Come through and I'll pour the wine.'

He follows me into the kitchen and leans against the counter, crossing his long legs in front of him. I put the flowers in water and open the wine.

'No Marcus tonight?' he asks, as I hand him a glass.

'He's gone to the cinema with Abi. Why?' I grin. 'Did you want to have dinner with him too?'

'Does he really have nowhere else to go,' Ben asks. 'Or is there another reason he's here?'

I decide to be honest. 'He came back here with the intention of trying to get back together with me.'

Ben doesn't say anything.

'I'd spent a lot of the last year trying to get over him. When he left for Thailand he broke my heart and it was so hard getting over him.'

'Ellie, I'm sorry,' Ben says. 'Ignore me, you don't have to tell me anything.'

'The thing is that even though I'd been wondering for months what it would be like if he came back, as soon as he did I knew we'd done the right thing when we broke up. I realised then that I'd already moved on.'

'Does he feel the same?'

I exhale. 'Honestly, I don't know how he feels. He keeps telling me that he's trying to prove he's changed and he's very clearly not OK about me seeing you.'

Ben raises an eyebrow. 'Really? Do I need to worry?'

I smile. 'No I don't think so. Although he did google you and found out you work for Moby's.'

'That's not exactly a secret,' Ben says.

'I know but Marcus seems to think you're here for nefarious reasons.'

Ben looks away from me for a moment, and I see that muscle twitch in his jaw – a sign of the tension he seems to feel every time I mention Moby's. Then he puts his wine glass down and looks at me again.

'And what do you think?' he asks, walking towards me and placing his hands on my waist.

'I think,' I say, standing on tiptoe so that my lips almost brush against his. 'That I'm just very glad you are here.'

'Me too,' he says quietly and he kisses me gently until we're interrupted by the oven timer letting us know that the lasagne is ready.

'Are you OK?' I ask as I turn away from him to take the dish out of the oven.

'Of course – why wouldn't I be?'

'Oh I don't know, I just keep thinking about how you must find this time of year as hard as I do and I know that you've been working all day.'

'Did Sascha tell you that?'

'Sascha is the eyes and ears of the neighbourhood,' I reply. 'Nothing gets past her.'

I set the lasagne on the side and as I do so Ben steps up to me and gently turns me towards him, his hands on my shoulders.

'I really am fine,' he says softly. 'Right now in this moment I'm more than fine, because I'm here with you.' Slowly he lowers his mouth to mine again kissing me gently as I let myself melt into him.

'So was Sascha right when she said you were working all day?' I ask as we sit down to eat.

Ben chuckles. 'Sascha's always right isn't she? Work is tough at the moment – Christmas doesn't really matter to a company like Moby's and there are things that need...' He pauses. 'I can't really talk about it.'

I hold up my hands. 'I completely understand,' I say. 'Confidentiality.'

He nods.

'I thought I was the only person mad enough to work seven days a week though.'

'No, there's a few of us about, burying our feelings in work.' He laughs. 'It's different for you though.'

'How?'

'Because this is all yours. The café is your kingdom and I can see how much you love it. Your eyes light up when you talk about tea, when you talk about your business. I think what you've done here is fantastic!'

'Thank you,' I say. 'That's high praise indeed coming from a coffee drinker.'

'I mean it,' he goes on. 'I wasn't here when your aunt and uncle owned this place but before them this was a really run-down old diner that hadn't been redecorated since the eighties.'

'My aunt and uncle did a lot of work here before I bought it off them.'

'But what you have now – this sort of apothecary of tea – that's all you, right?'

I smile, because he might prefer coffee, but he gets it. He gets exactly what I'm trying to do. 'The café is almost exactly how I always dreamed it would be,' I say. 'This last year has been a huge labour of love but I'm so pleased with what it's become, not just an apothecary of tea – which is exactly what I'm going for by the way – but a part of the community too.'

'You said that it was "almost exactly" how you wanted it to be. How would you change it if you could?'

I don't say anything for a minute.

'I'm sorry if I'm being too nosy,' he says. 'Tell me to shut up.'

'No,' I reply. 'But if I tell you, you must promise not to say anything to Sascha because she'll gloat about being right again.'

'Scout's honour,' he says.

'Were you a scout?'

'I was and a very cute one too.'

'I bet. I can imagine you in shorts and a woggle.'

'Stop changing the subject and tell me your secret dream for the café.'

'I'd like to open another one, maybe more than one. I'd like The Two Teas to be a chain – not a massive corporate chain like Moby's of course.'

'Of course,' he says. He's smiling but that tension is still there. What is going on with him and Moby's? 'Just a few select cafés in a few select places.'

'Exactly,' I reply. 'Maybe one in York, one in Harrogate, that sort of thing.'

'I think it's a wonderful idea. Do you have a business plan? A way to make it happen?'

I shake my head. 'Not yet,' I say. 'It's still just a dream.'

'But I'm guessing that Sascha is nagging you to get a business plan right?'

'You've come to understand Sascha very well in a short time,' I say, laughing.

'I could help,' he says quietly. 'If you wanted me to.'

'Can I trust a Moby's employee?' I say jokingly.

He leans across the table and takes my hand. 'You can trust this one,' he says and as he speaks the hairs on the back of my neck stand up on end and my stomach flips and fizzes in that way that's become almost familiar whenever Ben is in the vicinity.

When we've finished eating we go into the living room and I put on the Christmas piano playlist that Ben played on the day we put the Christmas tree up.

'Do you like it?' he asks.

'It's perfect.'

He sits on the sofa. 'Come here,' he says.

I sit beside him and he wraps his arms around me. I snuggle into his side and it feels comfortable. My overactive mind starts questioning how I can feel like this about someone who I still barely know.

Don't overthink it, Ellie.

We sit in comfortable silence, letting the music wash over us.

'I wish I had the guts to do what you did,' Ben says after a while.

'How do you mean?'

'Breaking away and setting up on your own like this.'

'You want to own your own café?' I ask.

He laughs gently and I can feel the vibrations as I rest against his chest.

'No, not a café just…' He pauses. 'Something,' he says.

'Do you have a business plan for that?'

'I mean it, Ellie, what you've done is brave.'

'I don't feel very brave,' I say. 'Coming to Sanderson Bay after I broke up with Marcus felt like a bit of a cop-out if I'm honest. This is the place I've always run to when things got tough. It's where I came when I ran away from school, where I came after Mum died.'

'But you walked away from your career to set up your dream café.'

'I love my café, don't get me wrong,' I say. 'But I grew

up here, I spent half of my holidays from school every year living above this very café, in this very flat. It feels comfortable not brave. There were so many brave things I could have done, but I chose not to.'

'Like what?'

'Like leaving York to do my PhD in Paris or New York. I had the grades to do it and it's what my father wanted, what my tutor wanted but I was too afraid to go.'

I feel him take a deep breath next to me, hear him let it go.

'I've stayed at Moby's all these years because I haven't been brave enough to do anything else. It pays well, it's a good job. It means I can get to Mum's at the weekend. My father always wanted me to work in a job like that.' I notice him flex the fingers of his right hand when he mentions his father. I want to get him to talk to me about it but I don't know how.

I turn towards him. 'Are you not happy?' I ask.

He shakes his head. 'Seeing you here in this café really brought it home to me how unhappy I've been at Moby's.'

'And yet still you've spent most of your Saturday working.'

'Pathetic isn't it?'

'I can hardly criticise anyone for staying in a job they didn't like for too long. I thought it was what other people – and by other people I mean my dad – expected of me.'

'What does your dad think of the café?' Ben asks.

'I don't know,' I say. 'We never really talk about it. When I was selling up in York he just told me that I was an adult now and didn't need his permission to do whatever I wanted. He always had some dream of me being like my mother; he wasn't particularly happy when I chose art history over English so I can't imagine he's over the moon about the café.'

Ben reaches over and cups my cheek with his hand. I lean into him, turning my head to kiss his wrist, and he pulls me close.

'I wish I could talk to my dad more,' I say. 'But since Mum died it's been so difficult and…' I trail off.

'And what?'

'I feel I've let him down. I feel as though I've always let my parents down and as though whatever happened between them when I was young was my fault.'

I feel his hand gently stroke my hair. 'It wasn't your fault,' he says quietly. 'But maybe it's time to be brave again and find out what happened, find out who your dad is now and what he really thinks.'

'Maybe,' I mutter reluctantly.

'And while we're on the subject of being brave, I want to ask you something.'

I pull myself up so I can see him properly. 'Go ahead,' I say.

'I really like you, Ellie, and I really want this to be more than a weekend thing.'

'I really like you too,' I say.

'I sense a but.'

I take a breath. 'It's just what you said in the restaurant last night, about your life – travelling between London and York. You made it sound as though you didn't have time for much else.'

He pinches the bridge of his nose between his thumb and forefinger. 'I'm not sure I want that life anymore,' he says. 'Coming back here and seeing how much it's changed, seeing you running this incredible business and talking to Sascha and Geoff about leaving the corporate rat race – all of it has made me reconsider a few things.'

'You want to leave Moby's?' I ask.

'I want to work up here, nearer Mum. In York or maybe Leeds,' he says. 'I've been trying to avoid thinking about all of this for far too long, burying myself in work to stop myself thinking about it. But coming back to Sanderson Bay has really hammered home how unhappy I am. I can't ignore it anymore.'

'Have you talked to anyone else about any of this?' I ask.

'Just Mum.'

'And what does she think?'

'She said that as long as I'm doing it for me and not for her then it's a good idea.'

'I agree with your mum,' I say.

He smiles. 'So with that in mind,' he says. 'I was wondering if we could see each other again after Christmas. You could come to York maybe?'

'It has been a while since I went to York,' I reply with a big grin on my face. 'And I do love York at this time of year.' I don't tell him I haven't been back to York since I left last Christmas. It will be good for me to go back; it'll be good practice for the day I feel ready to return to Paris.

'Is that a yes?' he asks.

'It's a yes,' I reply and he pulls me towards him again, his lips finding mine.

21

'I have to get up,' I say softly to the warm, naked body beside me early the next morning.

Ben makes a grumbling noise into the pillow next to me. 'You're really not into lie-ins are you?' he says.

'I don't want to get up,' I reply. 'But the café won't open itself. You can go back to sleep though. I don't mind.'

He pushes himself up onto his forearms. 'No,' he says. 'It's fine. I'm awake.'

He doesn't look awake and I remind myself how tired he looked when he first arrived in the Bay and how hard he seems to work. 'Go back to sleep,' I say, kissing him.

He pulls me towards him. 'Give me five more minutes with you and then I'll get up, get showered and help you open the café.'

We'd talked late into the night about work mostly. We'd talked about that fear that overcomes you when you know you need to change your life but you don't know how, and how that fear can paralyse you and leave you trapped.

'If Marcus hadn't gone to Thailand,' I'd said. 'I'm not sure if I'd have ever left. With him gone it felt as though my heart had broken and would never heal but now... now I feel as though he did me a favour.'

'I feel as though meeting you has been the same sort of trigger,' Ben had replied. 'A trigger to force me to work out what I want to do at long last.'

It had been easy to talk to him because even though he hasn't told me much about his father I know that he must understand so much of what I've been through – grief and loss and doing things for other people.

'Do you feel as though you've wasted years of your life?' he'd asked me.

'No,' I'd replied. 'Not really. You have to remember that those years of doing something that didn't light you up, those years of people-pleasing have got you to where you are now, they made you the person you are now, and they've allowed you to prepare for whatever it is that's coming next.'

'That's such a good way of looking at it.'

'It's the only way I can look at it.'

Ben's five more minutes in bed turns into twenty-five and we have to rush to get ready.

'I'll put a pot of coffee on for you,' I say as Ben follows me down the stairs into the café. 'You look as though you could do with the whole pot.'

'Thanks very much!'

There are two doors at the bottom of the stairs that lead up to my flat. One door, the door Ben arrived at the night before, leads directly out on to the High Street and the other leads into the storerooms of the café. Ben follows me through and I'm distracted as I walk into the café itself so I don't notice for a moment that somebody is sitting at a table with papers spread out in front of them.

'Marcus!' I say, alarmed, one hand on my chest. 'What

the hell are you doing here? You frightened me half to death.' I'm not sure if Marcus had come back to the flat last night. By the look of him he seems to have been up all night.

'Hi, Marcus,' Ben says from behind me.

But Marcus doesn't reply.

'Marcus?' I ask. 'How long have you been sitting there?'

'A while,' he replies, not taking his eyes off Ben.

'Did you have a good night last night with Abi?'

But Marcus just sits there and I take a step towards him to see what the papers are that he's looking at.

'What are you doing?' I ask. A strange and ominous silence has descended on the café and I have a creeping feeling that whatever Marcus is doing here and whatever he is looking at, no good will come of it.

I look over at Ben and see that he's looking at the papers on Marcus's table and his face has gone completely white.

'What's going on?' I ask again wondering why nobody but me is saying anything.

'I decided to have a look through that pile of post that you'd been ignoring,' Marcus says.

'I told you I'd deal with it.'

'I was interested in one envelope in particular,' Marcus goes on ignoring me. 'A large parcel of papers addressed to Ben.'

'What?'

'Good question,' Marcus says, an unpleasant smirk on his face. 'Why on earth would Ben be having post sent to The Two Teas I wonder?'

'You have no right to open that,' Ben says. His voice is hard and cold, his mouth thin, his eyes angry.

'You have no right to open my post,' I say to Marcus.

I turn to Ben but he's not looking at me. 'And I'd like to know why you're having post sent here. What is it?'

Ben ignores me and steps towards Marcus and tries to hide the documents from me.

'I don't think so,' Marcus says, snatching the papers back. 'Not until Ellie sees these.'

'What are they?' I ask, taking the pile of papers from Marcus.

'They're from Moby's,' he replies and my stomach drops. I suddenly feel as if all the joy has been sucked out of me, as if all the time I'd spent with Ben over the last couple of weeks was nothing but a lie.

'Moby's,' I hear myself repeating as I stare at the papers in front of me. My voice sounds very far away, as though it belongs to someone else.

'Ellie, this is not what you think,' Ben says.

'Really?' I say whipping my head around to look at Ben. 'Tell me how this doesn't look like somebody at Moby's thinks I'm about to sell my café to them?'

'Ellie,' Ben says quietly. 'Can we talk about—'

'And the only person I know at Moby's,' I interrupt. 'Is you.'

'He's bound to say this isn't what it looks like,' Marcus interrupts. 'As though none of this was his fault and he couldn't possibly have had an ulterior motive for hanging about the café all the time.'

'My ulterior motive,' Ben says. 'If you insist on calling it that, was to stop this happening and I don't understand—'

'Oh of course you don't,' Marcus jeers.

'Stop it!' I shout. 'Just be quiet both of you.'

'But, Ellie—' Marcus begins.

'I said be quiet.' Miraculously both of them shut up and I try to focus on the papers in front of me. First, a draft of a letter that Ben is supposed to sign and send to me offering me an eye-popping amount of money for the café, money not to be sniffed at as Miranda would say. Second, a handwritten compliments slip that simply says '*This should do it. See you soon, Mel*'. Third, oh God… third.

Third is an architect's drawing of a café. My café. A representation of what The Two Teas will look like when Moby's take it over, when it is no longer The Two Teas but just another black and cream Moby's café – exactly the same as all the other Moby's cafés up and down the country. From the plan it looks as though they'd take out the plate glass window at the front, from which my customers love watching the world go by, and extend out the back into the garden. They'd build over the herb garden that I'd been growing since I was fourteen years old – half my life.

The shapes of the drawings start to blur as my eyes fill with tears and I squeeze my eyes shut because I am absolutely not going to cry in front of either Ben or Marcus.

'What the hell have you done?' I ask looking over at Ben. His face is still white as a sheet.

'I tried to stop it, Ellie,' he replies. 'I thought I had stopped it. I don't understand how this happened.'

Marcus snorts loudly.

'What?' Ben asks, looking over at him.

'*I thought I'd stopped it*,' Marcus mimics. 'Why would you try to stop it? What would be in it for you to stop it?'

'This is between me and Ellie,' Ben says. 'It has nothing to do with you. I don't know who gave you the right to open other people's post in the first place.'

'How could you do this to me?' I ask before Marcus has a chance to say any more. 'I thought we had something... I thought we were...' I look away from him. 'Was that your plan?' I ask. 'To seduce me to get me to agree to sell up?'

'Of course that wasn't my plan,' Ben says walking over to me. He touches my arm but I move away from him. 'From the moment I first walked through that door and saw you and this café and how beautiful you'd made it and how much you loved it, my plan was to stop this from happening. To do whatever it took to stop Moby's doing this.' He gestures towards the paperwork.

Marcus snorts again.

'Stop snorting, Marcus, for God's sake,' I say.

'Well what possible power does he have to make Moby's change their mind?'

'I don't have any power,' Ben says sadly. 'Clearly or they wouldn't have gone ahead anyway.' He pauses. 'When did this letter arrive?'

I look at Marcus and he shrugs. 'Friday I think,' he says.

'What's the date on the letter, Ellie?' Ben asks.

'Thursday,' I say quietly.

Ben doesn't respond but when I look at him his jaw is tight, his eyebrows knotted. No wonder he tensed up every time I mentioned Moby's.

'I told you to look after her,' Marcus says into the silence.

'I was trying to look after her,' Ben replies. 'Her and the café.'

I watch Marcus open his mouth to say something else but I interrupt.

'Just shut up, both of you,' I say, throwing the papers

onto the counter. 'I've had enough of this. I don't need anyone to look after me.'

'I warned you about him...' Marcus begins.

I hold up my hand. 'I'm sick of hearing it, Marcus. I don't want to know about how good we were together and how we could be again. Just get the message.'

Marcus shuts up then, looking completely crestfallen but I don't care. I turn to Ben.

'And as for you I can't even look at you right now. I can't believe you didn't tell me about this. I shared stuff with you I'd never talked about with anyone before and this is how you repay me.'

'Ellie, please...' Ben begins.

'Get out,' I say, anger running through me. 'Get out of my café. I don't want to hear any more excuses and I don't want Moby's money or their horrible corporate tea.'

'I told you so,' Marcus sneers at Ben.

'You can get out too, Marcus.'

'But, Ellie...' Marcus whines.

'Leave,' I repeat. 'And if you want to help me, Marcus, could you phone Abi and ask her to come in as soon as she can. I need someone I can trust at the café today.'

22

Gossip is currency in Sanderson Bay and by the time I've walked through the fresh snowfall to my aunt and uncle's for Sunday lunch I can see by the way they look at me that they already know at least some of what happened early this morning.

Luckily for me Marcus must have called Abi almost straight away – more to tell her the gossip than to get her to come into work early I think, but at least she was there within an hour telling me to go and rest or go to my aunt's or whatever I needed, that Marcus wasn't far behind her and that between them they'd manage for the day.

'You know what's happened I'm guessing,' I said to Abi when she arrived. I'd already had several texts from Sascha demanding I ring her and tell her everything. I was fairly sure the whole Bay knew.

She nodded. 'I'm so sorry, Ellie.'

'Sympathy won't change anything,' I said as I walked away. I hadn't meant to sound so ungrateful, especially when she'd come into work early, but my mind was whirling and I had no idea what to think or say to anyone.

So when my aunt and uncle greet me with overly

enthusiastic smiles as though they are speaking to an upset child, I almost turn around and walk away.

'Come in, Ellie,' James says when he sees me hesitate on the doorstep. 'It's freezing out there.' It's the smell of Miranda's famous roast dinner that draws me in eventually.

After a lot of fussing about and pouring of wine, we sit down to dinner. My phone beeps again with another message from Sascha so I turn it off.

'You decided not to bring anyone with you today then, love,' Miranda says. I can't work out if she's alluding to Marcus's attendance last week or the fact that the whole town knows I've spent most of the last two days and nights with Ben. Either way it seems like a good time to address the elephant in the room.

'I'm assuming you've already heard on the Sanderson Bay grapevine what happened this morning,' I say.

My aunt and uncle exchange a meaningful glance before turning back to their plates.

'We heard there was some sort of misunderstanding,' my aunt mutters.

'Oh it was far from a misunderstanding,' I reply. 'It turns out that all this time Ben has been prepping me to announce that Moby's still want the café.'

'They what?' James says, putting down his knife and fork with a clatter. 'Over my dead body.' He looks furious. My uncle had always been more opposed the Moby's offer than Miranda who I knew had been drawn to the money more. I get why, of course I do, but I've always been glad they turned it down in the end.

'This has nothing to do with your body, love,' Miranda says, putting a calming hand on her husband's arm. 'Dead or otherwise.'

'They offered an eye-popping amount for it too,' I say.

'How much?' James asks.

I tell him and they look at each other again. It's significantly more than they were offered.

'They must be desperate,' Miranda says.

'Desperate to put another independent café out of business,' I reply. 'Anyway they're not getting it for any money.'

'Atta girl,' James says, going back to his dinner.

'But what has this got to do with Ben?' Miranda asks.

I tell them everything – about coming downstairs to see Marcus silently fuming in front of a stack of architect's drawings, about the slow realisation as I worked out what those drawings were, about Marcus's fury and Ben's stricken face.

'Did Ben not try to explain what had happened?' my aunt asks reasonably.

'He claimed he had been trying to stop the whole thing, but that's easy for him to say after the event. The envelope full of plans sent to him at the café address proves otherwise surely.'

'I wonder why they were sent to the café?' Miranda muses. 'You'd think they'd send them to him at the hotel.

I shrug and push my dinner around my plate. I've lost my appetite. 'Who cares?' I reply. 'Who cares where they were sent at all? All I care about is that they exist and Ben knew about them. You should have seen the look on his face and the way he was trying to hide the plans from me. His explanation sounded like an excuse and Marcus wasn't helping. I had to get away from both of them. I couldn't even look at them. They were still fighting when they left the café.'

'I don't know what Marcus has to get so upset about,' my uncle interjects.

'Really?' Miranda says to him rolling her eyes. 'You can't work out why Marcus is upset that Ellie has been seeing Ben?'

'I don't see what—' James begins.

'Well whatever happens I can't trust Ben again now,' I say before we get into a discussion about me and Ben and Marcus. 'Whatever his explanation is, the fact remains that he's been lying to me. I can't just let that pass.'

'It wasn't exactly a lie,' Miranda says. 'Just an omission of truth.'

'Whose side are you on?' I ask.

'Yours of course!'

'Plenty more fish in the sea,' my uncle says as he finishes his meal. 'After all you've only known Ben a couple of weeks.'

I feel a lump form in my throat and a burning sensation behind my eyes. I might have only known Ben a short while but I'd felt a connection there that I hadn't felt with anyone else for a long time. I'd felt as though he had understood me, understood my grief and my problems with my dad, understood why I'd had to leave my job in York to do something that my father thought was beneath me. I'd told him things I hadn't really talked about with anyone else. I'd trusted him.

I was a fool.

'Well it's just another case of someone rejecting me,' I say quietly, aware straight away how self-pitying it sounds.

Miranda and James don't say anything. My uncle just stands up and starts clearing away the plates even though I haven't finished mine.

'Rhubarb crumble and custard,' he announces as he leaves the room.

I feel myself deflate as though I haven't got any energy left in me.

'What did you mean just then when you said that it was just another case of rejection?' my aunt asks. 'Has Marcus's surprise arrival brought up some bad memories?'

I hesitate. I'd been thinking about this all morning and I don't know if I'm ready to talk about it yet, but what happened in the café with Ben and Marcus has triggered something in me, unravelled a lot of old memories, and now I can't stop my thoughts spiralling. I've been carrying around this feeling of rejection for years, this sense that I'm somehow not wanted. I started talking to Ben about it, last night – something else I mistakenly thought I could trust him with. The truth is I've felt as though people have rejected me my whole life – Marcus, my father, friends from school – but it started that first Christmas that my parents didn't come to collect me from boarding school and I was sent to Sanderson Bay instead.

'Whatever it is, Ellie,' Miranda says. 'You can talk to us about it.'

James comes in with three bowls of rhubarb crumble on a tray. 'Talk to us about what?' he asks as he hands the bowls out and tucks in.

I look at them both – at my uncle enjoying his pudding, at my aunt looking at me with concern – and I realise for the first time that they might know the truth, that they might be able to help me.

'It's about Mum,' I say quietly. 'All of this goes back to Mum.'

'To her death?' Miranda asks, reaching across the table for my hand and giving it a squeeze.

'Before that,' I say. 'Back to when she first rejected me.'

'Your mother never rejected you,' my aunt says, but there's something in her eyes that makes me think she doesn't fully believe that.

'Then why didn't she want me with her in the holidays? Why did she only want me in the summer? Why did she send me to you?' There's a flash of pain across my aunt's face and I remember that Mum was her sister, that she lost somebody too. And I remember how good she and James were to me. 'Not that I didn't have a wonderful time here with you guys every Christmas and Easter,' I hurriedly say. 'But it doesn't answer the question.'

Nobody says anything for a moment.

'We have to tell her,' my uncle says quietly.

'James no.' There's a warning in my aunt's voice.

'We should have told her years ago.'

'Tell me what?' I demand.

'Your mum didn't reject you, Ellie,' James says quietly.

'James, are you sure this is the right time?' Miranda interrupts.

'There was never going to be a right time, Manda,' he says placing his hand on my aunt's shoulder. 'I know you were trying to protect Ellie but you know I've never really agreed with that. We have to tell her.'

Miranda nods.

'She didn't reject you,' James repeats, pushing his bowl away from him. 'Your mum was ill and she wasn't always able to look after you.'

'What sort of ill?' I ask. 'Was it something to do with the aneurysm?'

James shakes his head. 'No,' he says. 'No that was a shock to us all.'

'Then what are you talking about?' I watch them share another of those glances and feel exasperated. Either they have something to tell me or they haven't.

'Your mother loved you so much, Ellie,' my aunt says. 'I need you to remember that.' There's a look in her eye that seems to dare me to contradict her.

I say nothing.

'I think she was surprised by motherhood,' Miranda goes on. 'She didn't know how she'd be as a mother and I think she was surprised by just how much she loved it, how much she loved you.'

I look away remembering the years before I went to boarding school, the fun I used to have with *Maman*, how happy we used to be.

'What happened?' I ask. Because something must have happened to change everything so much.

'Your parents wanted another child,' my aunt says and I watch my uncle reach over and place his hand on top of hers. I'd never asked why they hadn't had any children of their own – it wasn't my business – but I'm suddenly aware that this is a painful subject for Miranda, just as it clearly was for my parents.

'I always wanted a brother or sister,' I say quietly and I watch Miranda blink back tears.

'They tried for years but it never happened,' James takes up the story. 'And your mum became more and more desperate, more and more upset that she couldn't get pregnant.'

'Laurel became very depressed,' my aunt says. I can't remember the last time I heard somebody call my mother by her first name – Dad barely speaks of her and, up until now, James and Miranda only ever refer to her as "your mum". 'Do you remember the Christmas that we came to stay?'

'Yes, it was the only time you came to Paris. The only time I'd met you before you picked me up two years later.'

'Your father had asked us to come. He'd told us that Laurel wasn't coping well, that she was very unhappy and would we be able to come over to help make Christmas a happy time for you.'

'*Papa* asked you?'

James nods. 'Yes, he even paid for our flights.'

This is so unlike the father I know, I'm surprised.

'I do remember it being a very happy Christmas,' I say. 'Even if there was never any hot water.'

Miranda smiles. 'Yes, it was a very small apartment for all of us to squeeze into but you and your mum had a good time and that was all that mattered to us.'

'But it didn't help long term did it?' I ask. 'I'm guessing Mum was still depressed.'

'She tried everything,' my aunt says. 'Not just to get pregnant but to try to feel better in general – medication, therapy, meditation; she even started praying again but nothing was working. And then just before you went to boarding school she found out she was pregnant.'

My breath catches in my throat because if my mother had found out she was pregnant when I was thirteen and I'd never had a brother or sister there was only one other answer to what had happened and suddenly everything falls into place.

'She lost the baby,' I say quietly and Miranda nods, tears in her eyes.

'It happened in the November,' James says. 'Manda went to Paris to be with her. By then your parents' marriage was beginning to show the strain of what they had both been going through. I think you were probably at least a little aware of that, of how hard things were for them.'

'I don't think I realised at the time but as I've gotten older I've always thought that there was something I was missing,' I say. 'I never wanted to ask because I was scared.'

'Scared of what?'

'Scared that they might tell me the truth,' I admit. Because that had always been the reason. Even that last time in Marseilles airport when I accused my mother of not loving me, even then I knew I could just ask what was happening, push her to tell me the truth. But I didn't want to hear it. I didn't want to know about their problems. They were my parents and I wanted them to be there for me, not the other way around. 'I was so selfish,' I say.

'No, love,' Miranda says. 'We were the selfish ones keeping this from you for all this time. James is right, we should have told you years ago.'

'But none of this explains why she didn't want to see me,' I say. 'Was it too upsetting for her?'

'The first Christmas she was still healing from the

miscarriage,' Miranda says. 'When I went to Paris to see her Laurel asked if we could look after you at Christmas, just while she recovered. She didn't want you to know; she begged me not to tell you.'

'I can understand that. I was only thirteen.'

'We thought it would just be the one Christmas and then things would get back to normal,' my aunt continues. 'But unfortunately her depression got worse. Much worse.' She pauses, takes a breath and James squeezes her shoulder again. 'In the spring, a little while after she came to see you, she tried to take her own life.'

I gasp audibly. I hadn't expected this to be where the story led. 'My God,' I whisper. 'I had no idea, I...' I trail off. What can you say to that? How can you react? I felt as though everything I had taken for granted was being ripped out from underneath me.

'She took an overdose,' my aunt goes on. 'Mercifully your father found her in time, but it was the first of several attempts.' She stops and makes a little choking sound as though she can't go on.

'The doctors said that they were cries for help,' my uncle says. 'She never quite took enough to kill herself but she couldn't cope with her life as it was anymore and she was desperate I think. She had no idea what to do. Luckily, which I know is a strange word to use in this case, after one of her suicide attempts she found herself in a hospital that really seemed to help her.'

'When was this?' I ask.

'About a year before she died,' Miranda replies. 'That's the saddest part. She was really starting to make progress, really starting to seem like her old self.'

We are all quiet for a moment as I take in what I've heard. My mother was no dry, dusty academic. That was why her books were always so popular – she found a glamour in the feminist writers that she researched, a glamour that previous biographers had never found, and none of this makes sense to me. The story of depression and of suicide attempts doesn't fit with my flighty, intelligent, popular mother who always loved to laugh and drink a martini or four.

Or perhaps it does make sense if you think about it.

'I'm so sorry,' Miranda says. 'I know James is right, I know I should have told you this years ago. I…' She stops as the phone starts ringing. 'I'll get it,' she says hurriedly as though she wants to get away from this conversation, a conversation she's been putting off for so long, I suspect, because it is hurting her even more than it is hurting me. I can see the lines of pain in her face as she pushes herself up to standing and I wonder if it is her arthritis or the memories making her feel like that.

'Manda hates talking about this,' James says as my aunt leaves the room. 'It's one of the reasons I could never convince her to tell you. Because I know we should have told you a long time ago.'

'I'm not sure if you should though,' I say. 'I'm not sure if I could have handled this back when *Maman* died. It's only very recently I've even thought about making my peace with her memory. Ben helped me with that and I think it was Ben lying to me that made me think about how she abandoned me again.'

'She never abandoned you, Ellie,' James says to me. 'She loved you so much; she just wasn't able to look after you properly.'

'But she could in the summers?' I ask. 'When we went down to Provence?'

'If you remember there were a lot of families there in the summers.'

I nod. That was what had been so fun about it, the other families and the other children to hang out with.

'They were able to help, to look out for you,' James says.

'Did everybody know?' I ask. I can hear my aunt talking to whoever it was that rang. Who rings a landline anymore?

'They knew your parents were struggling but I don't think they knew the details.'

I blow a breath out of my mouth. 'I don't know what to say.'

'This is a lot for you to take in,' my uncle says softly. 'Especially after what you found out about Ben, but I wanted you to know.'

'Why suddenly now?' I ask. 'Why today?'

'Because I can't bear for you to keep thinking that these things are somehow your fault. That first your mother, then Marcus and now Ben have all abandoned you. I need you to know how special you are, Eloise, how brave you are. There aren't many women your age who would walk away from their whole life to set up a tea shop in the middle of nowhere and make such a success of it.'

'Oh it wasn't—' I begin to protest.

'It was,' James interrupts. 'It is a huge success and you know it.'

'Thank you,' I concede.

'But I also want you to know that there are always two sides to every story – I hope you realise that now you know the truth about your mother?'

'I do, and I am so grateful that you told me.'

'So perhaps,' my uncle goes on. 'There are two sides to this story with Ben as well.'

Before I get a chance to reply Miranda comes back into the dining room.

'Sascha's on the phone for you,' she says.

23

By the time I leave my aunt and uncle's house it's pouring with rain – that fine, cold rain that soaks you to the bone. It is quickly melting the snow and leaving grey slushy patches at the side of the street. The weather looks exactly how I feel.

I sigh and pull up the hood of my coat.

'Let me get you an umbrella,' James says.

'It's fine,' I reply. 'It won't help.'

Miranda puts a hand on my shoulder and turns me towards her. 'Are you going to be OK, love?' she asks. 'You can stay here tonight if you want.'

'I'll be OK,' I say, stepping away from her. 'I'll see you tomorrow for Knitting Club.'

'Think about what Sascha said,' Miranda goes on. 'Think about hearing Ben's side of the story.'

'I'll see you tomorrow,' I repeat as I walk down the front path towards the road giving a backhanded wave, the rain already soaking me.

I hear the front door shut behind me and I dig my hands into my pockets as I walk back to the café.

Sascha had heard everything by the time she had phoned me at my aunt and uncle's. I suspect she'd heard everything by the time she phoned for the first time this morning. Ben had gone straight back to the hotel after I asked him to leave the café and it seems that Marcus followed him.

'They were bickering so loudly in reception that a guest complained and Geoff had to split them up,' Sascha had said. 'So obviously I made them tell me exactly what was going on.'

'And?' I'd replied, unable to work up much enthusiasm.

'Well I think you should talk to Ben, let him tell you what he told me.'

'What did he tell you?'

She'd hesitated for a moment, knowing it wasn't really her business, before ploughing on anyway. 'He was trying to stop it, trying to stop Moby's buying the café. He said that as soon as he saw you in the café on that first night he knew he couldn't ask you to sell.'

'Is he still there?' I'd asked.

'He's been in the lounge all afternoon staring into space. He hasn't filled in a single crossword clue.'

I hadn't replied, hadn't known what to say. All I'd been able to think about was Ben standing in the café that morning begging me to let him explain and Marcus... Why had Marcus opened that envelope? Why was he so angry?

'Come and talk to him, Ellie,' Sascha had said gently.

'I can't. Not right now.'

I'd told Sascha I'd see her at Knitting Club and hung up. Now as I walk home I wonder if I've missed my chance. This rain means Ben isn't snowed in anymore. I know that he must be keen to get back to York, especially after all this, and there is every chance he'll leave tonight.

I hesitate outside the side door to my flat wondering if I

should go to the hotel and let him explain everything to me. I feel the tears burn the backs of my eyes as I remember the last two days that we've spent together, as I remember his kiss and the contours of his body. I remember everything we've talked about and everything we've shared and I remember that I can't trust him with any of that now, because he lied to me.

I can't do it. It's too late.

I'm about to open the door to the flat when I notice lights and movement in the café. I walk over to the café door and let myself in that way.

'What are you doing?' I ask. Marcus is in the middle of rearranging the whole café and he's moved the Christmas tree into the window at the front.

'It's better this way,' he says.

'Haven't you interfered enough for one day, Marcus?'

'I'm not going to apologise,' he replies. 'I knew Ben was up to something and I was right.'

'Do you have to be so sanctimonious about it?'

'Surely it's better to know in the long run.'

I slump against the door and press my forefinger and thumb into my eyes.

'I suppose,' I say quietly. 'It was better I found out now.'

I open my eyes and look around the café at the mess he's made.

'Why?' I ask gesturing at the Christmas tree.

'It was Abi's idea,' he says. 'We felt it needed to be more central to really show it off.'

I think about putting the tree up with Ben, about almost falling off the stepladder, about... I push the thought away.

'But there's no plug socket for the lights over here,' I say.

'I've used an extension.'

'But…'

'Stop worrying,' Marcus says. 'It's fine, I promise.'

I'm too tired to argue with him.

'I'm going to bed,' I say. 'It's been a long day.'

'Do you want to talk about it, El?'

'No,' I reply as I walk away. 'No I really don't.'

24

'He's not here,' Sascha says. 'He must have left really early because his key was on the reception desk when I came downstairs. I'm so sorry, Ellie.'

I look at the car park and see the space where his Audi used to be.

'I should have come last night,' I say.

'Come here,' Sascha says drawing me into a hug. 'Come inside and have some breakfast.'

It's freezing cold and looks as though it might start raining again any moment.

'Breakfast sounds good,' I say.

She leads me into the lounge and sits me down in front of the fire. There's nobody else here today but all I can think of is Ben sitting in here yesterday staring into space and not doing his crossword. I should have come then; I should have spoken to him before he left.

'Here you go,' Sascha says, putting a mug and plate in front of me. 'Earl Grey and hot buttery toast.' She sits down opposite me.

'You don't have to sit with me,' I say. 'You must have better things to do.'

Before Sascha can reply, Celia appears in the lounge doorway.

'Everything OK, Sascha?' she asks.

'Everything's fine thanks, Celia,' Sascha replies with a strange sort of fake merriment. 'I just need to talk to Ellie for a while.' She pauses. 'Privately,' she adds.

'Did you think any more about the uniforms?' Celia asks.

'No uniforms,' Sascha replies sternly.

Celia hovers for a moment longer and then drifts away.

'She's still here then?' I ask.

'I don't think she'll ever leave.' Sascha sighs. 'Do you know she suggested that Geoff and I should wear uniforms?'

'You and Geoff should? I thought she was talking about the staff?'

Sascha rolls her eyes. 'I'm trying really hard to get along with her but she is the most trying woman.'

I smile and pick up my cup of tea.

'Sorry, El, you don't want to hear about all this do you?'

'To be honest, anything that takes my mind off Ben is great.'

'I'm so sorry he's left. If I'd been up I would have forced him to stay.'

'It's OK, Sascha,' I say. 'It's probably for the best.'

'What makes you say that?'

'Because if I'd seen him I'd probably have believed any old lie that he told me. It's better if I don't see him again and just move on.'

'I don't think what he was saying was a lie,' Sascha says gently. 'I think this has all just been a terrible misunderstanding.'

'Oh don't you start. James was trying to get me to see things from Ben's point of view yesterday too.'

'Really?' Sascha looks surprised. 'I thought James hated anything to do with Moby's.'

I shrug. 'So did I,' I say.

'Look, Ellie, from what Ben told me and Marcus yesterday it does seem that he was genuinely trying to stop Moby's buying you out.'

'Right from the beginning?' I ask.

'Not right from the beginning,' Sascha says. 'But certainly from the point he saw the café, saw what you'd done here and how important it is to the community and the town.'

I don't say anything for a moment.

'You've changed so much, Ellie,' Sascha says quietly. 'You're so different from the woman who turned up here a year ago, so much stronger.'

'How do you mean?' I ask.

'Don't take this the wrong way but when I first met you I thought you were a flight risk.'

'A what?'

'When Miranda first introduced you to me and told me you were buying her and James out of the café I didn't think you'd stay for long. I thought perhaps you'd do the café up and sell it on. But you proved me wrong.'

'I had no idea you thought that,' I say. I can't work out whether I'm offended or not. I think probably not – I think she's closer to the truth than I'd like her to be.

'Lots of people thought it and you know what this town is like. Everybody gossips all the time. They said you were always on the verge of running away.'

'I always have run away,' I admit. 'From so many

things.' I think about what my aunt and uncle had told me yesterday lunchtime. Most of my life I've been running away from myself, from that feeling of being abandoned – that feeling that I felt all over again this morning when I saw the plans that Moby's had been making for the café. My café. 'But now I'm here I don't feel I need to run,' I continue. 'This was the place I always ran to but now it's my home. I don't need to go anywhere else.'

'Yesterday when Ben and Marcus turned up here and told me what had happened I was surprised.'

'It was a surprising turn of events,' I reply.

'Not just because of Moby's and the plans,' Sascha says. 'Although obviously I was shocked by that. I was surprised that you'd thrown them out instead of walking away yourself.'

'I'm not walking out of my own café,' I say.

'And that's exactly what I mean about you being stronger. I know you can handle anything.' She reaches over and squeezes my hand. 'If you want to see Ben again that's up to you, but don't run away from him. Face him and find out the truth.'

'I honestly don't know if I have the energy,' I admit.

'What's happened?' Sascha asks then, peering at me. 'This isn't just about Ben, is it?'

I need to tell somebody, to talk to somebody. I can't keep it all bottled up inside.

'No, it isn't just about Ben. Something else happened yesterday when I was at my aunt and uncle's.'

'Has your aunt deteriorated?' she asks.

'No, nothing like that. It was about my mother.' I look at Sascha across the table, if there is anyone I can tell the truth to it's her, the best friend I've ever had. And if there is anyone who will understand my mother's plight it's Sascha.

I tell her everything as we sit by the fire, her hand on mine. I tell her about how much my mother wanted another baby, how hard it had been for her to conceive and how, when she finally did she lost the baby and the grief sent her almost mad. I tell her about the suicide attempts and the hospitals and the therapy and as I do so she just sits there without interrupting, without judgement, without opinion.

'And you didn't know anything about this?' she asks when I finish.

'Not until yesterday, no.'

'Ellie, this is a lot to take on.'

'I know, I shouldn't have told you. This must be so triggering for you.'

'Don't be so ridiculous, sharing this stuff is what friends are for. It's what living in a place like Sanderson Bay is all about, isn't it? Being part of something and knowing that people have got your back.' She smiles. 'That's the payoff for everyone knowing your business I guess.'

'I don't know what to think or do,' I say.

'What made your aunt and uncle tell you now, after all these years?'

'We were talking about Ben,' I say. 'About the plans from Moby's and how I felt he'd lied to me, how I felt that he'd abandoned me just like everybody else, just like Marcus had. Just like my mother.'

'You think your mum abandoned you?'

'I've had this sense of being left behind, this sense of not having a home for such a long time and it stems back to when I was sent to boarding school. From my point of view it just felt as though my parents had left me in a cold, grey part of England and I only got to see them in the summer when they were surrounded by other people. I've carried that feeling around for so long that it became the truth and I think it became a mirror to my interactions with other people. It's almost as though I expect people to abandon me long before they do. Even in those few days I spent with Ben I was expecting it to be over, expecting him to leave.'

'Now you know the truth about your mum do you think it will change how you feel about other things, about other people?' Sascha doesn't say Ben's name but I know what she is getting at.

'Maybe, over time,' I say. 'But I'm not sure I'll ever be able to forgive myself for happened with my mother.'

'Why?'

'Because the last conversation I ever had with her I accused her of not loving me. How can I get past that? How can I think that wasn't my fault?'

'We can't change the past, Ellie,' Sascha says quietly. 'We all have things in our pasts that we're not proud of, stupid things we've said to people we love. But we can change our futures. You know that – you've already started changing yours after all.'

I think about The Two Teas café, about the shelves of tea and the carefully selected cups, saucers and teapots – each one with a story behind it – about the wooden tables and chairs that I'd painstakingly painted white, and the polished floor. About everything I'd dreamed of and made my reality.

'Can I make a suggestion?' Sascha asks.

'Go on then.'

'Try not to dwell on what you can't change. Instead think about what you can.'

'Like what?'

'It's not too late to change things with your dad,' she says. 'Talk to him, Ellie.'

25

'Do you think you'll see him again?' Lisa asks.

The last Knitting Club before Christmas meets that night. We sit by the light of the Christmas tree drinking champagne and nobody is even pretending to knit. We should just be called the Champagne Club these days.

'I don't know,' I reply. 'I have his number but...' I glance over at my aunt, remembering everything she had told me. 'I have a lot of other stuff going on at the moment.'

'What sort of stuff?' Bessie asks nosily.

'Just stuff. Stuff I need to deal with before I can think about Ben again.'

'So what are we all doing for Christmas?' Clara asks, changing the subject.

'Waiting in anticipation for the mother-in-law from hell to leave,' Sascha replies.

'When's she going?' Lisa asks.

'Boxing Day,' Sascha replies. 'And trust me she has already overstayed her welcome.'

'She's just worried about you after your scare the other week,' I say.

'Putting up notices in the bedrooms and moving everything around in the dining room and telling us to wear uniforms is not being worried about me. It's being interfering.'

'At least she'll be gone by New Year,' Lisa says. 'Look on the bright side.'

'Speaking of New Year,' Clara interrupts. 'How are plans for our champagne tea party? I'm looking forward to it.'

The rest of the group agree.

New Year's Eve had been in the back of my mind for days. I've kept meaning to be more proactive about it and to talk to Terry about the best way of doing things without taking custom away from each other, but with everything that has happened, I hadn't gotten around to it.

I'd been intending to invite Ben to come for New Year as well, but there was no way I could do that now and the disappointment I feel about that seems to have put me off wanting to celebrate at all. I'm finding it harder than usual to get into the seasonal spirit despite the Christmas music Sascha has put on in the café.

'I'd been meaning to speak to Terry about it all week,' I say. 'I don't want to tread on his toes or anything. To be honest I'm thinking of cancelling it.'

'Nooooo,' everyone choruses together.

'You can't cancel it, Ellie,' Sascha says. 'It's going to be lovely and you've sold loads of tickets.'

'I haven't sold that many,' I confess.

'I agree with Sascha,' Miranda says. 'I think we should go ahead with it.'

'Besides you've sold more tickets than you think you have,' Sascha says.

'I have?'

'Yup.' Sascha takes a sip of her non-alcoholic fizz. 'Abi

was telling me that she and Marcus sold loads but with everything that's been going on they haven't had a chance to tell you. Apparently even Terry and Mo have bought tickets.'

'Terry and Mo are coming?' I ask. 'Won't they be busy at the pub?'

'You might not have had a chance to talk to Terry about it but I think Marcus might have done,' Sascha goes on. 'You'll have to ask him about all the details.'

'I need to ask Marcus about why he's decided that he's running this café,' I mutter. 'You've seen how he's moved the whole café around as well,' I go on, gesturing to the Christmas tree in the window.

'Don't be too hard on him, love,' Miranda says. 'I think he's just trying to help.'

I don't know what I think about Marcus at the moment. I thought I'd made it quite clear that I didn't want his help but I don't have a chance to think about that because "I Want A Hippopotamus for Christmas", one of the songs we sung at the Model Village, has just come on the stereo.

'Oh my favourite,' Bessie exclaims and she takes our minds off everything else by getting us all to sing along. When it's over she gets Sascha to put it on again and we all sing along for a second time. By the end of that we're all laughing and red in the face and Bessie demands more champagne and just for a while I allow myself to stop thinking about Ben and Marcus and everything that has happened over the last few days.

I feel my shoulders release from around my ears as I allow myself to soak up another Christmas in Sanderson Bay and I realise that Sascha was right when she said I'd changed. Since I first went to boarding school when I was thirteen years old I have felt a need to be always looking for something else, something better. But when I made Ben and Marcus leave the café on Sunday morning instead of running away myself it was because the café, and the community I've built here, is my home now.

I have everything I want right here. I don't need to run anymore.

'Sascha tells me you've sold nearly all the tickets for the New Year champagne tea,' I say to Abi and Marcus early the next morning as we're setting up for Christmas Eve. It's going to be a busy day with lots of morning and afternoon tea bookings so it's all hands on deck.

'All of them now,' Abi says as she comes behind the counter to get an apron. 'I sold the last two in the shop just now.'

'Thank you,' I say, but I obviously don't sound very grateful as Marcus frowns at me.

'What's the matter?' he says.

'Nothing.'

I watch him and Abi exchange a look and Abi goes into the kitchen.

'Come on, Ellie, tell me what's wrong,' Marcus says sitting down and gesturing for me to join him.

'I was thinking of cancelling the New Year's Eve do,' I say. 'It doesn't seem like such a good idea as we get closer to the big day. I don't know if I've got it in me to sort out all those afternoon teas and—'

'Rubbish,' Marcus interrupts.

'Seriously, Marcus, I don't know if I've got the energy.'

'Is this because of Ben?'

I open my mouth to tell him of course it's not because of Ben, but then I close it again because he's right.

'It's partly because of Ben,' I say carefully.

'Look, Ellie, I'm in no position to judge. I didn't exactly treat you well when I left either but you cannot let him stop you living your dream, the dream you've made for yourself here.' He waves an arm at the café around us. 'This café is so amazing that even Moby's want it. What does that tell you?'

'It tells me that it's a prime property location and my aunt and uncle were idiots to let me buy it from them at such a knock-down price.'

'Better a knock-down price than a coffee chain taking over the High Street.'

I look at him. 'Since when did you care about Sanderson Bay?' I ask.

He looks away from me for a moment. 'I may have been wrong about this town,' he admits. 'I know I was always quite scathing about small-town life, and I'm fairly sure that the residents are never going to let me forget that, but now I'm here...' He hesitates as though he's not quite sure what to say next.

'I told you that Sanderson Bay gets under your skin' I say with a smile.

He nods, smiling back. 'It really does,' he says. 'Which is why you have to go ahead with New Year's Eve – everyone's looking forward to it.'

'People usually go to The Black Horse on New Year's Eve. I don't want to tread on anyone's toes.'

'Terry and Mo have bought tickets to your champagne tea and Terry and I have been talking about ways that people can go to your event and then to the pub afterwards.'

'You really are invested in this, aren't you?'

He takes a breath. 'I came back here looking for you, but I found something else, something I hadn't been able to find in Thailand.'

'What?' I ask.

'A sense of belonging,' he replies. 'I feel like I'm part of the town even though I've only been here a few weeks. Even though most people still treat me with barely concealed disdain.'

'Well you have treated their town with barely concealed disdain in the past,' I say.

He holds up his hands. 'Fair enough,' he says.

'You know it will take at least twenty years before they accept you as a local.'

'I know.'

'And...' I hesitate, not sure if now is the time but I have to say it eventually. 'You can't live here forever. There's no future in—'

'I know,' he replies. 'I'll look for somewhere to live as soon as Christmas is over.'

'One of my housemates is moving out after Christmas,' Abi says, coming back into the café with a tray of clean mugs. 'Perhaps you could move in there.'

'Perhaps I could,' Marcus says, and I notice a look pass between him and Abi that I can't quite make out.

'So are you going to do this New Year's Eve tea or not?' Abi asks.

'I don't have many excuses left thanks to you two.'

★

There's no Pilates class on Christmas Eve so I go to the penultimate pub quiz of the year a little bit early to talk to Terry, armed with a tin of gunpowder tea. It's time I told him which tea he is, I've been here over a year.

'Of course you're not treading on my toes, love,' he says, taking the tin of tea from me with a confused smile. 'Don't be ridiculous. Besides Mo's really looking forward to it.'

'Really?'

'Of course, everyone is. Sometimes I don't think you realise how much your little café has changed this community – Pilates classes for heaven's sake. I never thought we'd have them in Sanderson Bay and yet here we are.'

'Oh it's nothing…' I begin.

'Ellie,' he says. 'You have to start believing your own hype. What you've achieved in a year is fantastic and what better way is there to celebrate that than us all coming to the café for New Year's?'

'But what about the pub?' I ask.

'Well your Marcus suggested that we start early at the café and enjoy the food and champagne and then come here for midnight. After all the later it gets the messier it gets and I think the pub is a better location for the messier part of the evening. What do you think?'

I don't correct him on the "your Marcus" statement. 'That sounds fantastic,' I say, hugging him. 'Thank you, Terry, thank you so much.'

'Glad to help, love,' Terry says, embarrassed at my exuberant performance. 'Always glad to help and thanks for the tea.'

'You're welcome.'

'If I'm gunpowder, then what's Mo?'

'Oh,' I reply with a smile. 'I've always thought that she might be silver needle. It's a white tea from China that has a really complex flavour.'

'Sound about right.' Terry smiles.

We don't win the pub quiz, although we do get the final question right ('Ben must have taught you something,' Sascha says, winking lewdly at me), but I still walk home with a warm glow. I try not to think about walking back from the pub quiz with Ben at the beginning of the month; I try not to think about Ben at all.

Instead I think about everything I have got, and for the first time in my life I realise I have more than I'll ever need.

26

Talking to Terry is one thing but talking to my father is quite another. We do always try to speak on special occasions – birthdays, Easter, the anniversary of *Maman*'s death and Christmas of course. I decide to see if I can talk to him on my usual Christmas Day call.

I spend the day with Miranda and James as I have done every Christmas since I was thirteen and, just as I have done every year since then, I phone France just before lunch.

'*Bonjour, Papa*,' I say as he answers the video chat. '*Ça va?*'

It feels like every other conversation I've ever had with my father at first – slightly awkward and stilted, not really sure if we have anything in common anymore. My little sister comes onto the video chat and tells me about all the presents she got from *Papa Noël*.

When my father comes back on the call I know I need to tell him what I know, what James and Miranda have told me.

'Do you have to dash off?' I ask. 'Or can we talk about something?'

'I always have time for you,' he replies. I've never felt as though he always has time for me but perhaps that too was just my perception of events. My father must have been carrying so much sadness around with him over the years after all.

'Miranda and James told me...' I falter, I don't want to cry. 'They told me about *Maman* and the miscarriages and her depression and...' I falter again. I don't know how to do this. I don't know how to speak to my father at the best of times, let alone about something like this.

I watch him rub his hand over his face. 'I know,' he says. 'James emailed me to tell me he'd told you. I'm so sorry, Eloise, so sorry we kept this from you.'

'Why didn't you tell me?' I ask. 'Why didn't you tell me at the time?'

'You were so young and far away from home. We thought we were doing the best thing for you and then, after your mother died... well...'

'Well what?' I don't mean to sound harsh. I promised myself I wouldn't get upset or angry, but if Sascha is right and I do need to have this conversation with my dad (and let's be honest, when has Sascha ever been wrong?) then we need to be honest with each other once and for all.

'After your mother died we decided – that is James, Miranda and I decided – that it would be too much to tell you everything then, that we would let you grieve your mum for a while but after that it got harder and harder to tell you at all. There never seemed to be a right time. I didn't want to tell you on the phone. James thought you should know but in the end he conceded to Miranda and me who didn't think you needed to. But we were wrong and James was right. I should have found a way to tell you long ago. It should have been me you heard it from, not James.'

I think that is the most my father has said to me in one go since my mother died and, for a moment, I don't know how to reply.

'I'm sorry,' he says again.

'In a way you were right,' I say quietly. 'I don't think I would have been able to deal with it all right after *Maman* died but...'

'But you wish you'd known sooner?'

I nod, unable to blink back the tears now.

'Eloise, if I could turn back time I would, if I could do everything differently. I was a coward both with you and your mother. I should have been stronger, been there for both of you more.'

'I thought she didn't love me,' I say. 'I thought that's why she sent me away and only ever saw me in Provence in the summer.'

'She loved you so much,' my father says. 'It surprised her every day how much she loved you. And I love you too, Eloise. I know I'm not good at showing it but I do. I love you and I'm so proud of you.'

'You are?' I ask, wiping the tears from my eyes. 'I always thought I was a bit of a disappointment, especially when I dropped out of my PhD.'

He chuckles at that, a low rumble of a laugh that I remember from my childhood, a sound I haven't heard for years.

'Disappointed?' he says. 'Why would I be disappointed?

You went and did something very brave, Eloise. You left the comfort of the academia that you had known your whole life to set up in business on your own. That's something I would never have been able to do.'

'Thank you,' I say, shocked by his words and shocked by my own bad perception of my father.

'Miranda tells me the café is unrecognisable now, that you've turned it into a boutique of tea.'

'More of an apothecary,' I say with a smile, thinking of Ben again. Is Sascha right about him too? Do I need to hear his side of the story?

'Eloise, I really want to talk to you more about this, talk properly but not over the phone.'

My heart jumps for a moment. It's been so long since I saw my father in the flesh that the thought of it almost scares me.

'Perhaps I could come to England in the new year,' he goes on. 'I would love to see what you've done to the café and we could sit and talk properly.'

'That would be good,' I say slowly. 'But there's something else.' I think of Ben again. Whatever his ulterior motive for returning to Sanderson Bay, it was still the town he grew up in, a place where he spent time with his father before he died. Although Ben never told me anything much about his father's death other than it was eighteen years ago, coming back here took some guts. Regardless of Moby's, coming back must have been a big thing for him.

And going back to Paris will be a big thing for me too.

'Yes?' my father says, concern etched on his face.

'I want to go back to Paris,' I say. 'It's time. It's way past time if I'm honest.'

He nods slowly. 'Perhaps I could accompany you?' he asks tentatively.

'Perhaps you could come here and see the café and then we could go to Paris together,' I say. I hadn't expected the conversation with my father to take this turn. I just thought I would make more of an effort to call him more regularly, but it feels right. 'Just the two of us,' I say for clarity.

'Just the two of us,' he repeats.

We finish the call then. Marie is calling for him from another room and I know that Miranda has Christmas lunch ready. I put my phone in the pocket of my jeans and go into the kitchen to see what I can do to help, stopping to check myself in the hall mirror and wiping away any signs of the tears that I've just cried.

'Everything all right?' James asks as he gets ready to carve the turkey.

I smile. 'I think it's going to be,' I say.

'Happy Christmas, everyone,' Miranda says as she pours three more glasses of champagne.

'Ding dong the witch is gone,' Sascha says gleefully when I arrive at the hotel on Boxing Day. Almost everyone else is heading down to the marina for the start of the Brass Monkeys Yacht Race so we've decided to have brunch together.

'When did she leave?' I ask.

'First thing and it feels so good to have my hotel back.' Sascha bites into a fried egg sandwich, egg yolk spilling everywhere. I hand her a serviette. Geoff is taking his mother home and the few guests that the hotel does have are at the marina too, so we have the dining room to ourselves.

'You know she cares about you really,' I say. 'She only stayed so long because she was worried about you.'

Sascha puts her sandwich down and wipes her mouth. 'I know,' she says. 'And it didn't help that I didn't wake her the night we went the hospital. Families are great, but also they can be...' She hesitates.

'Complicated?'

'Exactly that.'

'I had a long conversation with my father yesterday,' I say.

'Really?'

'Well, long for us anyway.'

'That's great, Ellie.' She smiles at me.

'Turns out you were right again.'

'Obviously.'

'You were right about how much I've changed in the last year too,' I say.

'I know,' she replies with her mouth full. 'The scared, lost person who arrived here just over a year ago is long gone. Look at you now!'

'Maybe Sanderson Bay is magic.' I laugh.

'Well I never thought Geoff would do yoga,' she says. 'And I never thought I'd get pregnant so who knows? Maybe it is magic.'

'So much so that Marcus has become quite invested in it.'

'I thought he might have done,' Sascha says as she pours us both another cup of tea – Earl Grey for me and rooibos for her, 'from the way he was press-ganging everyone into buying tickets for the New Year's Eve champagne tea. But I didn't think he even liked it here.'

'I've got a feeling that Abi might have changed his mind on that one,' I reply.

'Really?' Sascha's eyes light up with the potential gossip.

'I don't know anything for sure,' I say. 'So don't go round spreading rumours. But apparently he's moving into her share house after Christmas.'

'How do you feel about that?'

'Gets him off my back,' I say. 'Maybe he's finally got the message that we're not getting back together again, even though Ben is out of the picture.'

'Is Ben completely out of the picture?' Sascha asks.

I hesitate for a moment before pulling out my phone. 'He texted me last night,' I say, showing her the message. 'I don't know whether to reply.'

I watch her read the message which simply reads: *I'm so sorry I didn't tell you truth. I thought I could stop it and I was wrong. I hope you had a lovely Christmas, Ellie. Thinking of you xx*. The two kisses sitting there reminding me of those two almost kisses we shared back before any of this had happened.

'Of course you should reply!' Sascha screeches and then she looks at me, her face a little calmer. 'If you want to of course,' she says.

'I do want to but I don't know what to say.'

'Why don't you invite him for New Year's Eve?'

'And what if he can't come? Or worse, what if he doesn't want to come?'

'Then at least you'd know,' Sascha replies.

Before I have a chance to think about that any more we

both look up because we've heard sirens in the distance, coming closer.

'I wonder what that's all about,' Sascha says getting up to look out of the window. 'I hope everything's OK at the marina.'

I'm about to go and join Sascha at the window when Eric bursts into the dining room.

'Oh, Ellie, there you are, thank God!' he says out of breath. 'I've been looking all over for you. The café is on fire!'

27

The fire trucks arrive at the same time as we do.

'Oh my God!' I hear myself scream. 'What happened?' Instinct makes me run towards the café, towards the door to try to do something to save my home and my livelihood, but somebody grabs my arm and pulls me back.

'Let the fire crew do their work,' Eric says calmly as he takes me back to where Sascha is standing.

'How did it happen?' I hear Sascha ask beside me. Everything feels as though I'm a character in a film, as though I'm looking down on the whole situation from above. I feel as though it's not really me watching my café burning down taking with it my home, my teas, my herb garden and everything I own in the world. I feel as though I will awaken from this hideous dream at any moment.

'We're not sure,' Eric says. 'It was Bessie who first spotted it and called the fire brigade. You weren't open today, love, I take it?'

I shake my head slowly. 'No,' I say. 'I didn't open today but...' Oh God no!

'Marcus,' I scream. 'Where the hell is Marcus?' When I left that morning to go and see Sascha, Marcus had still been in bed. He'd had Christmas lunch in the pub with Abi and I hadn't seen him since.

'Marcus!' I scream again as an ambulance arrives on the scene.

'Calm down, El,' Sascha says quietly and I feel her arm, warm around my waist. 'Everything's going to be all right.'

I spin round to face her. 'How can you say that?' I shout. 'Everything I ever worked for is in there, everything I've ever been able to call home is in there.' I pause for a moment, catching my breath as the smoke sticks in my throat. 'Marcus is in there.'

'Marcus isn't in there,' Eric says quietly from behind me. I turn and follow Eric's finger that is pointing towards Marcus, who thankfully seems very much alive. He's wrapped in a red blanket and is being led towards an ambulance by a paramedic. I break away from Sascha's firm grip and run towards him.

'Marcus,' I call breathlessly and he turns towards me and smiles. He looks pale and tired and is covered in black smuts of ash. He tries to say something but starts coughing instead.

'Don't try to talk,' the paramedic says to him.

'Is he OK?' I ask.

'Just some smoke inhalation, love,' she says as Marcus carries on coughing and wheezing alarmingly. 'We just need to give him some oxygen and get him checked out at the hospital but he should be fine. Are you a relative?'

'No, I... He... I own the café,' I say gesturing towards the mess that used to be my pride and joy. One of the windows is cracked and there's smoke pouring out of the door. Plus of course now the fire brigade are doing their job I can already see how much water damage there'll be. Oh God please don't let there be any structural damage. 'Marcus and I work together,' I go on. I turn to him then. 'Nobody else was in there were they?'

He shakes his head as the other paramedic fixes an oxygen mask over his nose and mouth.

'Do you know what happened?' I ask. 'Do you know how much damage there is to the building?'

'That's the fire department's call,' the paramedic says. 'You'll have to ask them. We have to get Marcus to the hospital.'

Marcus reaches out his hand and grabs my wrist. 'Come with me,' he says through the oxygen mask. I look at him properly then and can see how scared he must have been, how relieved he is to be in the fresh air. What the hell started this fire? Did I leave something on? Did I not unplug something?

'You can come with him but we need to leave now,' the paramedic tells me and I look from Marcus to the café wondering what to do? Should I go with Marcus or stay here?

'Ellie,' someone shouts from across the street. I turn and scan the growing crowd. The whole town must be here now, abandoning the yacht race for the more exciting entertainment of a fire. 'Ellie!'

It's my uncle James. He strides across the road and envelops me in a huge bear hug. 'Thank God you're all right,' he says. 'Eric called us and told us what was happening. I had to come down and check on you. Do you know what happened?'

I shake my head but suddenly I remember how Marcus had moved the café around and put the tree in the window for Christmas. He told me he'd used an extension lead but I'd never checked it to see if it was PAT tested, never checked to make sure he hadn't overloaded the plug. I remember leaving the Christmas lights on this morning when I left for the hotel. Part of me is suddenly furious with Marcus, for turning up here so suddenly, for taking over, for moving everything around, for shaking everything up. But part of me is just glad that he's all right.

James turns to Marcus then. 'Are you all right, mate?' he asks, his forehead crinkling in concern. Marcus nods and tries to talk but I stop him.

'Smoke inhalation,' I say. 'He needs to go to hospital and I don't know if I should go with him or wait here to see what the fire brigade say.'

'Go with Marcus,' James replies decisively. My uncle has always been a good decision maker, unlike me. 'I'll stay here and find out what's going on and call you when I can.'

I hug him again, tears falling down my cheeks now. 'Thank you,' I whisper. 'Thank you so much.'

The paramedic helps Marcus up into the back of the ambulance and I follow them in. The doors slam behind me and I turn to Marcus. I try not to keep crying but I can't stop myself and Marcus takes my hand as we drive away from the ruins of my beloved café.

'Thank you for giving me gave me a second chance,' Marcus says, his voice still a little croaky.

'Don't be so soft,' I reply, but I'm so relieved to see

him sitting up in bed with some colour in his face. We've been here about three hours now and he's been checked all over and his chest is clear, his oxygen levels back to normal and there's no soot in his nostrils. He definitely looks a lot better than he did when we first arrived and we're just waiting for the all clear to go back to Sanderson Bay.

'It's true, Ellie,' he goes on. 'Letting me stay at the café, letting me help out has been good for me – it's made me see the world and Sanderson Bay from a different perspective.'

'I almost let you burn to death, Marcus. That's hardly a second chance is it?'

He'd been asleep when the fire broke out I'd discovered, and he'd inhaled a lot of smoke by the time he'd managed to get out of the building. 'The fire didn't reach upstairs though,' he'd told me as a doctor listened to his chest. 'I don't think there'll be much damage.' Marcus always was overly optimistic about things. I'm fairly sure there'll be a lot of damage but I'm trying very hard not to think about that right now.

'Ellie,' he says quietly.

'Yes?' I reply even though I have a feeling that I know what he's going to say.

'The fire was my fault.'

I take a breath. 'You don't know that, Marcus,' I say. 'Not until the fire officer has checked everything.'

'I should never have moved that Christmas tree. I should never have used that extension lead. I don't know why I felt I had to interfere in everything like that. I just wanted you to—'

'Leave it, Marcus,' I say. 'Now isn't the time.'

'I've treated you so badly, El,' he goes on anyway. 'And now this.'

I shrug. 'It doesn't matter anymore. It was all for the best.'

'I was always looking for something else,' he says quietly. 'I didn't want to end up like my parents with all that material wealth but no happiness. But I had no idea what to do, which is why I came to York when the opportunity arose. I knew I wasn't going to find what I was looking for staying in New York. But whatever it was I was looking for still didn't come along, which is why I left.'

'Why Thailand?' I ask. 'I can't believe I never asked you that before but why there?'

'Do you really want to know?'

'Yes.'

'I stuck a pin in a map.'

'Really?'

'Really. I didn't know what else to do. I was desperate.' I feel my stomach drop a little and he touches my hand for a moment as though he knows what I'm thinking. 'Not desperate to get away from you. Just desperate to do something different.'

'I understand,' I say.

'I'm sorry about everything, Ellie. I'm sorry about just turning up like this and being horrible about Ben and opening his post.'

My stomach turns over at the thought of Ben, at the memory of that envelope of plans and blueprints.

'Why did you open it?' I ask.

'Because he was having his post sent here, because he seemed to be settling in too well.'

'Marcus—' I begin.

He holds a hand up. 'I know, I know. It sounds so jealous and possessive and I don't mean it to.'

'I've tried to explain, Marcus,' I say. 'I've tried to tell you from the moment you came back that we can't go backwards.'

He sighs and runs a hand through his hair, which he still hasn't had cut. 'I still care about you, Ellie,' he says. 'You know I do. Part of the reason I came back was for you.'

'Marcus,' I say again, warning in my voice.

'And you were right when you said there was no us. Breaking up with you was one of the hardest things I've ever done but it was also one of the best things.' He pauses. 'For both of us.'

I don't say anything but he's not wrong. I know that much.

'Neither of us was happy in York,' he says. 'And neither of us was prepared to admit it I don't think.'

'If you hadn't left I would never have come back here,' I say. 'I would never have bought the café, never have done any of it. I'd still be plodding through a thankless PhD that I was never going to finish.'

'And that's the thing, Ellie, I know how happy you are here. I can see it every time you talk about the café and about your herb garden and about the teas that you're making. I can see what a success you've made of this and Abi told me that you're thinking about opening a second one somewhere.'

I wave my hand at him. 'Oh that's just a pipe dream,' I say.

'Is it?'

I remember talking about it with Ben, how in those few moments it hadn't seemed like a pipe dream. It had seemed like something I could do.

But Ben isn't here and the café is ruined.

The doctor comes in then and does a few final checks before telling us we're free to go. He leaves us with a word of warning that if Marcus's cough gets any worse or if he has any trouble breathing at all then he's to call a doctor straight away.

'It's becoming a bit of a habit this, isn't it?' Marcus says.

'What is?'

'Ending up at the hospital like this. I don't have the car this time so we'll have to get a cab.'

'It's been a weird few weeks,' I say.

Marcus stops and turns towards me. 'Are you OK, Ellie?' he asks.

I smile, even though we both know it's fake. 'Of course I am!' I say.

'You don't have to pretend to me, El. I know Christmas is hard for you at the best of times.'

We walk towards the taxi rank but there aren't any taxis there. I remember that it's Boxing Day so there won't be many taxis about. I get out my phone to call one.

'I spoke to Dad,' I say as I fiddle with my phone.

'The usual Christmas pleasantries?' he asks.

'No actually, a proper conversation for once.'

'That's great, Ellie.' Marcus has always known how difficult I've found my relationship with my father.

'It was pretty great actually,' I say. 'I mean it was weird and awkward at first and I spent the whole conversation trying and failing not to cry and it was video chat of course so I looked a mess, but it was great. He says he's going to come and see the café.'

'Ah that's brilliant!'

'And I said…' I stop and take a breath. 'I said I'd go to Paris with him.' The thought of going back to Paris fills me with so much anxiety, it makes me feel like I've been trapped in a tiny room and the walls are closing in but I know I have to do it. Just like Ben coming back to Sanderson Bay.

'What brought this on?' he asks.

I almost start to tell him everything, about Mum and the miscarriages and her suicide attempts but then I realise that I don't need to. I don't need to share that story with him.

'It's just time to move on,' I say. Because it is.

'Ellie, that's amazing. How do you feel?'

'Scared and nervous. Worried that Dad and I won't have anything in common. But also relieved.' I look up at Marcus. 'Basically I'm just confused.'

'I think that's to be expected,' he says. He pauses for a moment and then he says, 'Am I allowed to ask about Ben?'

'He texted on Christmas Day. Nothing specific, just hoping I'd had a nice day. Sascha was trying to talk me into inviting him to the Bay for New Year's Eve when Eric came in and told us about the fire.' I stop and feel a lump in my throat as though I'm choking. 'I guess there won't be a champagne tea for New Year's Eve now,' I say. 'I'll have to refund everyone's money.'

'Don't think about that now,' he replies.

A taxi pulls up next to us then and we ask the driver if he'll take us to Sanderson Bay. He quotes an exorbitant price but we don't have much choice.

'Let's just go home,' Marcus says as he gets into the cab and slides along the back seat to let me in.

'Marcus, neither of us have a home to go to,' I reply suddenly realising that the fire has rendered us both homeless.

'Shit,' he says with a small smile.

'What will you do?'

'I think the room at Abi's place might be free by now and if not I'll have to sleep on the couch, but what about you? Will you stay with James and Miranda?'

I shake my head. 'No, they have enough to worry about. I'll stay at the hotel.'

'For what it's worth,' Marcus says as the taxi pulls away, 'I think Sascha's right. I think you should invite Ben for New Year.'

'There won't be a New Year now.'

'Just because there's been a fire at the café doesn't mean that New Year is cancelled. Phone him.'

'You've changed your tune.'

'I know I shouldn't have opened that envelope but I couldn't help it. I'd seen how happy you were here and it just felt…' He pauses as though he's looking for the right word.

'What?' I ask.

'I felt there was more to Ben's sudden arrival in town.'

'Which is why you were googling him?'

Marcus sighs. 'I google everyone and I'll admit I couldn't find much on him so when the envelope arrived, I needed to see what was in it. I guess I was hoping it would be something that would stop me being suspicious.'

'And instead it just proved your suspicions.'

'I thought that at first,' he says. 'And I was so angry – the plans showed that they were going to build over your herb garden.'

'I know,' I say, squeezing my eyes shut. 'That was the bit that got me the most too.'

'But now I'm not so sure that Ben is the bad guy after all.'

'You're not?' I'm surprised. It was normal, I suppose, for Marcus to not like the person I'm dating – an ex-boyfriend's prerogative – so I'm surprised he isn't gloating more to be honest.

'I haven't known how to tell you this, haven't really had a chance, but he said something to me after you kicked us out of the café that made me wonder if he might have been telling the truth when he said he'd been trying to stop the sale.'

'He did?' I ask. 'Sascha said he'd told her something similar, but how do I know I can believe him.'

'You don't,' he says. 'But what have you got to lose by just hearing him out?'

28

'Terry, are you sure?' I ask. 'I don't deserve this; the fire was all my fault.'

'You have to stop beating yourself up, love,' Terry replies. 'You should have checked the plug extension I'll agree but it was Marcus's mistake and, to be fair to him, it was a mistake that any of us could have easily made. It's not like you started the fire maliciously and Mo and I want to help you out, keep the spirit of the café going as it were.'

It's two days before New Year's Eve and Terry has come to find me at the hotel where I've been hiding out since I found out about the cause of the fire.

'Electrical,' the fire officer had said when he met me at the café – as if being in the ruin of my beloved business wasn't enough. 'Looks like it was a faulty plug maybe or...' He'd paused and glanced at me for a moment. 'An overloaded plug socket.'

I'd swallowed and been totally unable to think of anything to say.

'It happens a lot this time of year,' he'd said then, as though to make me feel better – as if anything could. 'You'd be surprised.'

After the fire officer had left I stood outside in the street for a long time looking at the blackened shell of what used to be The Two Teas thinking about the Christmas tree lights and the extension cable that I'd trusted Marcus with and hadn't checked because I'd been too tired and too upset about Ben.

What an idiot I'd been. I'd put myself before the safety of my business and my customers and I will always be grateful that nobody was seriously hurt.

After the inspection I'd been told that there was no structural damage to the building, which was a huge relief, and Marcus and I had been allowed to go back to the flat once to collect clothes and other stuff we might need. Clothes that I'd had to put through Sascha's washing machine twice to get rid of the smell of smoke.

Sascha had found me standing outside the café, shivering in the watery December sun.

'Come on,' she'd said. 'You can't stand here staring at it all day.'

'It's all gone though, hasn't it? Everything up in smoke. Literally.'

'Not everything, El – you're safe and so is Marcus and there's no structural damage. You'll be up and running again before you know it.'

'It's ruined in there,' I'd said. 'All the tea is ruined, everything stinks of smoke and there's so much water damage. I don't even know if my insurance will cover it seeing as it's all my fault.'

'How is it your fault?' she'd asked.

I'd told her about the extension lead and how I hadn't checked how Marcus had set it up. I hadn't been able to look at her as I'd said the words; I hadn't been able to take my eyes off the café.

'So it was Marcus's fault,' she'd said.

'It's my café and the buck stops with me.'

'You had a lot on your mind. So much on your mind of course the little things won't get done. It happens to all of us – that doesn't mean it's your fault. And if your insurance doesn't pay out then we'll fix it anyway.'

'How the hell will you and I fix that?'

'Not you and me, silly, the whole of Sanderson Bay. We're good in a crisis trust me. You weren't here when one of the ceilings at the hotel caved in and we didn't even have any insurance. The whole town got us up and running again.'

'Really?' Her words had given me a glimmer of hope, like a light at the end of a very long tunnel.

Sascha had taken my arm then and led me back to the hotel.

'I'll have to refund everyone for New Year's Eve,' I'd said as we walked.

'Don't think about that now, Ellie; you've been through enough these last few days – so many ups and downs. You need to rest. We'll talk about it tomorrow.'

But I haven't been able to sleep. I've barely slept at all since the fire. It was good luck rather than good management that the fire had happened on Boxing Day rather than on a day when the café had been packed. It was good luck that Marcus hadn't come to any harm and had recovered from his smoke inhalation so quickly.

'I'm made of tough stuff, El,' he'd said when I'd phoned him to see if he was all right. 'It'll take more than a little fire to get the better of me.'

I'd been holed up in the hotel ever since my meeting with the fire officer, speaking to my aunt on the phone each night, eating with Sascha and Geoff but I hadn't felt like doing anything else. So when Sascha had told me that Terry had come to see me I'd almost told her to tell him to leave. I didn't want to speak to anyone. But I'm glad Sascha forced me to see him because he was there to offer to hold the champagne tea at The Black Horse now the café wouldn't be open.

'I'd be lying if I told you the whole town wasn't talking about the fire,' he says as we sit in the hotel lounge – the only people there for which I'm grateful. 'But nobody is blaming you.'

'Do they know about the extension lead?' I ask.

'Of course they do and everyone is saying how easily done it is, how they've done it themselves, how it could have been them.'

I look at him doubtfully. 'Really?'

'Yes really. Besides we all know it was Marcus who moved the Christmas tree and the whole town already knows what an idiot he is.' Terry smiles at me. 'Why are you hiding in the hotel anyway when you've got a big New Year's Eve party to plan?' he asks.

'I can't do it, Terry,' I say. 'How can I after this? It seems inappropriate. That fire could have been really awful. It could have—'

'But it didn't,' Terry interrupts. 'Everyone is absolutely fine and looking forward to New Year. They don't want refunds; they want champagne and cake.'

'Are you sure?'

'Of course I'm sure, so are you in?'

I hesitate for a moment before agreeing. 'OK,' I say, uncertainty in my voice. 'I'll give it a go.'

'Come over and see me and Mo this afternoon,' Terry

says as he stands to leave. He leans forward and places a reassuring hand on my shoulder. 'Everything will be OK, Ellie,' he says. 'You'll see.'

'Come on,' Sascha calls from the front door of the hotel as I run back down the stairs, putting on my coat. 'We said we'd be there by two.'

'I don't think "we" said anything,' I reply. 'I remember telling Terry I'd pop into the pub this afternoon but I don't remember you being invited.'

'I'm just making sure you're OK,' she says, literally shoving me out of the door.

'I don't need chaperoning. I'm fine.'

She looks at me out of the corner of her eye. 'You're fine, are you?' she says. 'You've been sitting in that lounge moping for days.'

'Not for days, just—'

'What's done is done,' Sascha interrupts. Sometimes I feel like I can't get a full sentence out in front of her anymore. She's bossier than ever since she fell pregnant. 'You can't change what happened at the café but you have to stop blaming yourself. We all make mistakes; it's how we rectify them that counts.'

'Do you think this will work?' I ask.

'Having the champagne tea at the pub?'

I nod.

'I do actually, I think it's going to work perfectly.'

'And you don't think people will think it a bit much that I'm having a New Year celebration anyway, despite the fact I nearly burned the town down?'

Sascha sighs impatiently.

'You didn't burn the town down. There was a small but unfortunately timed fire at your café and anyway everybody wants cake and champagne and nobody will think it's too much – whatever that means.' She pauses, putting her hand on my arm. 'Look, Ellie, I know this feels like shit and I know how I'd feel if it was the hotel. I know it's so uncertain and you still don't know if the insurance will cover it. But I promise you that nobody thinks badly of you. The only person blaming you is you.' She pauses. 'We are all blaming Marcus though,' she says with a grin.

'Just as he was hoping people would start to accept him as well.'

She nudges me as we walk towards the pub. 'Everything will be OK you know,' she says. 'It always is in the end.'

I take a breath. I know she's right. I know I'm being way too hard on myself. I feel as though I've become complacent and settled in Sanderson Bay as it started to feel like the home I'd been looking for my whole life. I feel as though the fire happed to bring me back down to earth. But I know that's nonsense. I know this town is my home and that it has been since I was a teenager.

And I know that if I've got the backing of the town, if they really don't blame me, then I'll get through this somehow.

'You're right,' I say quietly.

'Of course I am,' she replies, squeezing my arm one last time. 'I always am. Now come on or we'll be late.'

'Late for what?' I ask as she marches on ahead of me.

She turns to look at me over her shoulder. 'You'll see.'

Half the town are at The Black Horse when we arrive – all the Knitting Club ladies are there, as is Geoff – who I thought was still at the hotel – and James, Abi and Marcus are sitting together deep in conversation, so even if the whole town does blame Marcus some people are still talking to him at least. Eric is at the back of the pub by the window having an animated conversation with somebody who I can't make out because the light is behind them. As I look around the pub, the person Eric is talking to turns around and my heart skips a beat.

Ben.

He grins at me and I can't help smiling back. What happened in the café just before Christmas fades away a little, because despite that, despite what I said to him, despite what he didn't say to me, he's here, right in the middle of my crisis, and he's smiling at me. I want to go over to him and rest my head on his shoulder. I want to hear him tell me everything will be OK. I want to talk to him, to hear his side of the story – if even Marcus thinks it's worth listening to then I owe Ben that much.

The fire and the long days sitting on my own in the hotel have helped me get some perspective on a lot of things. Finding out about my mother and talking to Dad have helped me understand that there are different sides to every story and that sometimes we think we're doing the right thing, even when other people might not see it that way.

I can't go over to him right now though, in front of half of Sanderson Bay.

'What are you all doing here?' I ask.

'Everyone's here for you, love,' Miranda says. 'To see what needs doing, to see how we can help and to make this the best New Year's Eve Sanderson Bay has ever seen!'

'Thank you,' I say quietly.

'And,' Terry says stepping out from behind the bar, 'we wanted to show you this.'

Everyone steps to one side as Terry leads me towards the alcove at the back of the pub. When I see what everyone has done, my breath catches in my throat and those tears threaten to make a comeback.

'What do you think?' Terry asks. 'Will it do?'

All the pub furniture has been moved from the large alcove and replaced with what can only be described as a mini version of The Two Teas.

'It's perfect,' I say. 'I can't believe you did this. How did you do it?'

'Well Bessie whipped up the bunting,' Terry says. 'Just like she did for the café and your aunt got the teapots and teacups.'

'Guilty as charged,' Miranda says from behind me. 'When they gave you and Marcus the all clear to go and collect some of your things I asked if I could get a few things too. I collected as may teapots and cups as I could and took them home and washed them thinking they might come in handy.'

'Which they have,' James says grinning.

'And what about the table and chairs?' I ask.

'That was young Ben,' Eric says from where he and Ben are still standing by the window. 'He got them on the internet and we all mucked in to paint them white first thing this morning. It's not the best paint job but it'll do in the circumstances.'

I press my hand to my mouth, speechless in the face of the kindness of this community I've become a part of.

And Ben. He didn't have to do a thing and yet...

'How did you know?' I ask. 'How did you know to get the table and chairs?'

Ben looks as though he's about to say something but Sascha butts in.

'That was me,' she says. 'I had his email address from when he stayed at the hotel and you weren't going to get in touch with him so I did.'

'Isn't that breaching all sorts of data protection laws?' I ask.

She shrugs, completely unconcerned. Ben says, 'I don't mind. I won't sue her I promise.'

There's a rumble of laughter through the pub, which turns into general chat, which in turn makes people thirsty and Terry is soon back behind the bar serving drinks. I want to go and talk to Ben, to ask him why he's here, where he got the chairs from and so many other things but I can't get to him. I feel Miranda's hand on my arm.

'What do you think?' she asks quietly.

'To this mini café in the pub idea or to Ben's arrival?' I ask.

'Either.'

'Overwhelmed to be honest. But in a good way.'

'Ellie!' someone calls from the other side of the pub. I turn around and see Mo gesturing at me to join her in the pub kitchen.

'I'd better go,' I say to my aunt. I walk over to Mo, a route that means I don't pass Ben. Sascha follows me.

'Right, you two,' Mo says to us. 'We need to talk about food for New Year's Eve and where it's all going to be prepared.' She leads the way into the pub kitchen, which is quiet, still and gleamingly clean after the lunch rush.

'Obviously I can store food in our fridges but I can't offer up the kitchens for prep as we've still got tomorrow's lunch and dinner and New Year's Eve lunch to do first.'

'We can use the hotel kitchen,' Sascha says. 'We're so quiet at the moment we're not offering evening meals, so we only have breakfast to do.'

'What needs doing, Ellie?' Mo asks.

My gaze flicks between the two of them. 'What do you mean?' I ask.

'For the champagne tea party on New Years' Eve,' Sascha says softly, her hand on the small of my back. 'What do we need to do to prepare?'

My stomach drops as I think about all the things I would have spent the last few days getting ready if I'd been in the café. I don't see how we can do this in time.

'Everything needs preparing,' I say. 'I was going to cancel the whole event so I haven't done anything and I don't see how we can get it done in time now.'

'Of course we can if we work together,' Sascha says and Mo nods in agreement.

'I really appreciate everything you've done and I can't believe you've all been painting furniture for me all morning but…' I trail off. 'And Ben's here, I should go…'

'Ellie, focus,' Sascha says. 'I know this is tough, I get it. But you have a whole town full of people who want to help so tell us what needs doing. Then you can go and talk to Ben.' She smiles at me and it's so reassuring I feel my shoulders melt away from my ears a centimetre or two for the first time since the fire.

'OK,' I say. 'Well we need to bake cakes and scones – at

least one of the cakes needs to be Christmassy. We need butter, jam and cream for the scones. We need to make sandwiches so we'll need bread, ham, cheese and eggs but we can get all of those from the shop. I need the three-tiered stands to serve the afternoon teas on so I hope Miranda salvaged them otherwise I'll need permission to go back to the café to get them. And of course I'll need tea and champagne.'

'We can provide the champagne,' Mo says.

'And I've got lots of your teas that we use at the hotel so you can have them,' Sascha says. 'It'll be a more limited selection than you're used to but needs must.'

'You and I can do an early morning trip to the cash and carry, Ellie,' Mo says. 'We can get everything you need so start making a list.'

'And the Knitting Club girls will all help with the baking that we can do in the hotel kitchens tomorrow,' Sascha says.

'Really?' I stare at them and feel a fizz of excitement in my stomach. Maybe we can actually pull this off.

'Really,' Sascha replies. 'Now go and talk to Ben.'

'I'll pick you up around seven tomorrow morning for the cash and carry,' Mo says as I start to walk away.

He's wearing a green and white striped shirt and a dark green pullover that makes his eyes look almost blue. He smiles at me as I walk towards him and my stomach turns somersaults.

'Ellie,' he says. His voice is barely more than a whisper. I feel as though everyone is staring at us.'

'What are you doing here, Ben?' I ask as we sit down. 'I mean I know Sascha called you but—'

'I wanted to be here, Ellie,' he says putting his hand over mine. 'When she told me about the fire I wanted to do something. I wanted to help.'

'The fire was all my fault,' I say. 'I don't deserve all this kindness.'

'The fire was Marcus's fault and nobody got hurt as I understand it,' he replies. 'People make stupid mistakes, Ellie, and I can hardly judge anyone after the stupid mistake I made with you.'

'This is different. Somebody nearly did get hurt. If Marcus hadn't—'

'Ellie,' he interrupts gently. 'It's not different. I hurt you.'

I don't say anything for a moment, because what he says is true. He did hurt me.

'I should have told you about Moby's plans right from the start.'

We stare at each other for a moment.

'It's good to see you,' I say.

'You too.'

'Thank you for the table and chairs – they're perfect.'

'You're welcome. Don't be angry with me but I didn't get them off the internet.'

'Where did you get them?' I ask.

'Well... I knew of a Moby's franchise just outside York that was having a refurb and I know how Moby's just tend to throw out any unwanted furniture so I went and collected them for you.' He pauses. 'Do you hate them now you know they're from Moby's?'

I laugh again. 'Of course not, I quite like the idea to be honest. But isn't that like stealing from work?'

'Nobody will know.'

'How long are you staying?' I ask.

'I have to go back to York this afternoon,' he says. 'Couple of things I promised I'd do for Mum. But I was wondering if you had some time before I leave. There's something I want to show you.'

29

'I owe you a huge apology, Ellie,' Ben says as we step out of the pub on to the High Street.

I want to wave his apologies away and avoid talking about this. I want to just hold on to the feeling I had when I first saw him, when he first smiled at me. But I know we have to have this conversation. Neither of us will be able to move on if we don't.

'I should never have allowed myself to get so close to you,' he goes on.

My stomach drops. It feels as though he regrets what happens between us.

I have no regrets, he'd said.

'No,' I say looking straight ahead as we walk down the street. I have no idea where we are heading. 'Perhaps you shouldn't. I don't want you to feel as though you regret the time we spent together.'

I hear him stop walking and I stop too, turning towards him.

'Is that what you think?' he asks. 'That I regret what happened between us?'

'You just said you should never have let it happen.'

'I should never have let it happen without telling you the truth, without telling you the full story about why I was really here.'

'To persuade me to sell the café to Moby's.'

'That wasn't the reason I came back,' he says. But his eyes flick away and I don't know whether he's telling the truth or not. I wonder what I was expecting. Did I expect him to be more apologetic? More contrite? In many ways he was just doing his job. But I had thought what happened between us had been special. Maybe I'm wrong?

I'm sure I'm not wrong though.

He turns and walks towards the promenade. I walk next to him just out of reach.

'I don't quite know how it happened,' he says as we walk. I have to strain to hear him as the cold wind whistles in off the sea and I wrap my coat more tightly around myself. 'I work in marketing not acquisitions. Persuading people to sell their cafés to us isn't in my job description, but my line manger found out that I came from Sanderson Bay and that I was planning to visit before Christmas.'

I turn slightly towards him. 'So you'd planned to visit anyway? You didn't come specifically for Moby's?'

'No,' he says. 'I'd been thinking about coming back for a while. I had some annual leave owing and it seemed as good a time as any. I didn't want Mum to know at first, I just wanted to see what it felt like being back here as an adult.'

I think about Paris and how I've avoided it for so long. It was brave of Ben to come back on his own. Paris is a huge city. I can pretend I'm just another tourist when I finally do go back, with or without my father, but Sanderson Bay is a different story entirely – people here still remember who he is and, presumably, how his father died.

'I was asked to check out the café whilst I was here,' he goes on. 'I was told that Moby's had been trying to buy it from a couple who were retiring but the sale fell through and Moby's wanted to know if the owners had changed their mind.'

'That's why you seemed so surprised when you found out that I was Eloise Caron,' I say.

He nods. 'They gave me your name but they'd given me the impression that you were…' He pauses, a half-smile on his lips. 'Somewhat older,' he finishes.

'Moby's had mixed up their facts,' I say, mostly to myself.

'So it would seem,' Ben replies. 'As soon as I saw you, as soon as I realised who you were and that the café was yours, I knew I couldn't do it. I couldn't possibly get you to sell to Moby's.'

'I'd never have said yes however hard you tried if that makes you feel any better.'

'It really doesn't,' he says with a sigh and carries on walking towards the green where the war memorial is and I follow.

'What did you want to show me?' I ask.

Next to the war memorial is a smaller sculpture that marks the lifeboat disaster of 2000 – several years before my aunt and uncle moved to Sanderson Bay, several years before I'd even heard of the place. Ben walks towards this smaller memorial and beckons me over. Six men lost their lives that afternoon when a storm came out of nowhere and a two-man yacht had got into trouble. Four of the lifeboat crew and the two people in the yacht never returned – Eric had been in the crew that night and had been one of the lucky ones. The bodies of those who died were never recovered. It happened two nights before Christmas and suddenly everything clicks into place as Ben runs his finger over one of the names on the memorial.

Alistair Christian Lawson.

'Was that your dad?' I ask.

Ben nods slowly and then goes to sit down on a nearby bench, wrapping his coat around him. After a moment I sit next to him.

'We'd had this enormous row,' he says quietly. 'That afternoon…' He pauses, rubs his eyes. 'Christ it all seems so stupid now. So pointless.'

'You don't have to tell me this,' I say.

He drops his hands and turns to me. He looks exhausted.

'I do,' he says. 'I should have told you this weeks ago. I should have told you when you first told me about your mum but I've never…' He stops, his breath hitching. 'I've never really known how to talk to anyone about any of this.'

I watch him take a breath and I wait for him to continue, a knot already forming in my stomach. I already know what he's going to tell me – that night changed Sanderson Bay forever. Even those of us who didn't live here then know that much.

'I'd wanted to go to this party,' Ben begins. 'A friend of mine had an older sister – only a couple of years older but that means a lot when you're fifteen – and she was having a pre-Christmas party, but my dad didn't want me to go, said I was too young. It was just an ordinary argument really, typical of teenagers and their parents when the kids are trying to push boundaries. A normal argument on a normal day. Except it wasn't a normal day...' He breaks off, pausing for a moment.

'It had been a beautiful morning,' he goes on. 'Cold and clear and still and lots of people were here practising for that ridiculous Brass Monkeys race. The storm hadn't been forecast to come this far south. All of the boats that had been out practising got back before the storm got really bad, all except one anyway. Apparently they were just kids, not very experienced. They probably didn't even see the storm coming until it was too late.'

He stops and leans forward, his elbows on his knees.

'The last words I said to him were "you needn't think I'm staying at home, spending another evening in with you".' Ben squeezes his eyes shut as though he's trying not to cry. 'And I never got to spend any time with him again.'

The knot in my stomach has moved up to my throat. The feelings Ben is talking about are so familiar to me – our stories so similar. Perhaps I'd always known that.

I know what it feels like when the last thing you said to somebody before they died was something you wish beyond all else that you could take back.

'That's why you got so upset at those customers in the café and why you went out and got drunk that evening,' I say.

He nods.

'And why you gave Eric so much money at the carol singing. They had record takings this year.'

'I had to do something,' he replies. 'It's all I could think of.'

'The local RNLI will be beyond grateful. You must know better than anyone how strapped for cash they can be.'

'I'm so sorry, Ellie.'

'You don't need to be,' I say. 'I understand.'

He turns to me. 'I thought you might.'

'My mum died of a brain aneurysm,' I say. 'It was totally out of the blue. One minute she was alive and writing her ground-breaking book on Mary Shelley and the next she was gone. When my father found her she was just sitting at her desk. At first he thought she was just thinking...' I break off at the thought, the lump in my throat making it hard for me to speak at all. 'It was a few days before her birthday and I hadn't seen her since I'd come back to England at the end of the summer. I'd never understood why my parents had abandoned me at boarding school and I'd tried to talk to my mother about it that summer but it had been so hard to get the truth out of her. When she took me to Marseilles airport on the last morning I saw her I asked her a question I wish I had never asked.'

Ben sits up and turns towards me.

'Ellie,' he says. 'It's OK.'

I shake my head. 'It's not though, is it? You know that as well as I do. We say these awful things to the people we love – horrible throwaway comments and then we never see them again and...' The tears that have been burning the backs of my eyes start to fall down my cheeks. I feel Ben shift in the seat next to me.

'I asked her if she had ever really loved me,' I say. 'She

said that of course she loved me and I told her she had a funny way of showing it. That was the last time I ever saw her. We spoke on the phone every week of course but neither of us ever acknowledged that conversation again and for the last ten years I haven't been able to get it out of my head.'

Ben doesn't say anything, but I'm very aware of his leg against mine, very aware of the proximity of him.

'Have you ever spoken to your mum about what happened?' I ask. 'You said you didn't tell her that you were coming to the Bay at first but have you ever talked about it?'

'Not really,' he replies. 'Not in any sort of meaningful way. She still gets so upset and when I told her that I'd come back here she was furious with me at first. We had this awful row. She seems to have come around a bit now but...' He trails off, shrugs.

'I found some stuff out about my mum at Christmas,' I say quietly. 'Some things about my parents that helped me understand what happened over the years.' I want to tell him everything but I know now isn't the time. Perhaps there will be another time in the future when I can tell him everything, perhaps there won't be. I know that finally talking to my dad has helped. Perhaps if Ben talks to his mum he'll feel the same. 'I had a proper talk to my father on Christmas Day – it was the first time we'd had a real conversation in years, perhaps since my mother died.'

'You think I should try to talk to Mum?' Ben asks.

'It might help,' I reply. 'You might be surprised.'

'Maybe,' he says quietly.

We sit staring at the lifeboat memorial for a while, neither of us speaking.

'Thank you for telling me about your dad,' I say eventually. 'I get it, I really do.'

'I should have told you right from the start.'

'You don't owe me any sort of explanation about your father or your grief,' I reply. 'But you should have told me about Moby's.'

'I thought I could fix it without you ever being the wiser, which was stupid of me. But when I saw you in the café on that first night, when I saw what you'd done to it, what you'd created, I knew you'd never sell and the more I got to know you, the more I realised what the café meant to both you and the community around you. I just couldn't bring myself to tell you that Moby's were still interested. So when I went back to London I tried to persuade the acquisitions department that it wasn't the right place for Moby's to open up, that it wasn't somewhere that liked chains or franchises. I spent days trying to find other places in the area that they might be more interested in, hours in meetings trying to tell them they were barking up the wrong tree with you.'

'Is that what you were working on?' I ask. 'Is that why you were so busy?'

'Yes, and by the time I took you out to dinner I thought I'd manged to convince them. I'd found somewhere else further up the coast.'

'Why did they send the plans then?' I ask. 'And why did they send them to the café?'

He rubs a hand over his face. 'Because I'm an idiot,' he

says. 'I naively thought they'd actually listened to me. But instead they upped the offer. They knew I was coming back to the Bay so they sent the whole sales pack again. I asked why they sent it to the café and they told me it was an oversight, a mistake but—'

'But what?' I ask.

'Knowing Moby's I suspect they sent it to the café on purpose so that you'd see it and I couldn't hide it from you.'

'Really? You think they'd be that underhand?'

'I've known them to do worse.'

I think about everything Sascha has told me about Moby's when she worked in their legal team. '*They have a way of taking over,*' she'd said.

'You should have told me, Ben,' I say. 'You should have told me right from the start but thank you anyway.'

'Thank you?' he says, his brow furrowing. 'What on earth do you have to thank me for?'

'Thank you for fighting for my little café. Thank you for persuading Moby's to leave me alone.'

'Sanderson Bay is not the right location for Moby's to open up,' he says. 'Even after Karol Bergenstein has made it famous.'

'They were going to build over my herb garden,' I say. This still upsets me more than anything. 'I've had that herb garden for over half of my life.'

'I know,' he says softly. He places his hand gently on my shoulder and for a moment I just want to melt into him, feel his arms around me, feel his lips on mine.

'I handed in my notice,' he says into the silence.

'You have?'

'I hated that job and I was doing it for all the wrong reasons. Seeing you here in the Bay and your incredible café made me realise that we don't have to stay in jobs we hate just to please other people.'

'Especially if those people are dead,' I say quietly.

'Especially then.'

'But don't you have to work out a notice or something?'

He shakes his head. 'No,' he says. 'They put me on immediate gardening leave. I don't think they were very happy with me.'

'I'm not surprised.' I smile. 'What with stealing furniture and stopping acquisitions.'

'Those tables and chairs aren't stolen!' He laughs and for moment the tension between us splinters.

'What will you do now?' I ask.

'I have no idea,' he replies and I look up towards him, his eyes locking on mine.

'Do you think you could ever trust me after all this?' he asks. 'Is there any chance we can start again?'

He looks as though he has lost everything, which in some ways I guess he has. I lean my head on his shoulder. He lied to me by omission but I'm so glad he came back and explained everything and I'm glad that Sascha and Marcus were right about Ben trying to stop Moby's interest in The Two Teas.

The feelings I had from him right from the start haven't gone away. If anything they've got stronger, but can I trust him?

'What are you doing on New Year's Eve?' I ask.

'Nothing planned,' he replies, pretending to act casually but I can feel the tension in his body again.

'Would you like to come to the champagne tea?'

I feel him relax and soften next to me, hear him puff out a laugh.

'I wouldn't miss it for the world.'

30

I spend most of the next day in the hotel kitchen with Sascha, Bessie, Miranda and various members of the Knitting Club getting the food ready for New Year's Eve.

'Right,' Sascha says to us all, clearly in her bossy element. 'You've all been allocated specific parts of the kitchen to do your baking so try and stay in your area and make sure you clean as you go.'

'Ready, get set, bake,' Bessie whispers to me, parodying a popular TV baking show. I try to hide my smile as I start preparing to make the scones we'll need for the champagne teas tomorrow.

'What are you baking, Sascha?' Bessie asks. Bessie is baking a "quick and easy" Christmas cake. I'd had a look at the recipe earlier, just after Mo and I got back from the cash and carry. I didn't think it looked easy at all but Bessie is a much better baker than me. For someone who specialises in afternoon teas I'm not a great baker– scones are pretty much my limit. 'It won't be as good as a real Christmas cake,' Bessie had said. 'But it should do the job.'

'I'm baking my infamous black bean brownies,' Sascha says. These aren't really Sascha's infamous brownies at all. She managed to get the recipe off a café owner in York who has been serving them for years and the story goes that she in turn got the recipe from her best friend's brother-in-law London. 'I'm giving them a Christmas twist.'

'What sort of Christmas twist?' I ask. Unlike everyone else she hasn't run her recipe by me, she's just taken matters into her own hands and I hope her twist isn't too *avant-garde*.

'I'm putting little sugar holly leaves on top of them,' she says.

'That's a twist I can live with,' I reply with a smile.

My aunt is making tiny sugar cookies in the shape of angels, which we used to make together when I was younger. Every now and then I glance over to where she is working to make sure she is OK and not in pain. She is working more slowly than she used to but she seems to be all right.

Halfway through the morning Lisa arrives with extra flour, sugar and eggs to make Christmas blondies.

'What are they?' Bessie asks.

'Like brownies but yellow,' Sascha says, not looking up from the bowl of black beans she seems to be mashing to death.

'Pretty much.' Lisa grins as she unpacks her ingredients. 'They use vanilla instead of cocoa powder but otherwise the recipe is similar to traditional brownies. As it's Christmas I'm adding some crushed M&Ms to the mix – but just the red and green ones.'

'Does that mean the other colours are going spare?' I ask hopefully as Lisa puts a bag of M&Ms – in all colours except red and green – on the counter.

'Sure does,' she says as we all help ourselves.

Between baking and gorging ourselves on M&Ms the morning passes quickly and it's not long before the glorious smell of baked goods is permeating from the two industrial ovens in the hotel kitchen.

'So tell me how the afternoon teas will be served,' Lisa says.

'Well I'll serve them on the three-tier plates as usual,' I reply. 'Each person will get one of Miranda's biscuits, a blondie, a brownie and a piece of Christmas cake on the top tier. The second tier will be scones – a choice of plain, fruit or cheese – and then the bottom tier will be the finger sandwiches – I think I'm going to do ham, cheese, egg, and cucumber.'

'And you're making them tomorrow?'

'Yes Mo and I will make them in the pub kitchen right before the tea takes place so they are nice and fresh. Nobody wants soggy sandwiches.' I pause for a moment and feel the familiar sinking feeling I get in my stomach every time I think about the café and what happened and the water and smoke-damaged walls. 'It's not ideal…' I say quietly.

'It's going to be brilliant,' Lisa says squeezing my arm and when I look up everyone nods in agreement.

'What about teas?' Bessie asks.

'Well it's going to be quite a limited selection,' I say, thinking again about the café and all the teas that are in there that eventually I'll have to throw away and start again. 'Darjeeling, Earl Grey and English breakfast for the black tea drinkers and I've got rooibos and camomile for people who want a decaf option.' I'd scavenged these few together from the hotel's tea selection. Sascha and Geoff buy their teas from me so at least I know they'll be top quality.

'I know it's not your usual extensive selection, love,'

Miranda says. 'But it's more than enough.' None of it feels enough to me and yet at the same time it feels too much, more than I deserve in the circumstances.

'What about coffee?' Bessie asks hopefully.

'We'll be at the pub, Bessie,' I reply. 'You can have all the fancy cappuccinos you desire!'

'And champagne,' Lisa says. 'Lots of champagne. It is New Year after all!'

I don't feel as though I have much to celebrate, but as I look around the kitchen at this incredible group of women who have helped me in so many ways, and not just today, I know that I am fortunate beyond measure.

'So you're going to leave it until January then?' Sascha asks later that day as we sit in her and Geoff's private apartment at the hotel eating stolen Christmas brownies and blondies that I hope we won't need tomorrow.

'James said there was no point getting into it all with the insurers in between Christmas and New Year as they'll be working on a skeleton staff and that he'd help me next week. He's right but I feel as though I'm in limbo.'

'In what way?'

'I just wish I knew what, if anything, will be covered. I'm terrified that the insurance won't cover it at all.'

'I've told you that the whole town will help you out if it doesn't,' Sascha says. 'What does your uncle say?'

Before he moved to the seaside and bought a café my uncle was as surveyor and what he doesn't know about buildings isn't worth knowing. When he and Miranda first moved to Sanderson Bay he renovated and rebuilt the café pretty much single-handed.

'He said that he built the café once and he'll do it again if he has to.'

'There you go then.'

'But he shouldn't have to. I should have checked that Marcus hadn't overloaded the plug socket. I shouldn't have left the Christmas tree lights on—'

'Oh my God, Ellie,' Sascha interrupts my spiralling thoughts. It's been happening a lot since the fire, as though I've taken a big step back and all the anxiety I had when I was in York has come back. I feel as though I'm not enough – not good enough, not clever enough, not successful enough. 'You have to stop blaming yourself for this. It was an accident. It says so in the fire officer's report.'

'I can't stop thinking about it,' I admit. 'Every time I close my eyes I see the smoke billowing out of the café door on Boxing Day. I feel like I did before I came to Sanderson Bay, as though nothing I do will ever be right.'

Sascha reaches over and puts her hand on top of mine.

'It's normal to feel like this,' she says. 'I'd be more worried if you didn't to be honest. Over the last week you've found out some truths about your family, finally had a proper conversation with your dad and watched your livelihood burn down.'

'Harsh,' I say quietly.

'But true. You're going to feel sad and anxious and angry. But you don't need to keep blaming yourself.' She pauses. 'It was Marcus's fault,' she says.

I open my mouth to protest but she holds up her hand. 'I

don't want to hear that guff about the buck stopping with you anymore. Marcus always was trouble and he's been nothing but trouble since he arrived here.'

'Without him I'd never have found out about Moby's,' I say.

'And would it have mattered if you didn't? Ben was trying to get them to look somewhere else, so while he might not have been entirely honest with you he was looking out for you. Marcus was just stirring because he couldn't bear to see you moving on with someone else.'

I take a breath. 'I know,' I say. 'I just like to see the best in everyone.'

'I know you do, El, but maybe letting Marcus stay wasn't your wisest idea.'

'Maybe not.'

'I hear he's getting on very well with your Abi,' Sascha goes on.

'Well he'd better not break her heart too,' I reply.

'Speaking of after New Year,' Sascha says. 'Have you spoken to your dad again about your plans? Have you told him about the fire?'

'Not yet. He was planning to come over in January. I was going to show him the café but now it's just a burnt-out shell.'

A bubble of laughter erupts out of her. 'A burnt-out shell,' she says. 'You do exaggerate – you've clearly been spending too much time with me. It's perfectly structurally sound, it just needs a bit of a refit – and your uncle will help with that, you know he will. And maybe your dad can help out too. What's he like with a hammer?'

I stare at her. If Sascha had ever met my father she'd know what a ridiculous question that was.

'I don't think my father has ever lifted a hammer in his life,' I say.

'Well maybe he can help some other way,' she replies. 'The point is that this is Sanderson Bay. We pull together when we need to and we make sure everybody is all right. This isn't any different.'

I rub my eyes with my other hand. 'Oh I'm sorry, Sash,' I say. 'I'm being ridiculous, I know, and in all this fuss I haven't asked how you are.'

'I'm fine,' she replies dismissively.

'Really?'

'I'm exhausted,' she admits. 'They say the first trimester is the worst so I'm hoping to start feeling full of second-trimester energy any day now. Plus my back hurts already so I'm looking forward to getting back to Pilates next week.'

'That's another thing,' I say. 'Where are we going to do Pilates?'

'Don't worry so much, Ellie – we'll find somewhere. Maybe we can do that in the pub too.'

I laugh at the thought of us on the floor of the pub practising Pilates. 'Well it would give the town something to talk about I guess.'

'Seriously, we'll find somewhere. We can move the furniture in the dining room – we won't be doing weekday evening meals until at least March and you'll be up and running again by then.'

I don't say anything. I hope she's right.

'Anyway, when's Ben coming back?'

'He didn't give me a time,' I reply. 'He just said he was going to be here for New Year. I know he and his mum find this time of year really hard.'

Sascha nods. I'd told her about Ben's father being one of the lifeboat volunteers in the storm of 2000.

'So are you going to forgive him for the whole Moby's thing?' she asks.

'I know he was trying to do the right thing,' I reply. 'And I know Marcus was stirring up trouble but—'

'So it's on?' Sascha interrupts.

'Me and Ben? I don't know.'

'You should give it a chance. It might be exactly what you need right now.'

'Really?' I look at her gleeful face. 'There's so much going on at the moment, so much I need to think about. It doesn't seem like the right time to start a new relationship, especially one that got off to such a rocky start.'

'You like him don't you?'

I nod. 'Yeah, I like him. A lot.'

'If you wait for the right time you'll be waiting forever,' Sascha says sagely. 'There's never a right time to start something new so you may as well go for it and see what happens.'

31

'Ready?' Mo asks as we put the finishing touches to the three-tier afternoon tea plates, which are now piled up with sandwiches, scones, butter, jam, cream and individual slices of Christmas cake, blondie and brownie. My aunt's angel biscuits take pride of place on the top tier.

'As I'll ever be,' I reply. Nothing about this is how I'd planned but I'm beginning to learn that life doesn't have a plan. Most of the time we don't seem to have any control so it's best to just try to go with the flow and make the most of every moment. Despite how beautiful Terry and Mo have made my corner of the pub look, it's not The Two Teas and there is a part of me that would have been much more comfortable cancelling this evening altogether, but I know that would have been a cop-out. Hiding away in the hotel burying my head in the sand and ignoring what has happened at the café wouldn't have helped. I need to be out here, showing that I'm still a part of the community, that I'm sorry for any trouble Marcus and I have caused, and that the café will be business as usual as soon as possible. Even if that doesn't feel as though it's true.

'Right,' Mo says. 'I'll start taking these plates out to the hungry hordes and you start bringing the tea. Once all that's done we'll start serving the champagne.'

The little alcove of the pub that has been transformed into The Two Teas for the occasion is buzzing with excited chat when I walk out into the pub with the first two teapots – Darjeeling for my aunt and, in the light of us not having any Assam, Earl Grey for Lisa. Everyone has pre-ordered their tea and sandwich fillings so all I have to do is make sure everyone has what they want. I feel a huge wave of relief wash over me when I see all the friendly faces smiling and chatting away. I can even almost tolerate the terrible tacky Christmas music that Terry has put on.

The champagne tea is taking place earlier than I'd originally planned so that Terry can get the pub ready for his New Year's Eve quiz, but it doesn't seem to have put anybody off – everyone who booked is here plus a few extras squeezed into the small space. I'm particularly surprised to see Celia back, sitting next to Sascha and chatting away as though the two of them are the best friends in the world. Sascha had mentioned feeling guilty about how she'd treated her mother-in-law; she'd even mentioned feeling bad that Celia would be on her own for New Year but she hadn't mentioned this. Clearly Sanderson Bay is weaving its magic once again.

But there is one person missing and when I realise my stomach drops.

Ben.

I wouldn't miss it for the world.

'Hello, Celia,' I say as I take her and Sascha's tea over. 'It's nice to see you again.'

'It's nice to be back,' Celia replies. 'I was just telling Sascha that she should do afternoon teas at the hotel and—'

'I've told you, Celia, I'm not treading on Ellie's toes,' Sascha snaps back. So Celia may be here for New Year but nothing has changed it seems.

As I move away Sascha touches my arm. 'He'll be here,' she whispers to me.

But I'm not here to moon over Ben, I'm here to work.

I spend the rest of the afternoon delivering more tea and sandwiches to everyone who wants them and stopping to chat to everyone, thanking them for supporting the café even when it's not open. I'm surrounded by a chorus of 'If there's anything I can do to help…' as everyone wants to do what they can to get the café up and running again as quickly as possible. The sense of support and community is so strong that it's almost overwhelming and, during a quiet moment I sneak into the ladies' just to have a few minutes to myself.

I lean my head against the cold tiles on the wall of the bathroom and take a few breaths. Everything is going to be all right, I tell myself. Nobody blames me for the fire except me and the whole town seems to have forgiven Marcus for his various misdemeanours, more interested in his near-death experience in the fire. I just have to forgive myself and move on.

'Are you OK, Ellie?' my aunt's voice interrupts my thoughts.

'I'm fine,' I say, turning towards her. 'So much has happened over the last week and I've had so much support from you and James and from the town in general. Everyone knows everybody's business here but it's worth it.'

'I've always thought so,' Miranda says holding out her arms to me. I step towards her and she envelops me in a hug. She smells of the lavender perfume she has always worn and it takes me back to being a lonely teenager who missed her mum.

'Thank you for telling me about *Maman*,' I say.

'Perhaps I should have told you sooner. I'm sorry, I was only trying to protect you.'

'Perhaps I don't need quite so much protection anymore,' I reply thinking again of Ben and how he didn't tell me about the plans that Moby's had for my café because he was trying to protect me. 'I'm stronger than everyone thinks, stronger than I think.'

'You're right,' Miranda says, stepping away from me. 'You are and your café are such an important part of this community. Everyone wants it back up and running as quickly as possible and we'll all help.'

I nod. 'I know,' I say. I notice a wince of pain flash across my aunt's face. 'Are you OK?' I ask.

'I'm as OK as I'll ever be, Ellie,' she replies. 'I have to learn to live with this condition and you and your uncle have to learn to stop fussing all the time. I have good days and bad days.'

'Do you need to go home to rest?'

'What did I just say about fussing?' Miranda laughs. 'No I'm in for the long haul. Do you think The Teacups can win the pub quiz tonight?'

Not without Ben, I think.

'No,' I reply. 'But we'll give it a good hard crack!'

'Why don't you go back to the hotel for a little while and have a rest?' Miranda says.

'I wouldn't mind getting a shower before the pub quiz, but I should stay and help Terry and Mo clear up.'

'Your uncle can do that. You've been working flat out for the last three days to get this ready. Go and have a rest. I need you on top form to beat The Brainboxes!'

My phone buzzes as I'm straightening my hair in my room in preparation for the continued New Year's Eve celebrations at the pub.

He's here, Sascha's text reads. *He had car trouble apparently, which is why he's so late but he's here. Where are you?*

My heart turns over in my chest and I look at my reflection in the mirror. He's here, Ben is here and I still haven't decided what I want to say to him.

On my way, I text back non-committally.

I finish doing my hair and add a swipe of red lipstick to contrast the black tea dress with a cherry pattern on it that I've chosen to wear for the evening.

If you wait for the right time you'll be waiting forever, Sascha had said. And Sascha is an expert at waiting forever, waiting patiently for years to fall pregnant. And then there's Marcus who went to the other side of the world to find something that wasn't there, something he only started to find when he came back to Sanderson Bay, a place he'd always disliked.

Maybe there isn't such a thing as the right time. Maybe there is just time. You can make all the plans in the world but the "right time" happens by chance when you turn up in the same place as somebody or something else. Some people call it fate.

I've never believed in fate, but when I look back at how

my life has turned out, the big things have always happened when I've least expected them.

When I'm at rock bottom.

And when I'm least ready.

Like taking over the café.

Like meeting Ben.

I take one last look at myself in the mirror, switch off my hair straighteners and pick up my coat.

I'm ready.

32

He's the first person, the only person, I see when I walk back into The Black Horse. Our eyes lock and he grins at me as my stomach fizzes. He's wearing a pale blue shirt, rolled up to the elbows, and dark jeans. For a moment he takes my breath away.

'Ellie,' he says softly as he walks up to me, placing his hands on my shoulders. 'I'm so sorry I was late. The car was playing up and—'

I place the flat of my hand on his chest and a rush of desire washes over me as I feel the planes of muscle under his clothes and remember the nights we spent together.

'It's OK,' I say. 'It doesn't matter. You're here now.'

'You look amazing,' he whispers, dropping his hands by his sides.

'Thank you. But are you ready?'

'Ready for what?'

'Ready to help The Teacups win this quiz of course. We haven't won since you were last on our team.'

'Won't I be seen as a plant?' He smiles at me, his grey eyes twinkling.

'Who cares? Everyone will be too drunk to notice.'

I gently wrap my fingers around his and we walk towards

the table where the other Teacups are waiting, pencils at the ready.

'Come on,' Sascha says. 'Terry's about to start. Thank God you're here, Ben, we might stand a chance of winning now.'

'So I understand,' Ben says as we sit down, our hands still interlocked. Sascha notices and raises her eyebrows at me but I look away. It doesn't matter if this isn't the right time, for tonight it just is.

The quiz questions start coming thick and fast and we all write down the answers that we know without discussion – partly so nobody else can overhear and partly because there simply isn't time for discussion as Terry is even faster than usual. He's probably eager to have a New Year's Eve drink himself.

Charlton Athletic, Oasis and Blur, Blue Peter, Edward Heath, we write in pencil on the answer sheet.

'And now it's time for the final question,' Terry announces with his usual drama.

There is a groan throughout the pub.

'Do you have to do this on New Year's Eve?' Eric shouts. 'These awful final questions that only Ben Lawson can answer.'

'Unfair advantage to The Teacups,' Clara shouts playfully at us.

'If you'd wanted him on your team you should have grabbed him before Ellie did,' Sascha calls back. Ben and I exchange a glance, dropping our heads to hide the colour in both our cheeks. I give Sascha a gentle kick under the table.

'What?' she says innocently.

'You know what,' I reply. Ben squeezes my hand.

'Quiet please for the final question,' Terry says, and the pub falls silent. Terry clears his throat loudly.

'Get on with it,' someone shouts.

'The final question is...' Terry pauses. 'Shopkeeper sounds ruder. I repeat, shopkeeper sounds ruder.'

We all turn to look at Ben who furrows his brow. Miranda pushes the answer sheet towards him.

'This shopkeeper will sound ruder if you don't quit these ridiculous questions,' Clara calls to Terry.

The Teacups wait in anticipation as Ben taps his pencil on the table.

We wait.

And we wait.

Hardly anyone in the pub makes a sound. I wonder if any of the other teams have worked it out.

Ben grins suddenly and writes a word on the answer sheet.

GROCER.

Grocer? I look at him quizzically.

'Trust me,' he says.

Those two words knock the breath out of me. I can trust him with Terry's final question but, as the quiz comes to an end and conversation starts up all around, I wonder if I can trust him in other ways too.

I look over at my aunt. Do I trust her?

Absolutely, is the automatic response in my mind. Even though she did exactly the same thing as Ben and kept something important from me in order to protect me.

If I can still trust Miranda then I can trust Ben can't I? Even though I've only known him a few weeks.

I take a breath. There's only one way to find out. I take his hand again and give it a squeeze and he turns to me, his eyes meeting mine. For a moment it feels like there is nobody else in the pub, just me and him.

'How on earth did you know the answer to that question, Ben?' my uncle asks.

'It's a homophone,' Ben says.

'A what?' Sascha asks.

'A word that sounds like another word,' Ben replies. 'Shopkeeper sounds ruder yeah?'

We all nod even though none of us understand.

'So we're looking for a word that sounds like shopkeeper and could mean ruder.'

'OK,' James says slowly.

'Another word for ruder could be grosser,' Ben goes on, writing GROSSER on a scrap of paper.

'And grosser becomes grocer!' Sascha crows as though it is her who worked out the answer.

'Well hopefully,' Ben says. 'I could be wrong.'

'You won't be,' I say quietly shuffling my chair closer to his. He wraps his arm around my waist and I rest my head on his shoulder. Sascha raises her eyebrows at me again but I just smile back. This is exactly where I want to be.

And we wait for the answers to Terry's New Year's Eve quiz.

Ben isn't wrong of course and The Teacups win by just one point.

'It was all in that final question,' James says holding out his hand to Ben. 'Well done, mate.' There's something about the way my uncle talks to Ben, the way he shakes his hand that makes me think he's somehow welcoming him to the family and my heart turns over again.

After the quiz is over and the usual complaints, swearing and accusations of "fixes" and "plants" have finished the rest of the evening becomes a blur of voices and people and glasses of wine. I talk to Marcus and Abi – who seem very much a couple tonight so that's something else Sascha was right about – to Eric and Bessie, to Clara and Lisa and every one of them asks me about Ben. Are we an item now? Will Ben be staying in Sanderson Bay? Will he help get the café back on its feet? Does he still work for Moby's?

Other than that last question I don't know the answers. I smile and nod and tell them that Ben and I still need to talk. Marcus tells me he's thinking of going back to Thailand in the new year and taking Abi with him.

'And what am I going to do for a waitress?' I ask. But I'm happy for him, happy he has someone to share his life with. It's not like the café is ready for business at the moment and, when it is, some of the local teenagers will be happy to help out.

'Are you still looking for something out in Thailand?' I ask, curious as to why he wants to go back.

He shakes his head. 'No,' he says. 'I think I found what I was looking for when I came here. Now I just want to share a beautiful country with Abi.'

I smile. 'It's funny how the two of you met here,' I say. 'The one place you always hated visiting.'

'Don't think that hadn't escaped my attention,' Marcus replies. 'And I'm not running away this time.'

'You're not?'

'No, we'll be back.'

RACHEL BURTON

'To Sanderson Bay?' I ask, surprised.

'I think everyone comes back to Sanderson Bay in the end, don't they?'

I look over towards Ben, who is chatting with Eric and Bessie, as Marcus says those words and I wonder if he will come back in the end. If he'll be able to face the tragedy of his father's death and live here happily.

It's nearly midnight before Ben and I catch a moment alone.

'We've barely had a chance to talk,' he breathes, his hands on my hips, his thumbs gently massaging my waist. I rest my hands on his forearms.

'Perhaps we don't need to talk,' I reply. 'Not tonight anyway.'

A Christmas song that I actually like starts playing, a slow one.

'I love this,' I say quietly as Ben pulls me towards him and my arms snake around his waist as we sway to the music.

'I've made such a mess of everything,' Ben says after a while. 'I'm so sorry.'

'It's been a messy few weeks for both of us, but in three minutes we get a whole new chapter to start over in.'

'To mess up all over again.' He smiles.

'Or maybe to stop seeing everything as a mess,' I reply. I know I have to change the way I see things, to stop living as though everything is my fault, as though everyone abandons me. I told myself that story for years but I know now that there's no truth in it. I have the choice to move forward differently. I have the choice to be happy.

'Not having a job feels like a bit of a mess.'

'Or it could be an opportunity,' I reply. 'The fire at the

294

café feels like a mess but perhaps I should see the fresh coat of paint it needs as an opportunity for something new.'

'A new beginning,' Ben says, his eyes sparkling again.

'A fresh start for both of us,' I say quietly, hoping I haven't said too much.

'Together?' he asks, his face a question.

Behind us I hear everyone begin to count down to the new year.

Ten, Nine, Eight, Seven, Six, Five…

'Is that what you want?'

Four, Three, Two…

'Yes,' he says, his lips so close to mine, his voice a whisper in the tension of the impending celebration.

One! Happy New Year.

He kisses me then as the clock strikes midnight, his arms holding me tight, his lips soft on mine and after a moment we realise together that the whole town that is squeezed into this pub tonight isn't clapping and cheering for the new year.

They are clapping and cheering for us.

Epilogue

One Year Later

'Ready?' Ben asks as he parks the car outside The Two Teas café in Sanderson Bay.

'As ready as I'll ever be,' I reply. 'I can't believe how nervous I am.'

'Worried that Marcus has messed everything up?' Ben asks with a smile.

'He'd better not have done.'

Ben gets out of the car and walks around to open the passenger door for me, something he's done since the night of our first date. He holds out his hand and I wrap my fingers around his as he leads me towards the café that was my whole life until Ben came along.

It had been Sascha's idea to open a new branch of The Two Teas in York. She'd even found a suitable property to rent.

'You know that I won't shut up about it until you start branching out,' she'd said, her hands on her ever-growing bump. 'You can't stay in Sanderson Bay forever.'

'I like Sanderson Bay,' I'd replied.

'But do you like living so far away from Ben?'

That swung it for me in the end. It was time to move on, time to take the next step. Even my father thought it was a good idea.

It took the best part of two months to get the café up and running again after the fire – the insurance came through in the end and the whole town pulled together to help with the repairs just as Sascha had promised they would, although Sascha herself took a supervisory capacity in proceedings what with being pregnant. My father surprised me by coming over to help as well, and being better with a hammer than I'd given him credit for. I'd told him about the fire in early January in an attempt to postpone his visit and our trip to Paris, but he came anyway and, in a few short days had become an honorary resident of Sanderson Bay.

'What you've done here is wonderful, Eloise,' he'd said. 'The café, the community… everything. And you seem so happy.'

'I am,' I'd replied.

'And Ben seems like a good man.'

'I'm glad you approve.'

When the work on the café was almost over James and Miranda insisted that they would put the finishing touches to the repairs while my father and I went on our planned trip to Paris before it was time to reopen. It had been a heart-wrenching trip but we were able to talk about things we'd never talked about before and remember *Maman* together.

It was while I was away that Sascha found the premises in York that she insisted would be the next Two Teas café.

'At least go and look at it,' she'd said on my return. 'I've booked an appointment for you and Ben to see it.'

I'd run out of excuses by then. Ben was as insistent on this as Sascha and together they were a force to be reckoned with. I'd known they were right though. I'd always known I needed to stop letting fear guide everything and opening a new café in York might be exactly the right thing to do that.

To give Sascha her due, the premises were perfect.

'You should set up as a commercial estate agent or something,' I'd told her when we'd called her from the car after our viewing. 'Matching clients to their perfect premises.'

'Does that mean you're taking it?' she'd asked.

I'd looked over at Ben and he'd grinned at me. 'Yup,' I'd said. 'Looks that way.'

Ben had been particularly excited at the prospect of my opening up another branch of The Two Teas, as it was him who had been driving back and forth between York and Sanderson Bay since New Year, him who was living with his mother whilst I'd been working on the café refit and swanning off to Paris, him who'd had the patience of a saint through it all whilst using every moment of his spare time to start setting up his own marketing company.

So you see me moving to York definitely worked in his favour.

Not that I'd minded. By the spring, by the time The Two Teas in Sanderson Bay reopened and we'd found the premises in York, I knew I wanted more than the snatched moments we'd been trying to find since New Year.

'It's big enough for two,' Ben had whispered in my ear

when the estate agent had showed us the flat above the potential new café.

'You'd give up your mum's home cooking to live above my café?' I'd asked.

'I want to be wherever you are, El,' he'd replied and then he'd smiled at me. 'Besides we can always go back to Mum's for a feed whenever we want.'

When Abi and Marcus came back from Thailand I bulldozed them with my proposition before they'd even slept off their jet lag.

'We would love to manage the café for you,' Abi had squealed. 'Wouldn't we, Marcus?'

Marcus had nodded, his eyes glazed with exhaustion, but the two of them have been running the original Two Teas for six months now and are making a very steady profit so he must have been more enthusiastic than he'd seemed.

I opened the York café in June, two days after Sascha gave birth to a healthy baby boy. She hadn't been there to see me off as she'd been in hospital, but it was still one of the hardest moves I've ever made, harder than when I'd moved from York to the Bay eighteen months earlier. I've come a long way since that day and I've learned that you have to follow your dreams, no matter how scary they might seem, because the other side of that fear is a magical place.

We're back in Sanderson Bay tonight for Abi and Marcus's New Year's champagne tea and I've never been so excited to see everyone, or so nervous to see my café again.

Ben pushes the café door open, holding it for me as I step inside to be greeted by a huge cheer. Everybody is here, raising their champagne glasses towards me – including all of the Knitting Club who carry on without me these days, with the addition of baby Davey who Sascha brings with her and who is dressed from head to toe in knitted items, no matter the weather.

I watch her now as she barges people out of the way to throw herself at me.

'I've missed you so much,' she says and I hug her back, too overwhelmed to speak. I love our life in York and I never thought it would be possible for me to be so blissfully happy in that city after what happened, but that doesn't mean I don't miss Sanderson Bay.

'*Bonjour, Eloise,*' says a small voice and I look down to see Marie standing next to me. I glance across the café to see my father smiling over at me and I wave. This is a surprise – I hadn't known they'd be coming.

Ben picks Marie up and twirls her around.

'How's my favourite girl?' he says to her in his rubbish French and she giggles, telling him that she knows English now. I think my half-sister has a little crush on Ben. I don't blame her.

The café is full of people and voices and questions as Abi and Marcus try to organise everyone enough to get them to sit at their tables.

'You sit next to me, Ben,' Marie demands and as I watch them together I think about the positive pregnancy test I took this morning, the test I haven't had a chance to talk to Ben about yet. I'd been terrified when I first saw those blue lines – we were too busy for a baby; we lived in a tiny flat with a narrow staircase. How on earth were we going to manage? But I know that I don't need to be scared about this, that together Ben and I will manage. My hand automatically goes to my stomach as I watch Marie wrap my boyfriend around her little finger. He's going to be an amazing dad.

I see Sascha watching me then, her eyes flicking down to the hand on my stomach. She raises her eyebrows at me knowingly and I press my index finger to my lips in an attempt to stop her from announcing something that doesn't need announcing yet.

She smiles and nods.

How does she always know everything?

Vegan Gluten-free Black Bean Brownies

These brownies have been mentioned in three of my books now, so I thought it was about time that I gave you the recipe. They were first baked by Rob Jones, brother of the hero in my debut novel *The Many Colours of Us* who passed the recipe on to Julia's best friend Pen. Pen and her husband Graeme moved to York and opened a café where the brownies were served in *The Pieces of You and Me* and it was from Pen that Sascha got the recipe she used to bake the Christmas brownies for Ellie's New Year's Eve champagne tea party. I believe that's called meta.

Ingredients

1 can of black beans, rinsed and drained
2 flax eggs (make these by mixing two tablespoons of ground flaxseed with 90ml of water – if you aren't vegan you can use two hens' eggs)

3 tablespoons of coconut oil (melted) or alternatively use olive oil for a nuttier flavour
100g of cocoa powder (I use Green & Blacks)
1 teaspoon of vanilla extract
75g of caster sugar
1.5 teaspoons of baking powder

Method

Preheat over to 180°C and lightly grease a standard muffin tin.
Put all the ingredients into a food processor and mix together. You can also put them in a bowl and mix with an electric whisk. You need to get it to the consistency of frosting – but definitely not runny.
Spoon the mix equally into the compartments of the muffin tin.
Sprinkle on an optional topping such as crushed nuts or chocolate chips.
Bake for 20–25 minutes until the tops are slightly crispy and the edges are pulling away from the sides of the tin.
Allow to cool and take out of the muffin tin.
Add optional candy Christmas trees.
The brownies will keep for 3 to 5 days in a cake tin or you can freeze them for up to a month.

Ben and Ellie's Playlist

These are the songs I was listening to when I was inside Ben and Ellie's heads. You can find Ben's 'Christmas Peaceful Piano' playlist on Spotify.

1. Dear Prudence – The Beatles
2. Pennyroyal Tea – Nirvana
3. Boom! There She Was – Scritti Politti
4. You Have Placed A Chill In My Heart – Eurythmics
5. All My Loving – The Beatles
6. Tender – Blur
7. Be More Kind – Frank Turner
8. Dignity – Deacon Blue
9. The Power of Love – Frankie Goes to Hollywood
10. For What It's Worth – Oui 3
11. Under the Bridge – Red Hot Chili Peppers
12. The Way You Used To Do – Queens of the Stone Age
13. Icarus – Bastille
14. Eloise – The Damned
15. You're The One – Greta Van Fleet
16. I Want A Hippopotamus For Christmas – Gayla Peevey

Acknowledgements

I wrote this book in seventy days during a pandemic. I suspect a lot of acknowledgements pages over the next few months will start in a similar way. It's a strange time to be writing about pubs and tearooms when all those places are closed and you have hardly left the house for weeks. But I write for the same reason that I read – to escape - and I hope, during these strange times we live in, that my books can provide a little bit of escape for you.

My thanks go to Hannah Smith at Aria for helping me wrestle my first draft into the book you have in front of you – it's a joy to be working with you again and all the other fabulous people at Aria Fiction. Thank you also to my agent Lina Langlee, who signed me when I was at my lowest ebb with my writing and gave me my confidence back.

Huge thanks to Katey Lovell for telling me I should write a book about tea and to Sarah Bennett for always being at the end of WhatsApp with a mad idea when I've written myself into a hole again. Thank you also to my writing crew - Maxine Morrey, Victoria Cooke, Mary Jayne Baker, Rachael Stewart and Rachel Dove – for cheering from the side lines (even though we haven't seen each other in months!). Thanks also to Jules Swain for advice on what happens when you inhale too much smoke!

Thank you to my husband for reading three drafts, telling me (as usual) how men would actually behave in any given situation and for always having an answer (however bizarre) when I ask 'what would happen if?'

Thanks to the bloggers and reviewers who help us writers in more ways than you know and thank you most of all to you, the reader. Thank you for buying this book and supporting authors and for allowing me to keep writing stories. I hope you enjoy!

About the Author

RACHEL BURTON has been making up stories for as long as she can remember and always dreamed of being a writer until life somehow got in the way. After reading for a degree in Classics and another in English Literature she accidentally fell into a career in law, but eventually managed to write her first book on her lunch breaks.

She has spent most of her life between Cambridge and London but now lives in Yorkshire with her husband and their three cats. She loves yoga, ice hockey, tea, The Beatles, dresses with pockets and very tall romantic heroes.

Find her on Twitter & Instagram as @RachelBWriter or follow her blog at rachelburtonwrites.com. She is always happy to talk books, writing, music, cats and how the weather in Yorkshire is rubbish. She is mostly dreaming of her next holiday....

Hello from Aria

We hope you enjoyed this book! If you did let us know, we'd love to hear from you.

We are Aria, a dynamic digital-first fiction imprint from award-winning independent publishers Head of Zeus. At heart, we're committed to publishing fantastic commercial fiction – from romance and sagas to crime, thrillers and historical fiction. Visit us online and discover a community of like-minded fiction fans!

We're also on the look out for tomorrow's superstar authors. So, if you're a budding writer looking for a publisher, we'd love to hear from you. You can submit your book online at ariafiction.com/ we-want-read-your-book

You can find us at:
Email: aria@headofzeus.com
Website: www.ariafiction.com
Submissions: www.ariafiction.com/ we-want-read-your-book

- **f** @ariafiction
- **𝕏** @Aria_Fiction
- **◎** @ariafiction